SHE'S MY RIDE HOME

Jackie Bushore

A MonkeyJohn Books Production

First Edition: April 2014
ISBN-13:
978-0615988078
(MonkeyJohn Books)

ISBN-10:
0615988075

For Mom
who gave me the gift of strength

and Dad
who gave me the gift of words

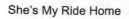

<u>One</u>

Green.

It was the first thing I noticed about her, from the lime-colored hoodie that covered her thin frame to the matching flip flops. Even her nails were painted green.

And her eyes. I caught them when she lifted her gaze to nervously scan the classroom. Maybe it was her pale complexion and bright blonde hair that made them stand out so much, but they made me think of emeralds. Beautiful.

She noticed me staring and I turned away maybe a bit too quickly. I felt my face begin to flush. *Girls don't check other girls out, Charlotte,* I reminded myself. Even so, I found my eyes drawn to her once more, as though something about her was magnetic.

I had decided the previous spring to take Theater as one of my last classes of my senior year in high school. At the time, I'd told myself it was because I needed to get over my massive stage fright. Well, that, and the slight catch that I needed an Art credit to graduate.

Now, however, as I glanced around the room at the handful of other students who all seemed so bubbly and excited, I felt out of place. Alone. I didn't know any of them. Worse yet, the desks were arranged in a circle so they could all see that I didn't have any friends.

"Alright, class." Our teacher was a plump little lady with a wave of red hair. I'd seen her around school before. She plopped down at one of the empty desks, grinning. "Welcome to Theater!"

Everyone grew quiet except for a few guys still talking animatedly a few seats away from me. From the corner of my eye, I watched the girl remove a pair of headphones and slip them into her bag. I hadn't even noticed she was wearing them.

"Let's start." She passed a syllabus around the circle. I glanced down to catch her name. Ms. Woodbridge. I was pretty sure I'd heard good things about her. "Icebreakers. I'd like each of you to tell us your name, year, and something we wouldn't know just by looking at you."

Oh, great. I hated this crap. Put us all on the spot, won't you? Then again, I guess Theater was made for that exact purpose. I sighed.

"We'll start with you, Zach." She obviously already knew the guy sitting next to her. He was one of the chatty ones.

A smile broke across his tan face and he rose. "Okay. I'm Zach Martin." He grinned. I was pretty sure he was gay. "And I'm a cheerleader. Go Grizzlies!" he yelled, pumping his arms above his head. Definitely gay. He quieted down after a moment, grinning sheepishly. "I'm a sophomore. And I love Ms. Woodbridge." He blew her a kiss, collapsing back into his seat. Woodbridge chuckled.

I counted off how many people were ahead of me. Four. I began thinking about what to say as my eyes drifted over to the girl in green. She was staring at her desk again, doodling with a pencil in her notebook. I wondered what she was drawing.

When it was my turn, I rose more hesitantly than the others. "I'm Charlotte Hayes." I forced a smile. "I'm a senior. I play on the Varsity soccer team." I paused, and then added, "And I have a dog named Wednesday." I sat back down, knowing my face was bright red. I felt her piercing green eyes on me. Watching me. *You could have said something more interesting,* I thought. Mentally bludgeoned myself.

"Do you have a nickname or anything?" Woodbridge asked.

"Uh, no. Just Charlotte."

"What kind of dog?"

"What?" I looked up. I hadn't expected more questions.

"What kind of dog is Wednesday?" Woodbridge's eyes were still locked on me.

"Oh." I was pretty sure my face was the darkest shade of red possible. "Siberian husky."

She smiled at me before moving on to the next person. I zoned through the next seven people, drawing a soccer ball on my hand with my ink pen. When the torch was passed to the green-eyed girl, I lifted my head with interest.

She nibbled her lip as she rose, shoving her hood off and running a hand through her wavy blonde hair. Looked about the same height as me, maybe a little bit shorter. And slight.

"Emma Pearson," she stated matter-of-factly in a voice that wasn't nearly as small as she was. "I just moved here."

"Oh?" Woodbridge looked interested. "From where?"

"North Carolina," Emma said, fiddling with her pencil and avoiding eye contact.

"Oh, wow. I bet it's nice there. What year are you?"

Emma sighed, as if bored. "Senior." She collapsed nonchalantly back into her chair.

Woodbridge said, "Well, welcome to Hidden Springs," with a huge grin. Emma just nodded. She went back to doodling in her notebook, ignoring Woodbridge, who had begun to discuss the syllabus.

My eyes trained on Emma long after she'd introduced herself. There was something about her that fascinated me. The bright eyes, the way the light caught her blonde hair at what seemed like just the right angle, the slight accent that made it obvious she wasn't born in the North…

"Now." Woodbridge clapped her hands together and my attention was immediately drawn to her. "I want to break you off into four groups. Within your groups, I want you to just chat and get to know each other. We're going to be doing a lot of work as a class, so I want everyone to be well acquainted. I'm going to give you a number one through four. Just arrange your desks together as a group."

She began counting off, starting with Zach. I was in group two. I took note of who else was in my group: Zach's friend, a small African American girl whose name I didn't catch, and Emma Pearson. I felt my skin tingling at the opportunity to get to know her better. What was going on with me? I wasn't normally like this.

As soon as Woodbridge finished assigning our groups, we all broke off. The four of us drew some desks together and took our seats.

We stated our names again. Justin was Zach's friend, the other girl was Jasmine. I scolded myself for being rude and not paying attention.

Justin was the first to begin speaking. "So." He kicked his feet out and leaned back against his chair, balancing his desk on two legs. "What year are you guys again?"

"I'm a freshman," Jasmine replied with a nervous smile. She brushed her long black hair out of her face.

"Senior," I told Justin. My eyes were drawn to Emma.

Justin looked at Emma for a moment. When she didn't respond, he dropped his desk back onto all fours with a loud clatter. Her head shot up. She glared.

"Are you awake?" He raised an eyebrow.

"Obviously," she retorted. She flicked the pencil in her hand across her notebook to make a harsh line.

Jasmine and I looked at one another, then back toward Justin and Emma.

"So." I quickly down the opportunity for Justin to mouth off to Emma. He looked peeved. "You're from North Carolina, right? Is it nice there?"

"Yeah," she said. She turned her eyes to briefly meet mine before looking back down at her desk.

"Did you live near the beach?" I asked. I didn't know what I was trying to do. Warm her up to us, maybe. Warm her up to me.

"Yeah, right near it. I lived in Corolla. It's sort of a beach town."

"Wow." Jasmine broke into a smile. "I bet the beach down there is so much nicer than the beaches up here."

Emma ran a hand through her soft hair, pushing it out of her face. A few freckles dotted her nose. I wished I had freckles. They were cute.

"So, why'd you move to Connecticut?" Jasmine asked. "If I lived by the beach, I don't think I'd ever move."

Emma looked up, her eyes piercing Jasmine from behind a few stray strands of blonde. "That's none of your business," she snapped.

"Damn." Justin narrowed his eyes at Emma. "No need to be such a bitch."

She opened her mouth, as if considering a response. Instead, she withdrew a little farther into her seat, lowered her eyes, and began sketching furiously in her notebook.

For the rest of the class period, Justin and Jasmine ignored Emma. I spaced out while they carried on the conversation. Emma didn't even look up.

I occasionally looked towards her, trying to make some sort of eye contact. She either didn't notice or didn't care.

Despite her attitude, I desperately wanted to get to know her. It was like a magnetic pull that I couldn't resist. And, honestly, I didn't know if I wanted to.

~~~

"Hey, dude, how were your classes?" Kenny asked when I met him at our lockers after Theater. I couldn't help but roll my eyes.

"Lame," I said.

Kenny Matheson had been my best friend since I moved to Hidden Springs, Connecticut from Philadelphia after my parents' divorce. We'd been inseparable since 7th grade. People often asked if we were brother and sister because we looked a lot alike: he had short, messy brown hair, brown eyes, and was only a few inches taller. Short for a guy. He'd prided himself on growing his first goatee over the summer, and was running his fingers through it as he waited for me to gather my books.

"What else are you taking besides History again?" He only knew I was in History because we were both in it. We always scheduled at least one class together each semester.

I sighed. "History, Photography, Lit, and Theater."

"Slacker."

Well, that was what I had been going for my first semester of my last year of high school. Had a pile of homework already, though, so it didn't really work out. "Whatever."

"Want to come over and play some Guitar Hero or something?"

"I can't," I said. "I have a soccer meeting."

"But you don't start practice for a few weeks," he pointed out.

"Yeah, but Reynolds still wants us to meet. I might be able to come over later tonight."

Kenny shouldered his bag. "Alright, well, whatever. See you, dude."

As he sauntered off, I turned just in time to see her walking in my direction. It was the green. She stood out like a butterfly in a beehive.

Her eyes caught mine. Did she smile? I couldn't tell. She looked away too quickly. I opened my mouth. Started to say hey. Something. Anything.

Nothing came out.

I could only watch as she disappeared into a crowd of students.

~~~

By the time I'd finished at my locker and made it to the cafeteria for the soccer meeting, I was late. Coach Reynolds had to stop talking.

"Glad you could join us," she called. I offered Coach a dismissive wave of my hand before taking a seat next to Sarah Callaghan, my main friend on the team and fellow forward.

"See all the newbies?" she whispered to me. Coach began speaking again. Something about practices. I glanced over at the girls. There were six of them. Each looked equally nervous. "We basically own this team," she added, shoving her dirty blonde hair over her shoulder.

Sarah and I had both been on the team since we were sophomores. There was only one other girl who had been on the team as long as we had and that was Brittany Osborne, our first string goalie. She was out for the entire season with a torn ACL. From what we'd heard, she was due for knee surgery sometime before practices started. That meant one of the new girls had to be a goalie, because our second stringer had just graduated.

"Practices this year will be Mondays, Wednesdays, and Thursdays after school," Coach was saying. "So make sure that's okay with your work, if you've got a job."

That was no problem for me. I'd been a hostess at a local Italian restaurant, Giovanni's, for about a year and a half and only worked on weekend nights.

I watched Coach pull our new uniforms out of a box at her feet and show them to us. They were Hidden Springs High colors: burgundy, gold, white. The school crest was emblazoned on the left breast of the jersey. Not bad. Professional looking. The shorts were bright gold, which was a lot flashier than the boring white we'd had the previous year.

"Nice," Sarah commented. I simply nodded in response.

"I'd like to finish off by introducing our new players for this year." Coach motioned to each girl as she told us their names, which I forgot in an instant. I'd have to play with them before I learned their names.

"And Corinne Knapp," Coach finished. My eyes stalled on her. She was shorter than me, dressed in baggy clothes with buzzed blonde hair. Around her neck, she wore a beaded rainbow necklace.

"Wow, you're kidding, right?" Sarah sneered. Her eyes swept judgmentally over Corinne.

I said nothing. I didn't really see anything wrong with the way she looked. Whatever happened to freedom of expression? The new girl turned to gaze at the two of us, passing a hand over her buzzed head.

"Here are the schedules for this season, as well as a team roster including phone numbers and e-mail addresses." Coach passed the papers down the table. "Don't forget to keep up with your exercise. See you all in two weeks."

Sarah and I rose simultaneously, glancing over the schedule together.

"We play Birchwood our first game? Are you serious?" Sarah made a face. Birchwood High was our toughest competitor. They had some of the best teams in the state. "That's suicide."

I shrugged. "Maybe we'll have a shot this year."

As Sarah gathered her belongings, I glanced up to see Corinne standing next to us.

"Hi." She stuck her hand out. "I'm Cor—"

"I don't care who you are," Sarah sneered. "C'mon, Charlotte. Let's leave this dyke to flock with her own kind."

The smile on Corinne's face faltered as Sarah slammed a shoulder into hers and began walking away.

I didn't know what to say. What to do. So I trailed after Sarah like a lost puppy, leaving Corinne in a wake of hatred.

<u>Two</u>

"Mom?" I stepped through the front door of my house. Wednesday came running at me full speed from my bedroom. I dropped my belongings at the door to throw my arms around her fluffy neck.

Mom appeared from the kitchen. "Hey, honey," she said. "You're home late. How was your first day?"

I followed her, pouring a glass of water and sitting down at the table. "I had a soccer meeting. And it was fine, I guess," I replied. "My Lit teacher is a real bitch, though."

"Witch," Mom corrected. "And is that really what you wore?"

Hurt, I glanced down at what I was wearing. A pair of grubby jeans and my Adidas sweatshirt. I hadn't seen anything wrong with it. I took a sip of my water and said, "Yeah."

Mom sighed. "The first day is for making a good impression. Couldn't you have put on a cute little dress or something? Maybe a skirt?"

I forced a laugh. Mom and I looked completely alike. Brown hair, brown eyes, same height. I even inherited her pale skin.

The likeness ended there, though. She was totally materialistic. I'm talking runner-up for homecoming queen kind of girl. She didn't even own a single pair of jeans. I, on the other hand, was a complete tomboy. Which was why the harassment about wearing a dress was a total joke. I couldn't be paid enough, and she knew it.

"Why are you off tonight?" I pushed her comment to the back of my mind. "Aren't you usually in the Psycho-Dome on Mondays?"

The Psycho-Dome, or the Hidden Springs Emergency Room, was where Mom worked as a nurse. Excuse me, she lived there. She had a pretty erratic schedule, and I rarely ever knew when she'd be home for sure.

She ruffled my hair and said, "I asked off. It's your last first day. I think it would go against the Code of Law for mothers if I worked."

"There are laws? I knew it!" I joked. "Is there a law in there that says mothers have to buy their daughters a new car for graduation?"

She grinned. "No, I don't think they had cars when they wrote it. What's wrong with Old Reliable?"

Old Reliable. My car. Sure, it was reliable. I could count on it to be the same bundle of junk every time I set eyes on it. It was a Ford Probe that was made before I was born. It used to be teal, but the paint was chipping so bad you couldn't really tell anymore, and the old leather interior was sun-bleached and torn. I'd thought about sending something in to Pimp My Ride, but I didn't think even West Coast Customs would touch it.

"Nothing," I said. "I'm going over to Kenny's, okay?"

"You don't have any homework?"

I frowned. "A little, but I'll just do it later. It's mostly forms and stuff anyways."

"Alright. Well, I trust you. You're driving, right?" She scratched Wednesday's head when the husky loped over to lick her hand.

I started to pull off my sweatshirt as I trekked down the hallway towards my room. "No, I'm going to jog." He only lived a few blocks away, and I needed to get my daily run out of the way. Might as well kill two birds with one stone, the way I saw it.

Mom didn't hesitate in rushing to my room. "You know how I feel about you jogging at night," she said. I could hear Wednesday's nails clicking against the floor as she followed. "Can't you drive?"

"Mom." I sighed. Slipped out of my jeans and threw on a pair of shorts. "I think I can outrun the crackheads." As if we had any. Hidden Springs was one of the nicer areas of Connecticut.

She looked at me for a long moment before saying, "Alright. Just carry your cell phone."

I pulled on my running shoes. "Alright. I'll call you if I get murdered on the street. I heard the Crips were cruising Shore Drive."

"Charlotte Nicole," she scolded. She was smiling. "Just be careful."

"Sure," I said as I made my way to the front door. I faked a jump of surprise when I opened it. "Well, wish me luck. I don't know if I'll make it past the crossfire."

Just as she started towards me, I bolted across the yard, turning around only to stick my tongue out in her direction.

~~~

Kenny lived a few blocks away, on the other side of my neighborhood. A few years ago, we would ride our bikes or walk to meet halfway and then play for hours on end. Now, we either drove to each other's house or I used going over there as an excuse to go jogging. So much had changed from when we were kids. I missed it.

"Gee, Charlotte. Why'd you dress up for me?" Kenny joked when he answered the front door.

"Shut it, Kendrick." I threw a punch to his shoulder, wiping a bead of sweat off my forehead and shoving my damp bangs out of my eyes.

"Don't..."

"Call you that, I know. But you deserved it." I followed him down to his room. Somehow, when he was 13, he convinced his parents to let him move his room to the basement and they accepted. My guess is that it was probably because they were sick of hearing his loud music. Parents weren't particularly fond of heavy metal bands.

"Glad we're seniors now?" he asked.

I rolled my eyes. "Sure. Another year of immature freshmen, bickering teachers, and piles of homework." That, and not knowing what exactly it was that I wanted even though I was 17.

"Well, at least we get to use the senior courtyard. That's a plus, right?" he pointed out. "Up for some Guitar Hero?"

Guitar Hero. His favorite game. Grinning, I said, "Sure."

He threw himself down on his rickety futon and I followed suit, letting my head fall against one of his pillows. As he grabbed the guitar off the ground and started to play, I asked, "So, any goals for this year?"

"Yeah," he said, sticking his tongue out of the side of his mouth in concentration. "Get a girlfriend."

I laughed. "You're joking, right? Not get good grades or into a college, but get a girlfriend?"

He swiveled his head toward me just as he finished the song and shoved the guitar over. "You can't tell me you never get lonely and wish you had a boyfriend. That you don't look at couples in the hallway and want the same thing. I mean, 80 percent of people meet the person they're going to marry in high school."

I clicked through the song list and chose one I knew was easy. "I mean, I guess I get lonely," I said. But I didn't ever find myself wishing for a boyfriend.

He smiled, swiping his bangs out of his eyes. "See? A girlfriend is a good goal, then. Your goal should be to get a boyfriend. We could totally do the American Pie thing."

I was about to answer when loud music began to spill from the television. Swallowing, I shifted the guitar in my hands and turned away, grateful for the distraction.

Grateful to forget the fact that I didn't feel normal.

~~~

"You're horrible at this game," he told me as he turned off the television and threw the guitar to the floor. For what seemed like the millionth time, I'd failed to pull off a decent score.

"I just don't get the chance to play it all day long like you." I reached for my shoes and slipped them onto my feet.

"You're just jealous I've beaten the game on advanced."

I tied my laces, rising to stretch for my run home. "Keep dreaming, Kenny. Anyway, I need to get going." I glanced at the clock. 9:30 already? I pulled my cell phone out of my pocket to look at the front screen. Two missed calls from her. I must not have heard my phone ring over Kenny's loud music. "Shoot, Mom's probably going to be pissed. She called a few times," I said.

"See you tomorrow," he told me before I dashed off. I ran as fast as I could the entire way home. When I finally burst through the front door I was panting like crazy.

Mom stepped out of the kitchen, her brows furrowed with irritation. "You're coming in late. It's a school night."

As if I didn't already know.

"Yeah, I'm sorry. I kind of lost track of time."

"Well, there's dinner in the fridge if you're interested. Meatloaf," she told me.

I wandered into the kitchen. Peering into the refrigerator, I pulled out the plate she left for me and popped it into the microwave.

"Don't forget to finish your homework," she called.

"I'll get it done. I promise." I'd be up until midnight, but I'd do it. I pulled my plate out of the microwave one second before the beep, knowing it irritated Mom, walking into the living room to fall into the loveseat.

"You're spending an awful lot of time with him." She glanced away from the television to look me over. "Anything going on that I should be aware of?"

I almost choked on a mouthful of meatloaf. "No, Mom," I said in between chews, shaking my head. "Really. He's my best friend, you know that."

"Well, it's just you haven't had a boyfriend since Jeremy, and that was two years ago." She turned her attention back to a re-run of Grey's Anatomy, which played at a low volume on the television screen.

I shoved another huge piece of meatloaf into my mouth, chewing slowly. It was true, I hadn't had a boyfriend since Jeremy, but it wasn't like I hadn't had a few guys ask me out. I just turned them down. They weren't my type. Not that I knew exactly what my type was.

"I know," I said, not really able to think of anything better to tell her.

"No boys you like at your school?" she asked. I wished she'd get off the subject. She brought it up every once in a while. It was so annoying. If I had a boyfriend, I would've told her. What would be the use in hiding that?

I sighed, setting my plate on my lap and staring intently at the television screen. "No. They're all obnoxious."

She nodded, picking up the remote and flicking through the channels until she landed on Fox News. The two anchors behind the desk were engaged in a thrilling discussion about the current economic condition of the United States. "Yeah. Most guys your age are incredibly immature. When I met your father, he was 24 and still in that stage." She paused, bringing her hand up to her face to rub her temple. "Come to think of it, I don't think he ever grew out of it." Which was partly the reason for their divorce.

We grew silent as I finished my dinner. Mom tuned in to all the news that Fox had to deliver to her: a double homicide in Hartford, a bomb threat at a Fairfield school, the crash of the Hidden Springs' court's online database. The entire time, I remained completely zoned out. I had lied to my mother. There were plenty of sweet, good-looking guys at my school. Kenny was one of the nicest, most mature guys that I knew. Why, then, couldn't I seem to find one that suited me?

<u>Three</u>

When I eased myself into the seat next to Emma on Friday, I felt my heart hammering against my chest. I'd been a chicken the entire week. It was time to grow some balls. Besides, what was the worst that could happen?

I wanted to break into her shell, to get to know her. Maybe open her up to the class.

"Hey," I said. It came out more like a squeak.

She was wearing her green sweatshirt again, but this time with a simple pair of jeans and white sneakers. Her hair fell gently around her pale face. I noticed the iPod earphones beneath the waves of blonde. I had thought she was cute before, but up close she was even more striking.

She lifted her head, emerald eyes catching my gaze. Up close, her skin appeared as though she hadn't seen the sun in ages, making the hue of her eyes even brighter. When she reached up with one hand to remove her earphones and lower them to her desk, I noticed her nails were bitten to the quick. The green nail polish that looked so fresh on the first day was chipped.

"Charlotte," I reminded her. Held out my hand in greeting.

"I know," she replied. When she didn't take my hand, I was thrown. I nibbled at my lip and looked away to pull my binder out of my backpack.

I could hear the music blasting from her earphones. She was listening to a song I'd heard recently on the radio. I didn't know who the singer was, but I liked it.

"So, I take it you don't really like it here?" I asked.

"What makes you think that?" She captured my gaze once more. My eyes followed her movement as she picked up a pen with her right hand and began twirling it in her thin fingers.

"You just don't seem like you do."

Emma turned her attention to Woodbridge. The teacher had taken a seat in the circle. "I'm not here because I want to be."

There was venom in her voice, and I didn't want to unleash it again. I decided not to speak to her for the rest of the class. Occasionally, I would glance over to see her off in her own world, hardly acknowledging her surroundings. I wished she'd look at me, speak to me. Maybe even smile.

She didn't.

~~~

"Have you heard back from any colleges yet?" Kenny asked as he sprawled out on the grass beside me. It was a nice Saturday. Warm for September in Connecticut. Wednesday, enjoying the open space of the park, bolted after squirrels.

College was a subject I had been dreading. I'd been guided for so long that I was nervous about venturing off to an entirely new environment where I'd be on my own.

I leaned back in the grass to balance on my elbows. "No. I doubt I'll be accepted anyway." I'd applied to Fairfield and Wesleyan, but I wasn't sure what I'd been thinking. I would never get in. My grades weren't that great.

He nodded, plucking a blade of grass between his index finger and thumb and shredding it slowly. "Well, at least you've still got that soccer scholarship to UConn," he pointed out. "Capital accepted me. I think I'm just going to go there." Capital. A community college. I wasn't surprised. Kenny wasn't exactly a die-hard academic.

"You're not going to apply anywhere else?"

"Nope." Kenny dropped the piece of grass back to the ground: once alive and thriving, now mercilessly mutilated.

Wednesday plodded over and jumped on top of me. I laughed, throwing my arms around her neck. She began attacking my face and neck with her tongue, huge paws dancing around my body.

"Come on, girl," I urged the husky, pushing her heavy body off of my thin frame. At 70 pounds, she weighed over half of what I did, and her playfulness could sometimes get painful. I picked up her slobber-coated tennis ball and chucked it across the clearing where it landed and bounced between some trees. She took off toward it, tongue dangling merrily from the side of her mouth.

"You work at four tonight, right?" Kenny asked. He ran a hand through his shaggy brown hair before messing it up more with his fingers.

I groaned, letting my head fall back to the soft earth. "Yeah," I grumbled. Kenny and I both worked at Giovanni's. I was a hostess, he was a line cook. He'd gotten me the job. It was a pretty nice place to work. The pay wasn't that great, but the owners were decent. "You too?"

"Yep. Want to just ride together?"

"Yeah, I guess so," I replied. I was scheduled to get off about an hour before him, but I could do homework or something while I was waiting.

We continued chatting. Yet, even while he moved the conversation on to a different subject, I couldn't help but let my mind train on the prospect of college.

Kenny wanted to go to Capital. I had my mind set beyond that. I was worried. Scared to be alone in a place so new. Besides, I didn't even know who I was yet. How was I expected to grow up so quickly? Couldn't I just give life a rain check?

~~~

Giovanni's was slow. I sat quietly in a chair behind the host stand, doing a word search out of sheer boredom. *Broomstick, where's broomstick?* I ran through all the B's I could see, unsuccessfully trying to find the word. It was the last one on the page, too.

The front door opened. I shoved the small book into an open drawer and looked up. "Hi, welcome to Giovanni's," I said casually before realizing who I was speaking to.

When I saw her, my breath caught.

Emma appeared in the doorway, accompanied by an older man and a smaller boy. Her father and brother, I assumed.

"Hi," Emma's father said, flashing me a friendly smile. His face was lined with wrinkles, black hair just beginning to gray out. I vaguely wondered how Emma's hair was so blonde. "Three, please? Non-smoking?"

We didn't have a smoking section in the entire restaurant, so his request wasn't a problem. I made an ordeal about looking at the sections outlined on my host stand even though we were dead as a doornail.

I glanced at Emma. She was looking away from me, through one of the windows of our front entrance towards the busy road that the restaurant sat off of.

"You can follow me," I told them, scooping up three menus and leading them to a nearby booth. I placed the menus on the table and backed up, allowing them to take a seat. Emma's dad and brother sat next to each other. She slid in across from them.

I faked a smile and said, "Enjoy your meal."

"Thanks, Charlotte." I heard Emma say.

My eyes shot back to meet her gaze. I couldn't believe she acknowledged me. Even more so, I couldn't believe that she was smiling at me. I returned the smile, genuine now, and didn't say anything as I returned to the front of the restaurant. I caught her dad asking how she knew my name, but I didn't hear her response.

I couldn't help but think of how much cuter she was when she was smiling. I also noticed, whether I realized it or not, that I had placed her family at the only booth that was visible from the host stand.

~~~

"Mom?" I called. I slipped through my front door, dropping my backpack next to the wall. The sound of paws against the floor reached my ears as Wednesday rushed from my room to greet me.

School had been terrible. I just wanted to relax for the rest of the night. Not only had I been ten minutes late for my first class because of traffic, but I had completely forgotten my lunch money and Woodbridge gave us a pop quiz that I definitely failed.

Walking into the kitchen, I searched through the refrigerator and finally pulled out a cup of strawberry yogurt. When I went to get a spoon out of our silverware drawer, I noticed the note Mom had left for me.

Charlotte,

Got called into the Psycho-Dome. Probably won't be home until late.

Love you,
Mom

Poor Mom, it was supposed to be her only day off. I gave Wednesday a pat on the head and threw her a cookie before going into my room to change into my pajamas and crash in bed. Grabbing my remote off my nightstand, I turned on my television and began flipping through the channels. Wednesday clambered up onto the bed a few minutes later, nuzzling up against my back.

I paused briefly on MTV, but it was playing old re-runs of *Made*. Whatever happened to it being *Music* Television instead of *Horrible Reality* Television? I clicked to the next channel. A bunch of girls were gathered around a table in a coffee shop, chatting.

I pressed the info button. *The L Word*. I'd never heard of this show. As I began to watch, it became quickly apparent that a few of the girls in the group were lesbians. My heart started to beat faster. Was this what the show was about?

The scene cut to two girls, who hardly spoke before becoming engaged in a deep lip-lock and answering my question. My hand froze on the remote as I watched, swallowing hard. It didn't take long for the two girls to end up in bed, where much more of the human anatomy was shown than I would have seen watching ABC Family.

As I began to feel a soft burn pulse through my body, my index finger struck the "off" button. The scene disappeared instantly, leaving nothing but black where there was once the unabashed nudity of two girls together.

Rolling over, I wrapped an arm around Wednesday's soft back, the scene playing itself over and over again in my mind. I didn't find it gross, like I felt I should have. Instead, I found something mesmerizing about it.

It wasn't normal. A normal girl would be disgusted.

What was wrong with me?

<u>Four</u>

"The Triangular Trade was a trade route that connected three countries: Africa, the West Indies, and Europe," Mrs. Lancaster, my History teacher, was tracing the triangle on the overhead map with her finger. She was an older lady. Nice, though. Not strict like other older teachers. "Can anyone tell me what goods were most commonly traded on this route?"

I was on the verge of sleep, struggling to keep my eyes open as I rested my chin on my arms and stared at the front of the class through my messy bangs. Kenny had mastered the art of sleeping with his eyes open and was dozing next to me.

"Slaves?" A girl in the front row, the only one who ever seemed to be engaged in the lecture, spoke up. My guess was the rest of the class was half asleep as well.

Mrs. Lancaster nodded and began scribbling a list of items on the whiteboard. "Not only slaves, but other goods such as copper, cloth, sugar, and molasses. Guns and ammunition, too."

She sent the map hurtling back to its home in the ceiling with a loud crash.

I jumped. So did everybody else. Seth Michaels, a guy who had been in nearly all of my classes since sophomore year, nearly fell out of his desk. I noticed him swipe at some drool that had formed at the corner of his mouth. He caught me looking, offering a goofy grin as he fixed his glasses. Faking a dramatic yawn, he collapsed across his desk.

"Well, I guess it's a good thing we're almost out of time for today, anyways." Mrs. Lancaster laughed, shaking her head and walking to her desk. "You all can use the time left to do whatever. Don't forget the worksheet that's due tomorrow."

"This class is boring." Seth ran a hand through his short blonde hair. He was kind of dorky, with a crooked nose and large, round glasses. Kind of made me think of Harry Potter. All the same, he was down to earth and as nice as could be.

"It's not so bad," I replied. I glanced at Kenny. His forehead had hit the desk.

Seth shrugged. "If you say so. I'm pretty sure you were nearly in Dreamland, too, Hayes." Removing his glasses, he began to wipe the lenses with the bottom of his black t-shirt. My eyes followed his movement. I noticed the quote on the front of his shirt that said, *Out of my mind... be back in five minutes.*

"Nice shirt." I shoved my bangs out of my eyes and began sliding my binder into my bag.

Before he could respond, the school bell pierced the loudspeakers. A chorus of scraping chairs followed as each student shot up and made a beeline for the door.

"C'mon, Kenny," I told my friend, reaching over to tug on his hair. He responded with a grunt, lifting his head and wiping his bloodshot eyes with the backs of his fists.

"Too much Guitar Hero last night?" I rose.

He yawned, grabbing his binder and lumbering from his chair to follow Seth and me out of the classroom. "Shut up."

Waving to Seth, Kenny and I fought our way through the crowd of students towards our lockers. As we were replacing books and binders, a flash of green caught my eye and I spun on my heel. Kenny followed my gaze.

Emma was walking slowly toward us, bright green sweatshirt making her stand out against the students around her. Her black shoulder bag was thrown over her neck and fell at her side, one hand resting on the strap. The glazed look on her face told me that her iPod was sending sound waves into her ears.

As she passed us, I caught her gaze. Her green eyes flickered back and forth between Kenny and me. Throwing on an awkward smile, I began to fidget with the binder in my hand. "Hi," I mouthed, not bothering to make a sound. She probably couldn't even hear me.

Without so much as a blink, she turned away and strode on by as though she'd never seen me before in her life. My face grew hot. Why did she have to be such a bitch to someone who was just trying to be nice?

I turned away, shoving my binder into my locker with a bit more force than I otherwise would have given.

"Damn, that girl's cute," Kenny said, shutting his locker door and leaning against the cold metal. His eyes followed Emma's backside.

"She's in my Theater class," I said, grabbing my camera box and my Photography notebook to drop into my bag. "And she's a total bitch." I slammed my locker shut.

"What a shame. I could see myself with a girl like that," he said.

I swallowed a grapefruit.

It didn't bother me that Kenny thought that. What bothered me is that I had thought the same thing.

~~~

In Theater, I didn't bother sitting next to Emma again. Instead, I returned to the seat I had originally chosen. But even though she still wasn't paying attention to Woodbridge, Emma didn't doodle endlessly in her notebook. Instead, her gaze was fastened on the air in front of her, her expression zoned. She broke her locked stare only occasionally to glance at her desk, seemingly lost in thought.

What is your problem? I focused my eyes on the top of her blonde head, trying to maybe penetrate her thick skull and read her thoughts. *Why are you so cold?*

Despite my intense efforts, I didn't get anything out of staring but a headache that took a trip to the nurse's office and three Ibuprofen to fix.

~~~

As assignments in History and Lit began to pile up, a new distraction returned to my weekly routine: soccer practice. After school the next Monday, I met Sarah at the entrance to the locker room and we both threw on our gear while we chatted about our classes.

"Oh, guess what?" Sarah grinned as she wrapped her long black laces around the bottom of her cleats to tie them. "I have a new boyfriend."

It wasn't surprising. Sarah was one of those girls that seemed to always have a boyfriend. I'd been perfectly happy being single for most of my teenage years, but she acted completely miserable without a guy to complete her.

"Yeah? Who?"

I tried my hardest to sound interested as I tugged a bright purple sock over my shin guard. I couldn't find its matching counterpart, so I'd figured I would just look like a complete idiot running around with one purple sock and one gold one.

"Bryan. He goes to Capital." She threw her bag into her locker and slammed it shut in one quick movement. "I met him at a party a couple weeks ago."

I just nodded as she continued to drag on about how wonderful, sweet, and cute he was. Not to mention, he played lacrosse, which was apparently supposed to be pretty sexy. I must've been alone in thinking that dirty, sweaty guys running around trying to catch a ball in a tiny net wasn't much of a turn on.

I tossed my ball gently in my arms as we walked from the gym and out onto the soccer field where most of the girls were already stretching.

"And, guess what?" she said while we sat down with the others.

"What?" I noted how exasperated I sounded, but Sarah didn't seem to notice.

"He wants to be a lawyer!"

"Neat." Attending Capital with an ambition to become a lawyer. Sure. More like restaurant manager, at best. I twisted my body over my legs and began concentrating on stretching out my muscles. Unconsciously, my eyes fell on Corinne, who was sporting her new goalie gear and stretching her arms over her head by the net. Her eyes slipped down to my mismatched attire, then back to my face with a chuckle. *Nice socks,* she mouthed. I turned away, bringing my hands to my hair to tug it back into a ponytail. I felt her gaze on me even when I wasn't looking, though, and it made me feel awkward and jittery.

Coach Reynolds blew her whistle and we moved to gather in front of her, sitting down either cross legged or sprawled across the lush grass. I picked at a loose thread from my gold sock while Coach told us about the drills we were going to be working on and about how our first game was in only three weeks.

We ran a few laps before doing a bunch of different passing drills. I could easily pick out the girls who hadn't been keeping up with an accurate workout routine. By the end of practice, most of them, including Sarah, were breathing as though they'd never run before in their life. I was proud to be one of the few who didn't have a heaving chest.

At least the hard practice shut Sarah up. The only thing she said as we returned to the locker room was how she was exhausted. There was no more mention of Bryan and how fabulous he was until we were waving goodbye to the girls and heading through the locker room doors.

"So, Bryan has this really cute friend, and if you're interested I think you two will click," Sarah told me as we pushed through the gymnasium door and walked towards the front entrance. "He's way gorgeous, I promise," she added, throwing me a wink before scurrying off ahead of me. "Anyway, I've got to fly, I'm supposed to meet Bryan in half an hour. See you, Charlotte. Think about it!"

I heard her words, but I didn't acknowledge them. I didn't even wave goodbye when she left. A figure leaning against the wall outside had triggered my attention.

I slowed my stride as I pushed through the front doors.

Emma was half standing, half sitting against the long stretch of brick wall that lined the front of the building. Her hood was on, long waves of blonde billowing from the sides. I could see her ever-present iPod cord. Her lifeline.

I glanced at my watch. 5:30. School had let out hours ago. Why was she still here? Maybe she had some sort of after school activity.

Shifting my Adidas bag on my shoulder, I took a few steps towards her. As I grew closer, I noticed the cigarette dangling from the corner of her lip. Gross. I guess she hadn't gotten the memo that smoking wasn't allowed on school grounds. Or maybe she just didn't care.

She expelled a breath, a cloud of smoke billowing out in front of her.

"Those'll kill you, you know."

"Yeah. Whatever." Her chin crooked upwards and her gaze met mine. Her eyes were puffy. She'd been crying. There was no mistaking it.

I slipped my hand around the strap of my bag as I narrowed my eyes at her. "You alright?" I asked.

Emma nodded, tossing the butt of the cigarette onto the ground and stomping it with her foot. "Yeah. Just waiting for my dad to pick me up."

"How long have you been waiting?"

"What time is it?" Emma peered at me from behind thin golden bangs.

"Five-thirty."

"Two hours, then," she said.

I felt a spark of sympathy for her. How could her father keep her waiting two hours? I couldn't even believe she'd been standing outside for that long.

"Do you need a ride home?" I twisted the toe of my cleat on the ground.

Emma turned her face hopefully back to mine. I felt any resentment I had toward her melt away. "Would you mind?"

I shook my head and waited for her to pick her bag up before beginning the trek to my car. When we finally arrived at Old Reliable, Emma breathed out a sigh of relief. "Long enough walk," she announced as she made her way over to the passenger side.

I unlocked my door and shoved everything from the passenger seat into the back. My car was disgusting, littered with clothes, trash, and schoolbooks. It was embarrassing.

"Sorry about the mess," I told Emma as I unlocked the door for her to climb inside.

She looked at me like I was stupid. "It's alright," she said. "Really. I probably wouldn't turn down a ride home in the back of a Perdue truck right now."

"Gee, that makes me feel special," I said.

Emma grew quiet as I sped out of the school parking lot.

"So, where do you live?" I asked. My eyes flickered over as I watched her push the hood off her head and run a hand through her hair.

"318 Swallowtail Road," she recited, before adding, "It's over near—"

"I know where it is," I interrupted. The expression on her face changed to one of bewilderment. "I actually live in the neighborhood across from you."

I shifted into neutral to stop at a red light, leaning back against my seat and tapping my index finger on the wheel. I could feel Emma's eyes on me, but pretended not to notice by looking through the window at a couple of guys in a pick-up truck in the lane to the left.

"So, you play soccer?" Emma asked. She sounded shy, tentative. Different from her usual affronted attitude.

My gaze shifted from the guys in the truck to the lifted tires that were caked with dry mud. "What gave you that idea?" I replied sarcastically, realizing a moment too late it came out pretty mean.

"I guess I deserved that." She shoved a few stray strands of hair behind her ear as she fidgeted with her backpack. I glimpsed over. She was wearing pearl earrings. They looked nice.

I slammed my foot on the brakes when I nearly rear ended another car. "Sorry. Yeah, I play Varsity."

"That's neat." She traced her finger along the inside of my window. "I like your socks, by the way."

"Yeah, I have a pretty amazing sense of smile, huh?" I lifted my foot off the accelerator to show her my bright gold sock. She smiled. She was so pretty when she looked happy.

By the time I pulled into her neighborhood, I'd come to the conclusion that she wasn't such a cold bitch after all.

She guided me through the neighborhood by pointing out street signs. I shifted into neutral and let my car idle in her driveway next to an older truck. Her dad's, I guessed. He was home, and yet he didn't have the time to pick his daughter up? Irritated, I glanced over the outside of her house. It was small, with an unkempt front lawn and a rickety bike on the front porch.

"Thanks for the ride." Emma brought my attention back to her. She grabbed her bag off the floor and pushed the door open.

I nodded. Smiled.

"See you, Charlie." A small smirk tugged at the corners of her lips. Before I had a chance to respond, she slammed my door shut and disappeared into her house.

I remained in the driveway for a moment, eyes locked on the now empty passenger seat, her last three words ringing in my ears. For some reason, the idea of Emma calling me by a name that no one else did made my stomach jump.

~~~

Mom was at the Psycho-Dome. As usual. Which was good, because I couldn't contain my excitement.

Could Emma and I be friends? The idea made me jittery. As though I'd just thrown back a double espresso.

Shoving past an excited Wednesday, I slid into my room and shut the door behind me. I leaned against it for a minute, letting out a long breath and grinning to myself.

Until something on my bed caught my eye.

I stepped forward, gaze locking on the envelope leaning against my pillow. Mail? I never got mail. I definitely wasn't behind on my cell phone payment. Besides, I had paperless billing for that.

Picking it up, my eyes fell on the name in the top left corner. My stomach wrenched inside of me. My head started to spin.

Dad.

Five

I was angry. No, understatement. I was livid. I clutched the letter from Dad in my hand, feeling my heartbeat quicken as I read it for the millionth time.

I miss you so much. I can understand why you're not writing me, but I'd love to hear from you. How are you? How's your mother? How's school? I think about you constantly.

I shut my eyes. He missed me? Could've fooled me. It'd been five years since he left us, and he'd never even bothered with a single letter or phone call until now. I'd moved on, erased him from my life. He was in the past.

Until now.

I looked up when Emma slid into the seat next to me. Shoving her iPod into her bag, she pulled out a pack of Starburst and offered me one. I shook my head.

"Thanks again for the ride last night." She popped an orange Starburst into her mouth. "My dad had fallen asleep on the couch." A weak laugh escaped her lips, which I quickly interpreted as fake. "Hey, are you alright? You don't look so well."

"Fine," I said, shoving the letter unceremoniously into my bag. "And you're welcome," I added, thinking at the same time that I would give her a ride home any time she needed.

Before we could say anything more, Woodbridge's bellowing voice brought order to the class. "Okay, guys! I have some exciting news for you."

Everyone grew silent, even Zach, who usually continued chatting regardless.

"I know you all have been dying to get out on the stage. I think it's about time we did so myself. For the next few weeks, I'm going to have you all practice some voice and diction in preparation for your very first stage assignment."

Zach squealed and acted like he was about to cheer, but hushed when he realized he was the only one.

"For the first assignment, we're going to be doing a skit with a partner. I'm going to allow you to choose your partner, so long as you don't goof off too much." She sent a meaningful look to Zach and Justin. "You'll have three weeks to prepare and will have to work together out of class. By the end of the week, I'd like to have submissions for what piece you'll be using."

Grabbing a stack of papers from her desk, she began passing them around. I looked over the huge list of plays to choose from and felt a knot rise in my throat. Why had I taken this class again? Oh yeah, because I apparently wanted to torture myself.

I picked up my pen and jotted at the top of my paper, *want to be partners*? Swallowing hard, I shoved it towards Emma as Woodbridge began reading the criteria from the paper.

Emma looked up, bright green eyes catching my inquisitive gaze. I noticed the unmistakable surprise on her face. She must not have expected anyone to want to work with her.

She wrote a response and pushed the paper back to me, twirling her pen in her fingers. I looked down at the paper on my desk.

Only if you promise not to fall in love with me, she'd written. Her script was tidy, with the slight loopiness that most girls' handwriting seemed to possess. It was a beautiful contrast next to my messy penmanship. I gulped, raising my gaze to meet hers. She laughed. It was a joke. I let out a relieved sigh.

We exchanged numbers on the same piece of paper. My insides felt jittery. I attributed it to the nerves of the upcoming stage performance, but knew deep in my mind that wasn't it.

And by the time class let out, I was pretty sure I had those seven digits permanently engrained in my mind.

~~~

It rained the rest of the week, which made soccer absolutely miserable. At the end of practice on Thursday, I came off the field not only soaked to the bone, but with the entire right side of my body covered in mud from taking a dive while trying to steal the ball from another girl.

Before Sarah and I reached the locker room, I caught a flash of green in the bleachers. I was shocked to see Emma scurrying through the benches. Her sweatshirt was nearly soaked through as if she'd been sitting for quite some time.

"Hey, Charlie," she yelled, breathing hard as she jogged over. Water from the grass sloshed around her ankles and sprayed against the bottom of her jeans.

Sarah came to a stop next to me, looking curiously towards Emma. "Who's that?"

"A girl from my class," I replied. "What are you doing out here?" I said to Emma, raising my voice a notch.

She looked pissed off. "Can I get a ride? Dad forgot again." She rolled her eyes.

"Yeah," I said. "Come on."

"I'm sorry," she told me when we reached my car. I went around to the passenger side to let her in first. The rain was pouring more heavily now, and for some reason it only seemed right that she got out of the rain before I did. "You're the only person I really know here," she added as she slid into the seat.

"Don't apologize." I climbed into the driver's seat, grimacing as I got mud all over the fabric. "I can't believe your dad keeps forgetting, though."

I started the car and cranked up the heat. Searching through my backseat, I found a relatively clean beach towel from when Sarah and I had ventured to the beaches in Fairfield over the summer. I handed it to Emma.

"Thanks." Her voice cracked. She turned away, but not before I noticed the tears streaking down her face.

"It's really not a big deal," I told her in my most reassuring voice. "I don't mind giving you a ride at all."

She slid her soaked hood off her head, dabbing at her eyes with the towel. "It's just embarrassing."

I pulled out of the school parking lot and was immediately greeted with bumper-to-bumper traffic. *Great, there must be an accident*, I thought. With a heavy sigh, I put Old Reliable into neutral so I didn't have to hold my foot on the clutch.

"Why don't you have your mom pick you up?" I leaned back against my seat.

Emma turned her head to look through the foggy windshield, the brake lights from ahead reflecting in her moist eyes. "My mom passed away this summer."

Wow, now I felt like an asshole. Loosening my grip on the steering wheel, I lowered my eyes. What do you say to that? "I'm sorry," I spat out uselessly. It was so cliché and expected, but I couldn't seem to think of anything better.

She shrugged, sighing as she pivoted her face towards me. "At least you match today," she pointed out, offering me a weak smile.

"What?" I followed her gaze. She was referring to my socks. "Oh. Yeah." I grinned, grateful for the change of subject.

"Hey, Charlie, do you mind if I smoke in here?"

My eyes met hers. I hesitated before saying, "No, go ahead." I don't know why. If it had been anybody else, I would have said no in a heartbeat.

But this was Emma.

A smile spread across her lips as she reached into her pack of Marlboro Lights and plucked a cigarette out. She flicked her small pink Zippo and lit it with ease. Clearly, she was no amateur to smoking.

"You want one?" she asked, tilting the pack towards me. I shook my head. She shrugged.

Even though she cracked the window, the smell of nicotine and tobacco flooded the air. I coughed. She didn't seem to notice.

I was almost grateful when we pulled into her driveway and she put the cigarette out. The smell of smoke seemed to linger, permeating the fabric of my seats and clinging to my clothes. If Mom smelled it, she'd kill me.

"Thanks again," Emma said as she pushed the door open.

"You know, I wouldn't mind giving you a ride every day," I blurted. "But I know you probably don't want to wait so long for practice—"

"No, that would be awesome," she cut me off. "I don't mind. I could study or something."

"Okay." I smiled.

"Thanks, Charlie," she said as she slid out of her seat. She paused outside of the car before poking her head back in. "You don't mind if I call you that, do you?"

I listened to the rain hammering against my roof, holding Emma's eyes with my own. "No," I answered. "I like it."

~~~

"Holy cow, Charlotte!" Mom exclaimed as I walked through the door. "I thought you were at soccer practice, not mud wrestling."

I dropped my Adidas bag, ignoring her.

"Mom, what is this?" I dug through my bag to pull out the crumpled letter, shoved it into her hands.

She looked down at the abused letter, her face blanching. "I thought you might want it," she replied. "I got it in the mail yesterday."

"Why now?" I couldn't hide the annoyance in my voice. "Five years, Mom."

"He's your dad, Charlotte," she said. "I honestly don't know how his mind works. You know that."

"He's *not* my dad. He stopped being my dad the moment he left us for that Playboy bitch." I couldn't help it. The words, which had been bubbling on my tongue for years, slid from my lips before I could stop them. I snatched the paper out of her hand, ripping it in half. "I hate him!"

Mom bent down and scooped up the papers, trying to straighten them out. "Charlotte, you don't mean that."

I meant it. With every fiber of my being. As I stormed off to my room, I made sure to slam my door to show it.

~~~

"That's weird," Kenny was saying. "Why would he just now be writing you a letter?"

"I don't know." I shrugged. "I don't think I'm going to write him back, though. He's got some nerve."

Kenny leaned against his locker. "I think you should. I mean, he is your dad."

I felt my face grow hot. Whose side was he on?

"Hey, Charlie," Emma said from behind me.

I spun, forcing a smile. My stomach did a flip and I quickly shoved my bangs out of my eyes. Kenny swiveled his head, glancing back and forth from me to Emma with a confused look on his face.

"Hey," I replied as I shoved my History binder into my locker.

"Ride tonight?" Emma asked, raising her eyebrows hopefully. "I told my dad not to pick me up," she added.

"Oh, yeah," I said, flushed. I felt my hands grabbing blindly at books to shove them into my bag. "Definitely. I don't have practice, so we can leave right after school."

"Okay, awesome. See you in Theater." I watched her saunter off down the hallway.

Slamming my locker shut, I turned to see Kenny staring at me with a look of complete bewilderment. "I thought you said she was a bitch?" He gently shut his locker.

"Not so much," I replied with a shrug. "I guess I was wrong."

Later, in Photography, I found myself confused and surprised as I pulled out my Literature textbook and Theater binder.

<u>Six</u>

I needed to forget about Dad. So when Kenny asked if I wanted to spend the night watching horror movies and playing Scrabble, I gratefully accepted.

RGLAMNE. I scoped out a place to put my letters, resting my chin in my hands. Kenny's head was turned to look at the movie he'd picked out for the night, *The Hills Have Eyes*.

Using the word *GAMBLE*, I arranged a few of my letters to spell out *LAMB*.

"Your turn," I said.

I grimaced as I looked at the screen to see one of the creepy guys eating a dead German shepherd. "Tell me why you picked this disgusting movie again?"

He turned back towards me, raising an eyebrow and blowing a few strands of messy brown hair from his eyes. "It's a classic," he said, using a few letters to connect *LONER* to my *LAMB*.

"Whatever you say." I looked over my new letters. *RGMEXNI*. I would never use the *X*.

"So, about that Emma chick," Kenny began. "Do you think maybe you can introduce me or something? She's really cute." He waggled his eyebrows.

Nibbling at my bottom lip, I narrowed my eyes to scrutinize the scrabble board.

"Charlotte?" he piped up, reaching over to poke me on the nose.

"Huh?" I jumped, tugging the corner of my lip into a small frown. "Oh, yeah, sure," I grunted. Using the E in *GAMBLE*, I shuffled my letters to spell out *GREEN*, which immediately brought Emma's image to the foreground in my mind.

~~~

The next day after history class, Emma stopped by my locker as usual to say a brief hello.

"Hey," she greeted as she approached, a huge smile on her slightly freckled face.

"Hey, Emma." I shut my locker door. Kenny was immediately at my side, brown eyes glued to my friend.

"Oh, yeah." I tried to act as though his presence was a complete surprise to me. Definite fail. It was a good thing I was taking Theater. "By the way, this is my friend Kenny. Kenny, Emma. I don't think you've met yet." *Mostly because I didn't want you to meet,* I thought. I faked a smile.

"Hi," Kenny said, pushing his hand forward and putting on his most charismatic smile. "Nice to meet you."

"Oh." Emma threw me a confused look before taking his hand. "Hi."

I turned away, making a big deal out of digging in my bag to see if I had gotten everything, even though I knew I already did.

"So, where are you headed?" I heard him ask.

"Biology, unfortunately." She sighed.

"Oh, really? I'm actually going to the Science hall too. Want to walk together?"

I turned around to stare at Kenny, confused. He had study hall next period, which was on the opposite side of the school.

Emma's green eyes floated to meet mine, as if trying to send me some message that I just couldn't receive. Maybe the receptors in my brain had been blocked off by the serious annoyance I was feeling.

"Sure," she said, breaking our gaze to look back at Kenny. "That'd be cool. See you later I guess, Charlie," she said.

I watched as the two sauntered off down the hallway together. Kenny twisted his head around to mouth, *Thank you.*

Yeah, I thought as I sulked off to Photography. *You're not welcome.*

~~~

My cleats struck the soft grass in a steady rhythm, propelling me ahead of the rest of the girls. I didn't look back. I didn't care if I was going too fast for them, and I didn't care if I would use my energy up a bit more quickly. The breeze cool against my face, the swish of my soccer shorts against my legs, the feeling of power as my leg muscles swelled to accommodate my speed. I was in the zone.

Until Sarah's voice broke it.

"Hey, Charlotte. Wait up a second!" she shouted. Glancing over my shoulder, I tightened my lips before slowing my pace to allow her to catch up to me.

"I have really good news." She grinned.

"Oh, yeah? What's that?" Probably something about Bryan.

"I got you a date for Friday."

Coach blew her whistle for us to gather, and it was a damn good thing. The feeling of shock could have floored me right there. I stumbled over to where Coach stood and plopped down on the grass. Sarah took a cross-legged seat next to me.

"What are you talking about?" I finally managed to ask.

"Remember? I told you he had that cute friend. And, it so happens that this said cute friend agreed to double up." She was so excited.

I couldn't even hide my annoyance.

Coach began to give us all a pep talk, so I lowered my voice to a whisper. "You didn't even ask, Sarah," I said angrily.

"That's because I'm not giving you an option," she replied, hitching her chin a bit to try to seem more convincing. "Besides, it's already set up. We're picking you up at seven."

I sighed. There was no way out of this. Arguing with Sarah was like trying to tell a brick wall to move out of the way. "Fine," I said, "but don't expect to play Dr. Hitch."

~~~

After practice, I found Emma sitting on a bench outside of school, waiting for me. It was an unusually warm day for late September, and she was wearing a plain white t-shirt instead of her usual hoodie.

Looking up from behind her book, she broke into a smile when she noticed me. "Hey," she greeted, shoving the book into her bag.

I couldn't help but smile back. "Hi," I replied. "What were you reading?"

"Oh, nothing. Just some dumb book my English teacher is making us read." She rose, tossing her bag over her shoulder. We walked out to my car in complete silence. I tried to think of something to say as I twirled my keys with my index finger.

"We need to start working on our skit," I told Emma as I backed my car out of its parking space. "I think we only have, like, two weeks."

"Yeah." Emma began digging through her bag. She pulled out the assignment sheet that Woodbridge gave us. "I think we signed up for October 17th. That's a Wednesday."

I grunted in response, scanning the main road from the school for traffic. None. "What piece are we doing again?" I asked.

"Abbott and Costello. Who's On First," she said. I glimpsed over to see her scanning the dialogue.

"What's it about?"

She read for a moment longer and finally glanced over at me with a shrug. "Baseball, I guess." She pulled out a cigarette and lit it. "It seems funny."

"So when should we start getting together to work on it?"

"We should probably start pretty soon." She shoved the sheet back into her bag. "It seems pretty long, so maybe every day after school?"

"Okay. Sure," I replied. "It'll probably take me a while to learn the lines. I'm not that great at remembering things."

She laughed, white smoke billowing from her mouth. "That's okay."

I smiled as I scanned her face. *I wish she would laugh more*, I thought to myself. "Alright," I said, snapping out of my thoughts. "So, we'll start tomorrow after school?"

"Right. It's a date." She threw me a wink as she shoved the passenger side door open and clambered out of the car. "See you tomorrow."

"Wait," I said. Her book had slipped from her bag and onto the floor of the car. "You dropped your book."

I picked it up. Glanced at the cover. *Annie On My Mind.* I'd never heard of it.

Blushing furiously, she snatched the book out of my hands and shoved it into her bag. "Th-thanks," she stuttered. "See you tomorrow."

I watched, dazed, as she slammed my door and bolted off towards her front porch. My pulse was racing.

Maybe I wasn't alone in the world. Maybe Emma was going through the same thing I was.

~~~

"I want a bite of your pizza."

I looked longingly at Kenny's lunch. I had completely forgotten to grab money in a rush to get to school on time, and was wishing I had been a few minutes late for the sake of getting a couple of dollars.

"Oh, this pizza?" Kenny took a bite off the tip, exaggerating a look of delight and sighing heavily. "Mmm, it's good."

"Shut up, I'm starving," I grumbled.

He chuckled and handed it to me. After taking a large bite, I returned it to him and snagged a couple of his fries to shove in my mouth as well. With my cheeks full, I gave him a grin. "Thanks."

Making a face, he set his pizza down and glanced over at a few rowdy football players on the other side of the courtyard.

"So, Friday," Kenny began, "do you want to go play laser tag or something? There's this sweet new place across town."

"Can't," I replied. "Sarah's dragging me on this stupid double date with her."

Kenny nearly choked on a fry. "What'd you say?"

I laughed. "A double date."

"No way," he said with a disbelieving shake of his head. "You? A date? Who is this poor guy?"

"Oh, shut up." I punched his arm from across the table. "And I don't even know him. He's a friend of Sarah's boyfriend."

Kenny broke into a grin. "So, want to make it a triple date? I can take Emma."

"You're kidding, right?"

He shook his head. "No. Would you be able to work it out?"

I stared off into space, my mind running over a thousand possible excuses. But I couldn't lie to my best friend. "I'll ask her," I said. "But no guarantees."

"Awesome." He smirked. Picked up a fry and smacked my nose with it. "You're the best friend ever. I'll totally have to work on my charm before Friday. Or, well, the lack thereof," he added with a laugh.

I tried to laugh back, but to me it seemed as strangled as I felt.

~~~

"Your house is really nice," Emma said when I was through giving her a tour of the place. Wednesday trailed behind us, tail wagging furiously as she desperately tried to get Emma's attention. She loved meeting new people.

"Thanks," I replied. "Want to just do this in the living room? My mom's at work, so we have the place to ourselves."

"Sure." Without hesitation, she collapsed on the couch and began digging through her school bag.

I stroked Wednesday's head. "Do you want something to drink? We have Coke, water, juice…" I trailed off.

She turned, blonde hair falling across her eyes. "Coke is good. Thanks."

Grabbing two sodas from the fridge, I returned to find Wednesday lying on the couch next to Emma, still attempting to earn attention by putting on her cutest face. Not that her cutest face was any different than any other face she made.

"Sorry," I said, placing both cans of Coke on the coffee table to shove Wednesday off the couch. "She can be such a whore."

"It's alright." Emma giggled as Wednesday started licking her hand.

I growled at the husky and she stalked off to lie down across the room. Sitting on the other end of the couch, I heaved a sigh.

Emma looked up. "So, who's going to be Abbott and who's going to be Costello?"

"I don't know," I said, watching her read the dialogue. *She's really cute,* I thought fleetingly. "You pick."

"Okay. How about you're Abbott? The lines aren't as long. I'm pretty good at memorizing, so I'll take Costello."

"That's fine." I pulled out my copy of the dialogue to look over the first few lines. "I guess we could just do a read through today?"

"Sure." Her green eyes flickered to my face and she smiled. I couldn't help but grin back, looking down as I ran a few fingers through my hair.

"I wish I had your hair," Emma said, drawing my eyes back to her. The corner of her mouth cricked upwards in a weak smile.

"It's a mess," I replied.

"It looks cute like that, though."

My heart skipped. I felt my face turn red.

"Thanks," I finally managed to mumble. Emma nodded, quickly turning her attention back to the paper in her hands and filling the space between us with an awkward silence. Was she blushing?

We spent the next 45 minutes reading through our lines. The dialogue wasn't too in depth. It was actually pretty funny. Even if we forgot a line, we could pretty much guess based on how repetitive the speech was.

"I'm getting a headache." Emma let herself fall back against the armrest with a groan. "Let's take a break or something."

Grateful for the suggestion, I tossed the paper to the floor and took a sip of my relatively ignored soda. My eyes trailed over Emma's relaxed frame. I couldn't help but notice the soft skin that outlined her collarbone.

Knock it off, Charlotte. I wondered if she could tell how awkward I felt.

"So, how long have you been playing soccer?" Emma closed her eyes and folded her hands over her stomach.

"I think about 10 years or so, now. I've played on the school team since middle school. Do you play any sports?"

She shook her head. "I tried dancing when I was a kid, but I'm just not cut out for something that requires that much coordination . I used to ride horses, though. But not anymore."

"Really?" I'd never met anyone who rode horses before. "Why'd you stop?"

"I'd rather not talk about it, to be honest," she said. "I shouldn't have brought it up."

Weird. Blushing, I gazed at the far wall, letting silence fall between us. I still needed to ask her about Friday. Without allowing myself to hesitate any longer, I said, "I have a question."

"Yeah?" She perked up, lowering her Coke.

"KennywantedtoknowifyouwouldgoonadatewithhimFridaynight," I blurted.

"What is this about a date?" Emma chuckled. "Geez, take a breath."

I forced a smile. Drew a deep breath. "Kenny wanted to know if you would go on a date with him Friday night. Sarah and I are doing a double date with some other guys. It would be like a triple date, I guess."

Her smile disappeared. "With Kenny?"

"Yeah." I nodded.

"Sure. I mean, I guess so."

Wednesday plodded over and started licking my hand. I turned my attention to my dog, biting my lip. "Sounds great," I lied.

I had wished harder than anything that she would say no.

<u>Seven</u>

"So, I think we should shoot for having the entire thing memorized by next Wednesday. What do you think?" Emma asked.

I brought Old Reliable to a stop in her driveway. It was nearly 9:00. We'd spent the entire night working on our skit. Well, some of the night, anyways.

"Yeah, that sounds good. And don't forget our date tomorrow." Our date. With other people.

"Who are you going with, by the way?"

"You wouldn't know him," I said, adding, "I mean, I don't even know him. He's a friend of Sarah's boyfriend. You know, the girl on my soccer team."

"Oh. Okay. Well, that's cool. Is he cute, I hope?" She waggled her eyebrows, smirking.

I looked toward Emma's front porch where the outdoor lights were still on, seemingly beckoning her inside. "I hope he's at least that much. I mean, I don't really care though. I'm not really interested in a boyfriend right now."

She nodded. I turned in time to see her lower her gaze. "I didn't figure you were the type, anyway," she said.

"What do you mean?" I felt my heartbeat quicken.

Emma tucked a lock of hair behind her ear. "I just mean that you seem independent." She paused for a moment, as though searching for the right words to say, before continuing. "It's like you don't need a man on your arm to be complete, you know? It seems like all most girls in high school care about is getting a boyfriend."

I let out an audible sigh. Emma pushed open the passenger door and hopped out, dragging her shoulder bag with her. "Hey." She stopped, dropping her bag next to the side of the car. "Do you have Instant Messenger?"

"On the computer?" Stupid question, Charlotte. Of course on the computer. "Uh, yeah. I don't get on much, though."

She pulled a piece of paper out of a binder and scribbled something before handing it to me. "Well, here's my screen name anyways. Goodnight, Charlie."

I watched her disappear into her house before looking at the piece of paper. *Shes a Dilemma.* I wondered what it meant.

~~~

As soon as I got home, I blew by an excited Wednesday and into my room to plop down in front of the computer. *She's probably not even on,* I thought as I waited for the PC to boot up.

Logging on to my instant messenger, I plugged her name into my buddy list. It immediately appeared on the bottom. She was on. My heart began to pound furiously against my ribcage. I double clicked the name to bring up the message window.

But what would I even say?

I looked at the screen for the next five minutes before finally deciding to close it. Instead of messaging her, I dragged her screen name to the very top of my buddy list and signed off.

As I went to shove my keyboard back, I noticed a piece of paper sticking out from between a couple of books on the edge of my desk. Lifting the books up, I felt anger starting to gnaw at my insides.

Dad's letter. Mom had taped it back together.

I could be too much of a chicken to message Emma, but I wasn't going to hide from Dad anymore. I pulled out my stationery.

Dear Dad, I began. *I hate you.*

~~~

"So, are you excited about the big date tonight?" Kenny asked, winking. Lancaster paced the front of the classroom, lecturing about the War of 1812.

"Shut up," I grumbled. I couldn't have been dreading it more. Not only did I have to endure Sarah, her boyfriend, and this guy I'd never even met before, but I'd also have to watch Kenny and Emma have a great time together. It was wrong, but a part of me was hoping something happened to cancel the date. World destruction, maybe? No, that wouldn't work. Sarah and Kenny would still probably want to go.

"What's this guy's name, even?" Kenny stretched across his desk, bored.

"Preston," I told him. "I think."

"Excuse me," Mrs. Lancaster stopped mid-sentence to turn toward the two of us. "Would you two like to take the stage so you can finish your conversation? Or do you mind if I continue?"

"Sorry, Mrs. L," Kenny apologized. She began speaking again with a forced smile.

I was tempted to be rude and continue talking. I couldn't go on a date if I had detention, after all. The only thing that kept me from going through with such an absurd idea was the knowledge that Emma would have to wait after school for me.

~~~

The doorbell rang.

"Are you ready?" Sarah asked when I opened the door. I returned a pained nod.

She bustled past me, making a bee-line for the bathroom. I trailed after and watched as she fixed her hair in the mirror, wondering how some girls could be so eager to impress.

"Is that what you're wearing?" Sarah asked when she turned around to see me standing in the doorway.

Jeans and a grey hooded sweatshirt. That was as dressed up as I was going to get for this. I nodded. "Is that okay with you, mom?"

Sarah shrugged, grabbing my arm to tug me along with her. "Alright, let's go then. Bryan and Preston are waiting."

I trudged out of the house after her. Sarah hopped into the passenger seat of the Suburban. That was my cue to get in the back.

"Preston." Sarah twisted her body to look at us. "This is Charlotte. Charlotte, Preston."

I smiled. He returned it.

"Nice to meet you," he said. He sounded just as excited as me.

The entire way to the movie theater, Bryan and Sarah talked animatedly in the front of the vehicle. Preston and I, on the other hand, could hardly think of two words to say to one another.

"What kind of music do you like?" he asked after nearly five minutes of silence.

Fidgeting with my seat belt strap, I leaned back against the seat cushions to look at him. He was kind of cute: short blonde hair, blue-grey eyes, pretty muscular. Typical jock.

"Alternative, mostly," I said. "You?"

"I really like classical, actually. But, some hip-hop too." He turned to look through the window.

"So, you play lacrosse?" I asked, trying to keep the conversation going for fear of an awkward silence.

"Yeah. Do you play any sports?" Turning back towards me, he ran a hand through his hair.

I nodded. "Soccer. I play on the school team."

"Senior, right?"

"Yeah." I saw Sarah swivel in her seat and mouth, *do you like him?* I threw a mocking glare at her. "So, what year are you in?" I asked Preston.

"I'm a third year sophomore. I'll be a junior when I get..." He paused, staring at the ceiling of the car as he counted in his head. "Nine more credits." He grinned at me. His teeth were really white. He must've bleached them. How metro.

When the car finally pulled to a stop, he and I were quick to jump out.

Kenny and Emma were already waiting at the front of the theater. I straightened up. Drew a deep breath. She looked so pretty.

My nerves started kicking in. Why was I more nervous about seeing Emma than Preston? This was stupid. I tried giving my arms a shake to get rid of the butterflies.

"What in the world are you doing?" Sarah was looking at me as though I was crazy.

I felt myself blush. "Uh. . ."

"Oh, never mind." Sarah grabbed my arm and began steering me towards the theater. "How do you like him?"

"He's alright." I shrugged.

"Alright? Are you kidding me?" Her eyes widened with shock. "He's gorgeous! If I wasn't dating Bryan, I'd be all over him."

"That's because you're a whore," I mumbled under my breath.

She narrowed her eyes at me. "What was that?"

"I agreed with you," I lied.

"Charlie!" Emma flashed me a grin when I reached her. She acted like she was going to hug me, but at the last second, stepped away. I felt my heart throb with disappointment. *Cut it out*, I thought to myself. *There's no reason to be jealous. You've got a cute guy. She's with your best friend. It's all good.*

Emma turned her head. Blushed. I did the same.

I zoned as everyone bought tickets. Stared at the back of Emma's blonde head. At Kenny's delighted smile. It wasn't until Preston spoke that I snapped back to reality.

"Here," he said, shoving my ticket into my hand. "You alright?"

I nodded. "Yeah. I'm good. Thanks," I said. My eyes never left her. Preston frowned.

We chose some open seats in the back. Even though we were arranged by couples, Emma made a point of sitting next to me. I smiled at her when she slid into the chair.

She leaned in so close I could feel her breath on the side of my face. "Ever heard of this movie before?"

Shaking my head, I said, "No." It was some horror movie that had received awful ratings. The only reason we were watching it was because Bryan and Preston were given choosing rights.

As soon as the movie started, Sarah and Bryan's lips were attached like magnets. I cringed. Preston glanced in my direction with a raised eyebrow. "Awkward," he mouthed.

Preston and I started picking out which characters would die at the beginning. But, as hard as I tried, I couldn't draw my attention away from Kenny and Emma. I held them in corner of my eye. Watched as Kenny inched closer. As he snaked his arm around her shoulder. As she tensed, but slowly settled against him.

Emma glimpsed over. Caught me staring. "Are you feeling alright? You're really pale."

"Yeah. Well, no. I feel kind of sick. I don't know."

She reached over. I felt the back of her hand press against my forehead. I stiffened, swallowing hard. "You don't feel hot," she whispered. Her touch lingered before finally, to my dismay, withdrawing back to her lap. My nerves still tingled beneath my skin.

I didn't speak to her for the rest of the movie.

But when I looked over to find her hand rested on top of his, my heart sank to the pit of my stomach.

~~~

Preston and I talked less on the way home than we did on the way to the theater. For some reason, he seemed more awkward and uncomfortable than when the date began. Shoving Kenny and Emma out of my mind, I tried to ask him a few questions about lacrosse and college. He only threw back monosyllabic answers.

Bryan put the car in neutral as we reached my house. Preston and I jumped out. He seemed nervous, jittery.

Was he expecting to kiss me? I began to panic.

The porch light was on. A beacon. We stopped beneath it, facing each other awkwardly. I knew Bryan and Sarah were probably watching intently, waiting to see if their little hook-up was successful.

"Look, Charlotte. I had a great time—"

"Me too," I interrupted, swallowing hard.

"But there's something I have to tell you." He looked up. I noticed how pale his skin was. He glanced towards my front door before saying, "I'm actually gay."

I was shocked. That was the last thing I expected. He was so masculine. Such a jock.

"But, the thing is, Bryan doesn't know. In fact, a lot of people don't. It would kind of ruin me, you know? With the team and all." He looked upset. I felt a pang of sympathy.

I reached out, placing a hand on his arm and smiling. "That's alright," I assured him, smile breaking into a laugh. "I was kind of wondering about the classical music thing."

He smiled. It instantly made me feel better. He opened his mouth and glanced at the car before turning back to me, his eyes troubled.

"You can kiss me," I told him, confirming what I knew he wanted to ask. "Bryan won't even know."

"Thanks, Charlotte." He let out a sigh of relief.

I met him halfway, kissing him gingerly. It lasted only a second, but I was sure it was enough to keep Bryan convinced that his all-star friend was straight.

"Give me your phone," I demanded. He looked confused, but pulled it out of his back pocket to hand to me. I plugged my phone number into his contacts list before giving it back to him.

"That's my number. Call me sometime. I'd really like to hang out again." I met his eyes, grinning. "As friends, I mean," I added, chuckling. Giving his arm a squeeze, I opened the front door to my house.

"Thank you, I will." He returned my grin. "Nice meeting you, Charlotte."

I paused with my hand on the door, taking a deep breath before turning back around. "Hey, Preston?" I called. He stopped in his tracks and whirled around to face me.

I bit my lip, feeling the blood rush to my face. Emma's face flooded my mind. "How did you know?"

His expression melted into one of understanding, a small smile etching across his features. "You just know, Charlotte," he said. "You just know."

I watched him go, my mind racing, my heart thudding.

He saw right through me. Who else could?

~~~

I shut my bedroom door quietly behind me. Drawing a sharp breath, I took a seat in my chair to log onto the internet.

Emma's name glared at me from the top of my buddy list. She was already home.

I hesitated with my mouse hovered over her name before clicking it. Typing a simple *hey*, I hit the enter key before I could even think to second guess myself.

Shes a Dilemma: Who is this?

Her font was small and bold. Green, of course.

CNHHATTRICK: Charlotte.

Shes a Dilemma: Hey!

Not knowing what to say, I typed *hey* once again. Lame.

Shes a Dilemma: Thanks 4 inviting me tonight. It was fun.

CNHHATTRICK: I didn't. Kenny did.

Shes a Dilemma: Well, u invited both of us. How'd u like ur date? He was cute.

CNHHATTRICK: He's gay.

Shes a Dilemma: LOL, he couldn't have been that bad.

CNHHATTRICK: No, I'm serious. He told me he's gay.

Shes a Dilemma: Wow.

CNHHATTRICK: Yeah. I felt bad 4 him. I think his friend kind of forced him 2 go.

Shes a Dilemma: Well at least ur still single. That's what u wanted, right?

I let my hands sit over the keyboard for a moment before answering.

CNHHATTRICK: Yeah. Sure.

CNHHATTRICK: What did u think of Kenny?

Shes a Dilemma: He's really nice.

I felt a lump work into my throat.

CNHHATTRICK: Do u like him?

Shes a Dilemma: I don't know. I mean, I just met him. But he was way sweet. I can see why he's ur best friend.

I couldn't take it anymore. I changed the subject.

CNHHATTRICK: What does ur name mean?

Shes a Dilemma: My mom always called me Dilemma. Lame, I know.

CNHHATTRICK: lol. No, that's cute.

Like you, I wanted to add. I didn't. That was Kenny's line.

Shes a Dilemma: What does urs mean?

CNHHATTRICK: My initials. And a hat trick is when u score 3 goals in 1 game.

Shes a Dilemma: Have u ever done that?

CNHHATTRICK: Only once before.

Shes a Dilemma: Ur really good.

CNHHATTRICK: How do u know?

Shes a Dilemma: I watch u play sometimes while I'm waiting.

I felt my heart start to race as though I'd just run a mile. She'd been watching me? What did that mean? I'd never seen her around the practices, aside from the one time she'd asked for a ride.

CNHHATTRICK: Really?

Shes a Dilemma: Yeah.

Shes a Dilemma: Um, I've g2g. I'll see u Monday, ok?

My once pounding heart sank into my stomach. Already? I just started talking to her.

CNHHATTRICK: Oh, ok. Nite.

Shes a Dilemma: Later.

Shes a Dilemma has logged off.

Sighing, I turned my computer off and changed into my pajamas. As I settled into bed, I could only stare at the wall, lost in thought. She watched me play? From where? And why? I imagined her sitting in an obscure place in the bleachers: hood on, iPod blaring, watching me practice without my knowledge. I couldn't help but smile into my pillow.

Eight

"What do you think about Charlotte's new boyfriend?" Mom shouted excitedly as she barreled into the living room for the hundredth time. I knew she was just trying to be friendly and all, but I hated it when she kept coming in and out to talk about pointless things.

It was late Sunday evening, and Kenny and I had decided to ride home from work together to watch a movie at my house.

"Mom!" I shrieked.

Kenny's face broke into a grin. I'd told him what Preston had admitted to me.

"He's not my boyfriend," I groaned, taking a pillow from the edge of the couch to smother my face in embarrassment.

"Sure, hon—" Mom stopped mid-sentence. "What in the world are you watching? Disgusting!" I heard her gasp and flee the room. Tossing the pillow to the floor, I looked to the television screen. A young Asian woman was seated in a chair, screaming at the top of her lungs as a blowtorch was pressed against her eye.

I turned to Kenny and we both started laughing simultaneously. Not because the scene was funny, it was gruesome actually, but because of Mom's reaction.

"Maybe we should watch horror movies all the time," I told him. He nodded in agreement.

"It's like Mom Repellant." He smirked. "Kudos to Eli Roth, for sure."

We sank into silence for the next few minutes, eyes glued to the scene as the main character came to the rescue. I had to keep turning my head away. I knew everything was fake, but the amount of gore in the movie was still pretty hard to bear.

"So, I wanted to thank you again," Kenny said. "Really. I had a lot of fun. I've never met a girl like Emma before."

Me either, I thought. I felt my body stiffen at the subject.

"I think I might ask her out again."

I raised my eyes to meet his.

"I really like her. She's sweet. Funny. Gorgeous." He waggled his eyebrows. "Did you ask what she thinks about me?"

I hesitated. "No." It wasn't a lie. I hadn't *asked*.

"Oh." He sounded disappointed.

He was my best friend. What was wrong with me? I was being so selfish. "But I think she really liked you," I said.

He flashed me a smile. "So do you think it would be worth it to ask her out again?"

I clenched my teeth. Forced a tight smile. "Yeah. Sure."

"Dude, awesome." He leaned forward. Lightly punched my shoulder. "You're the best for hooking us up."

I lowered my eyes. As much as I didn't want the two to be together, I couldn't stop it from happening.

After all, maybe if Emma developed an interest in Kenny, it'd dispel whatever it was that I felt for her.

~~~

My cleats ripped at the soft grass as I forced myself to run faster. The defender in front of me, a girl I didn't recognize, was dribbling the ball in preparation to pass it to a teammate.

I started to move to the left, but, faking her out, stole the ball with the outside of my right foot to break away down the field. I was blowing by players left and right and doing moves with my head and feet that I didn't even know I had in me.

But when I looked up, my eyes caught something that threw me completely off guard. Emma and Kenny were standing on the side lines. They weren't cheering for me. Instead, their arms were around each other, lips locked together. Kenny broke the kiss to look towards me. "Thanks again, Charlotte!" he yelled across the field.

Furious, I turned my focus back to the game. There was only one person between me and the goal now, and that was Corinne. She was bouncing back and forth on her toes, gloved hands held in front of her.

Digging my right foot into the ground, I pulled my left leg back to kick the ball as hard as I could to the corner of the net.

Corinne made a leap. Her fist struck the ball, sending it hurtling out of bounds. I missed.

I came to a stop, breathing heavily as Corinne crossed her arms and sneered at me. "You should have known you weren't going to get that one," she told me with a chuckle, glancing over towards Emma and Kenny before walking off the field.

~~~

"Charlotte Hayes!"

I nearly tumbled out of my desk in surprise. At the last second, I managed to grab the corner of my chair and haul myself back into a sitting position.

Looking up, I found myself inches from my teacher's annoyed face. Mrs. Norris was possibly one of the bitchiest teachers in the school. I had lucked out by getting her for Lit.

I noticed the huge puddle of drool on my desk and quickly swiped it away with the sleeve of my sweatshirt. I could feel the eyes of every other student in the class burning into me.

"Take your belongings and wait for me outside." She was fuming. Great.

I dejectedly grabbed my things and rose, heading across the classroom and looking towards the other students to see their gazes following my every move. A girl in the front row gave me a sympathetic smile.

I didn't even have to wait a minute before Mrs. Norris was in my face.

"Do you sleep through the rest of your classes?" She inspected me from behind her thick glasses.

"No," I answered. "I'm sorry—" I was going to try to explain, but she cut me off by shoving a piece of yellow paper in my hand.

"Detention, after school tomorrow. You can spend the rest of this class period in the Principal's office."

I felt my mouth drop. "Detention? But, I—"

"Don't even try it. I won't have any student being disrespectful in my classroom." She glared at me. "Especially when we're reading a story as complex and fascinating as *Medea*. Now, I expect—"

With a sigh, I turned and made my way to the Principal's office, not even bothering to listen to what she had to say.

~~~

In Theater, I told Emma about how I fell asleep in class and received a detention from Mrs. Norris.

"Yeah, so, I probably won't be out of detention until around six or so," I said, looking over the handout Ms. Woodbridge had given us on different blocking techniques. "I'm sure Kenny will probably give you a ride home if you don't feel like waiting."

She didn't reply, and for some reason that made me feel worse than if she had actually said something.

~~~

The next day after school, I trudged into the designated detention classroom as though I was headed to a funeral. I'd never had detention in my entire high school career, and to start now over something as silly as falling asleep in class seemed completely irrational to me.

I chose a seat in the far back and pulled out my notebooks. The white board read all the things that we couldn't do, which pretty much encompassed everything but study. I glanced around the room, taking note of the handful of other people that were there as well. I didn't know any of them, but they all seemed as though they were there on a regular basis. They laughed under their breath and threw each other notes, and when the supervisor wasn't looking they made goofy faces at his back.

I heard another person walk in and didn't even bother to look up. Probably another delinquent. I stared at the text of *Medea*, trying my hardest to understand the ancient words.

"Can I sit here?"

My head shot up in surprise. Emma was standing next to me. Confused, I nodded.

"What are you doing here?" I whispered.

"No talking!" the supervisor yelled, glaring around the room. Frowning, I pulled out a piece of paper and wrote, *what are you doing here?*

She scribbled back: *I got caught smoking in the bathroom.*

I swallowed hard, staring at her to try to read whatever was floating through her mind. She pulled out her books and began doing homework. I went back to reading *Medea*, but my gaze was drawn to her so often that I couldn't even concentrate on what the story was about.

She grabbed the torn sheet of paper off my desk and scribbled something on it before handing it back to me.

Want to practice at my house tonight? It read.

I wrote back, *Sure*, and went to place it back on her desk. It floated to the floor.

We both reached for the paper at the same time. I felt my hand graze against hers. It lingered for a moment before I drew it away. My breath lodged in my throat.

Her green eyes flickered upwards to burn into mine. Biting my lip, I looked away and straightened in my chair. I watched Emma from the corner of my eye as she pulled the paper back onto her desk and shoved it in her notebook.

For the rest of detention, it felt like the two of us went out of our way not to look in each other's directions.

~~~

"I think we're doing pretty well," Emma told me when we finished reading through our script once again. She had the entire thing memorized. I wasn't far behind.

I nodded. I was stretched out on the carpeted floor of her room on my back. She was lying on the edge of her bed, picking at a small hole in her wall.

"So, why were you smoking in the bathroom?" I asked. It had been on my mind all day. "You know that everyone who does that lands in detention."

She shifted her head to look down at me, blonde hair falling in waves across her face. "I don't know." She smirked. "What do you think?"

I shrugged. "You forgot?"

Emma exaggerated a roll of her eyes, making me chuckle. "Gee, Charlie. I thought you knew me pretty well by now."

"Do I?" I raised my eyebrows.

"Not everything, I suppose," she replied.

"Well," I met her eyes. "I'd like to."

She grew quiet. Did I say the wrong thing? I searched her face for an answer, but she looked away to glue her gaze on the wall.

After a moment, she looked back towards me and broke into a grin. I felt her press her palm against my forehead.

"I'll just transfer it all to you through osmosis, then," she joked.

Laughing, I instinctively reached up to place my hand on hers. I felt her palm loosen from my forehead as she intertwined her fingers into mine. We stayed that way for a few minutes, not talking, until we both realized what we were doing and broke away.

<u>Nine</u>

I tossed my soccer ball in my hands, scanning the bleachers for any sight of Emma. Ever since she'd told me she watched my practices, I'd been trying to find wherever it was that she hid.

"Hey, Charlotte!" Regina, one of our new midfielders, yelled from across the field. My concentration broken, I turned to see that the rest of the girls had gone for our after practice lap as instructed by Coach. Dropping the ball, I took off after and fell in behind them.

Corinne dropped back a step to run at my side. "Hey, Hayes," she said, grinning.

"Hey, Corinne," I said. She irked me. It wasn't the fact that she was gay. I think it was just that she felt like she had to flaunt it.

"Cory," she corrected. I rolled my eyes. Concentrated on keeping my breathing under control as I trailed the other girls.

"So," she began, speaking between breaths, "do you like running back here for the same reason?"

I looked over to see a suggestive smirk on her face. "No," I said, feeling myself growing defensive. "I don't."

When we finished our lap and pulled up in front of Coach, I was grateful. Corinne, or Cory, broke off to chat with a girl named Felicia and Sarah jumped over to my side. For once, I was actually happy to have Sarah start blabbing in my ear about Bryan.

"Alright, girls!" Coach brought us to her attention with a blow of her whistle. "Who knows what Saturday is?"

"Our first game!" Hannah shouted. I looked over to her and chuckled. She was a short girl with flaming red hair. An absolute hilarity. She was the type of person that just seemed to love life, and I admired her for that.

A firm expression crossed Coach's face and she placed her hands on her hips. "Right. But against who?"

"Bitchwood," Hannah added with a huge grin. The rest of the girls, including me, erupted into laughter. Even Coach couldn't help but to chuckle.

"Okay." Coach shrugged. "I guess you can call them that, but only if we win. I need you all in your best shape for Saturday, so make sure you're eating right. Tomorrow's our last practice before the game, so we'll probably scrimmage. Alright, girls. Go home."

We all broke off, chatting energetically about the game.

"So, do you think we'll win?" Sarah asked.

I shrugged. "I hope." Birchwood was a tough group. Each year, we were the top two school teams. We never knew which of us would come out ahead.

I spotted Emma across the field, waving, and broke into a grin. "Alright, Sarah. See you," I said.

Just as I was about to make my way over to Emma, I was brought to a stop by the sound of Cory's voice.

"Is that your girlfriend?" She jogged over, running a hand through her spiky hair and looking towards Emma with a smile. "She's cute, Hayes."

"She's not my girlfriend," I insisted, annoyed. "She's just a friend."

"Oh?" Cory raised an eyebrow. "What's your type, then?"

I sighed. "Cory, I'm not—" I lowered my voice to a whisper. "I'm not gay."

"Yeah, okay," she said. "Whatever you say."

"I'm not," I repeated. Instead of responding, she simply turned on her heel and trudged back to the locker room.

"I'm not," I said again, speaking only to myself. Maybe if I said it enough, it would be true.

~~~

"What'cha doin'?" Trevor, Emma's 12 year old brother, poked his head into her room, curly blonde hair bouncing around his freckled face.

Emma sighed, pausing in the middle of a line to turn her attention to her kid brother. "We're doing homework, Trev."

"That doesn't look like homework." He stepped further into the room and closed the door behind him.

I looked towards Emma, noticing the irritation that was crossing over her expression. "It's okay," I told her. "He can be here."

We continued our act. I was proud that I only looked down at the script three times to jog my memory. Trevor flopped down on Emma's bed, intrigued. When we finished, we bowed dramatically towards him.

"Bravo!" he yelled, clapping. "That was funny."

Emma and I both laughed.

"How come I don't have a class with homework this easy?" He nibbled his fingernail as he looked back and forth between us.

Emma and I both burst into a new wave of laughter. "This isn't easy homework," I said, flipping through the script to show him. "We had to memorize all of this."

His mouth dropped open. "Are you kidding me? What class is this?"

"Theater," Emma and I said at the same time.

"Remind me never to take this class." He looked pointedly at his sister before leaving the room.

Our eyes met and we laughed. I almost wished I hadn't decided to take it, but if I hadn't, I wouldn't have been sitting there with Emma.

I wouldn't have been more content than I could ever remember.

The next day, instead of turning when I should have to reach my house, I traveled straight through the neighborhood to the local park.

We both hopped out, scripts in hand, and I followed her through the gates. It was one of the nicer parks in our area, filled with trees and even a natural creek that cut straight down the middle. A man-made pond was located on the south side, spotted with mallards, geese, and other ducks.

"It's such a nice day." Emma grinned. I felt my own smile spreading across my face. She was wearing a grey argyle sweater which hugged her small frame. Her blonde hair was pulled into a loose ponytail, leaving a few locks to fall tousled around her pale cheeks.

I nodded and said, "Beautiful," but I wasn't talking about the weather.

"Alright then, Abbott," she said.

"Alright then, Costello," I mocked.

"I'll race you to that clearing?" She pointed a finger, tilting her eyebrow upwards in a challenging appearance.

"You're on." Just as the words escaped my mouth, she bolted off towards our destination. I took off after her, catching up effortlessly. I stuck my tongue out at her as I flew by, coming to a stop in the clearing and collapsing onto my knees. "I win!" I announced, turning to look towards her just as she nearly tripped over me and went flying to the side.

Giggling, I watched her roll over onto her side and unconsciously took note of the new grass stains on her jeans. She grinned back, blowing her hair out of her face.

"You only won because you have all that soccer stuff on." She pushed herself into a cross-legged position and folded her arms against her chest.

"Oh, yeah, you're right." I rolled my eyes, brushing off my sleeves. "My shorts are aerodynamic, and I actually hide batteries under my shin guards for the jet packs attached to my cleats."

"Yup." She smirked as she tossed her script to the side. "I knew you had all that stuff. See, if you didn't have your uniform, I would have definitely beat you."

We sprawled out in the grass and ran through our lines only once. I didn't have to look at my script at all.

"So, I don't think we need to really do blocking or anything," Emma told me, rolling onto her side. I was on my back, watching the multi-colored leaves wave gently above.

"I don't either," I agreed. "I mean, we can probably just pull up chairs and sit. Abbott and Costello were probably sitting, right? As baseball announcers?"

"Yeah."

She grew quiet. I turned my head to the side to see her looking back at me. I couldn't help but smile.

"Kenny asked me out again," she finally said.

My heart skipped a beat. "Yeah? What'd you say?" I tried to sound casual, but inside, I was pleading for her to tell me she said no.

"He wants me to go with him to see your game on Saturday and then get lunch afterwards. I said yes."

I looked at the side of her face. A piece of hair was caught in the corner of her mouth, and I fought the urge to push it away for her. "Oh."

Her head tilted back towards me, worry in her eyes. "That's okay, right? I mean, I felt bad saying no. He's a really sweet guy. And I want to see your game, so it's kind of a ride there."

I forced a fake smile. "Oh, yeah. That's cool. You and Kenny are kind of cute together, I guess."

She raised her hand to wrap a lock of blonde around her finger. "It's not like we're together, Charlie. It's not even a date, really. Just hanging out."

"I know." I swallowed hard as I pushed myself up, leaving my hands out behind me for balance. "He really likes you, you know."

She stared at me, as if taking it in. Then, out of nowhere, her right hand flew out from behind her to fling grass right in my face.

"I'm declaring war, Hayes." She laughed, scrambling to her feet to take off at a run. I grinned as I leapt to my feet, grabbing a few dead leaves in my hand to throw at her back when I was a few strides away.

We spent the next few minutes tossing leaves on one another and laughing hysterically before collapsing onto the ground side-by-side and giggling like a couple of children. And I realized, suddenly, that I was just like a kid around Emma. I forgot words, confused emotions. I felt like I was stumbling through complete and void darkness and she was the only thing that could guide me.

~~~

I wondered if anyone else was feeling the same butterflies that I was.

It was the day of the big game, and I couldn't tell if it was first game jitters or the knowledge that Emma and Kenny were sitting somewhere in the bleachers, ready to watch my every grandeur and my every mistake.

"Okay, girls," Coach called. We all gathered in a circle around her. "Don't forget, this is Bitchwood we're playing." Her comment sparked nervous laughter throughout the group. Hannah's was the loudest. "Play hard, play fair."

We all stuck our hands together, shouting "Go Grizzlies!" before jogging out to the field to get into our positions. The second string girls simply walked over to the sideline, plopping down among a forest of water bottles and bags.

Sarah and I high-fived each other in the middle of the field before I took my respective left side. She floated over to the right.

I did a jig in place to try to keep the butterflies at bay, but to no avail. Rebecca, our center forward, and a player from Birchwood did a coin flip for possession of the ball. Birchwood took it.

As soon as their forward made the first kick, I was off like a rocket, the ball my target. Overzealous, I tried to steal the ball from one of their forwards, but the other girl did a swift maneuver to the side which nearly sent me hurtling over.

Come on, Charlotte, I told myself. *Emma's watching you.*

I back peddled for a moment to get my gusto back, shaking my head before retreating to the side. Our defenders managed to salvage the ball and sent it flying towards Rebecca, who began hurtling down the center of the field. Sarah and I ran parallel to her, waiting for whenever she needed to forfeit the ball to one of us.

Which came pretty quickly. Just as a Birchwood midfielder made a strike for the ball, Rebecca passed it to me. Taking it with the outside of my foot, I made my way for the goal, flying by a few girls who tried to take the ball back into Birchwood possession.

Instead of trying to score for myself, I kicked the ball to Sarah, who took her own shot. A miss to the outside of the goal post. I shook my head, wondering if I could have made it.

The ball went back and forth down the field for the first fifteen minutes of the game before Birchwood finally managed to hit the net. Our team groaned, and, sulking, we retreated back to our positions. Coach Reynolds took a moment to make a few substitutions; Sarah and I remained on the field, and Rebecca was replaced with Miranda, a new girl.

Vengeful, Sarah and I took matters into our own hands: as soon as she got the ball, we were off down the center of the field, passing the ball strategically between the two of us. It wasn't long before we found that there was no one between us and the goal. Sarah passed the ball to me. I sent the ball soaring past the Birchwood goalie's hands and into the corner of the net.

Score!

Our team erupted into cheers. Sarah and I were immediately overwhelmed by our team-mates tackling us with congratulations.

Looking up into the bleachers, I spotted Emma and Kenny at the very top. Kenny was grinning from side to side. I couldn't help but think it had more to do with Emma than my goal. Emma waved when she saw me looking. I stupidly returned a rock-on sign.

Coach Reynolds pulled Sarah and me out of the game for the rest of the half. Grateful for the break, I drank nearly half of my water bottle, watching the game and periodically glancing up at Emma and Kenny. They both seemed so into the game, cheering wildly and doing a dance every time Hidden Springs took the ball.

I wished desperately that I was the one dancing in a circle with Emma.

~~~

In the second half, Sarah, Rebecca, and I were placed back into the game. We attacked full force. After about ten minutes Rebecca was able to successfully score with an assist from Sarah. Even so, our glory was short-lived when Birchwood scored again within a matter of minutes.

The ball was thrown back and forth between our players and theirs. There were a ton of shots, but no goals.

Birchwood called a time-out. Our team groaned. They were just trying to buy themselves time.

The whistle blew to restart the game. I kicked grass as I wandered back onto the left side of the field and looked up to the bleachers to see Emma and Kenny. His hand was resting on her shoulder, which made my stomach curl. She waved hysterically when she saw me looking. I simply looked away to spit on the ground.

As soon as the ball was back in play, I was drawn to it like a magnet. After a small duel, I was able to break away to bolt down the side of the field. Rebecca called for me to pass to her, but I obstinately pressed on until I was one-on-one with the Birchwood goalie. As I dug my cleats into the ground, I slammed the ball into the back of the net.

Breathing hard, I turned to look back up at the bleachers. Kenny's hand was no longer on Emma's shoulder but instead waving above his head. Emma celebrated with a small jig at his side. I turned away, scuffing the ground with my shoe and ignoring the congratulations.

There was only a minute left in the game and I knew I had to score again. As soon as the Birchwood center made a pass to their right wing, I was on top of the ball. I used all the force in my body to hurl myself through midfielders and defenders, passing the ball only briefly to Sarah when I ran into a mess with a girl nearly half a foot taller than me.

When she passed the ball back, I was directly in front of the goal. I drew my foot back, ready for the strike.

But instead of meeting the soft flesh of the ball, my cleat met grass and dirt and I tripped. I had missed. It was my chance to shine and I had completely screwed up.

The goalkeeper scooped the slowly rolling ball into her arms and cracked up laughing. I felt my face turn red.

"Way to miss, loser," she sneered. It took a lot not to just punch her in her face and take a red card from the referee.

We didn't have time for any more plays in the game. Not even five seconds after being back in play, the whistle blew to end the game. We'd won, 3-2, but I still felt like a failure. I jogged over to the sideline with Sarah at my heels, who kept patting me on the back in reassurance. I ignored her. With the back of my hand, I wiped the sweat from my forehead and gathered my belongings as I listened to Reynolds congratulate us and tell us how proud she was that we won our first game of the season, especially against Birchwood.

"Nice game," Rebecca said after the coach's speech was finished. She congratulated me with a hug. "You still won the game for us, regardless of that last shot."

I shrugged, wiping my eyes with my hand as Emma and Kenny approached. They were both wearing the biggest grins imaginable. I couldn't even seem to muster a smile.

"You were awesome," Kenny said, throwing a punch to my shoulder. I frowned, pulling away.

Emma folded her arms across her chest, smiling. "So, was that a hat trick?" She kicked at a random soccer ball.

"No," I said. "It would have been if I hadn't screwed up the last shot."

"That doesn't matter. You were amazing," she said. I looked away.

"So, we're going to go get lunch. Do you want to come? I'm buying. You totally deserve it," Kenny offered.

"No," I replied, shaking my head and throwing my Adidas bag over my shoulder. "I don't want to intrude."

"You wouldn't be," Emma tried to explain, but I was already walking away.

~~~

"How was your game, sweetie?" Mom asked as soon as she got home from work. She tried to dance her way past Wednesday, who was whining like she hadn't seen Mom in forever.

"It was fine," I said. I was sitting on the couch staring at the ceiling, tossing my soccer ball up and down. "We won."

I could sense the enthusiasm from the hallway. She burst into the living room, grinning.

"Did you score?"

"Yeah. Twice."

"Wow, honey!" She leaned down and gave me a hug. "Are you alright? You don't really seem too happy about it."

"I've just got other things on my mind," I said, tossing the ball into the air once more to catch it and let it fall to the ground beside the couch.

She ran a few fingers through my hair. I turned my head away, cringing jokingly.

"Boy stuff?" she asked.

I sighed, looking at the black television screen and listening to our grandfather clock tick for a few seconds. "I guess you could say that."

I wanted to tell her about the letter I sent to Dad. I wanted to tell her about Emma. About a lot of things.

But I couldn't.

~~~

Shes a Dilemma: Hey. Congrats again on the game!

I saw her instant message pop up as soon as I logged onto my computer. Wednesday sat next to me, wagging her tail as she nudged me with her muzzle.

Shes a Dilemma: R u there?

Don't be a bitch, I scolded myself as I started typing a response.

CNHHATTRICK: Yeah.

Shes a Dilemma: Ur really awesome. U definitely won the game 4 Hidden Springs.

CNHHATTRICK: I guess so.

Shes a Dilemma: U should have joined us 4 lunch.

I clicked away from the message for a moment to log into my e-mail box. Nothing new that wasn't spam.

Shes a Dilemma: Kenny is a really nice guy.
CNHHATTRICK: Do u like him?
Shes a Dilemma: I don't know. Should I?
CNHHATTRICK: I don't know.
Shes a Dilemma: R u okay?
CNHHATTRICK: I'm fine.
Shes a Dilemma: U really were amazing today.
CNHHATTRICK: Thanks.
Shes a Dilemma: I was really impressed.
CNHHATTRICK: I'm gonna go. TTYL.
Shes a Dilemma: Oh, okay. Goodnight.

I logged off and climbed into bed. Yet, even though I was exhausted from the game, I found it impossible to sleep with images of Kenny and Emma together running through my mind.

<u>Ten</u>

"Oh my God, Charlie, stop!"

I slammed on my brakes, frightened, adrenaline racing through my veins. The person behind me had to swerve to miss rear-ending me and flipped me off as they sped by.

My heart pounded against my chest. I looked towards Emma to find her pointing at a store in a shopping center. "What?" I asked.

"Look!" She tugged my sleeve. My gaze followed where she was indicating.

"You nearly got me in an accident over a hat store?" I was peeved.

"Can we go? Please?"

"Emma, we need to practice."

Her eyes were pleading. "Just for a minute?"

I sighed. Pulling my car into the parking lot, I stopped in front of the store.

She leapt out of the car before I even had a chance to turn it off. Still grumbling, I got out and followed her.

As confused and irritated as I was, I couldn't help but realize I had never noticed the store in all my years of living in Hidden Springs.

Emma bumped my shoulder gently, lifting her head to scan the store windows. After pausing briefly to look at the display, the two of us entered the store.

The walls were lined with hats. There were visors, ball caps, and fedoras. Reds, blues, whites, greens. Every color and style imaginable. Emma floated over to the wall to snatch a top hat off a hook and pop it onto her head. She whirled towards me with a giggle, striking a pose with her hands on her hips. "How do I look? Gentlemanly?"

"You look cute," I told her, crossing my arms.

She plucked it off her head and placed it gently back on the hook before grabbing the gray fedora next to it. Sliding it on, she posed once more, this time throwing a made up gang sign out in front of her. I chuckled, searching her face. Her hair billowed in waves from the sides of the hat, which was so large on her that it fell down over her forehead and nearly shielded her eyes. So cute.

"Do I look gangster in this?" She smirked.

I stood for a long moment, hugging my chest a little tighter as my smile faded. She dropped her stance, tilting her head to the side in an attempt to look at me from beneath the large gray hat.

"You okay, Charlie?"

"Yeah," I replied, tightening my lips. "I just—" I paused. I didn't want to lose her. I didn't want to tell her that.

Emma began to smile slowly. There were a few other people in the store, but Emma didn't seem to care. Wrapping her arms around my shoulders, she pulled me into a tight embrace. The brim of the fedora pressed into my forehead, but I was only conscious of her body against mine and the feeling of my heart dropping into my stomach. She pulled away, leaving her hand wrapped around my fingers.

"You're an amazing friend," she said, plucking the fedora from her head to toss onto mine. It sat awkwardly on my head, so I pulled my hair from its ponytail to let it sink down over my forehead. It was much too large for me, too. "Really," she added. I felt her hand give mine a small squeeze before releasing it.

I watched as Emma resumed trying on every hat she could reach, posing differently with each one. She was like a kid in a candy shop, not caring who turned a head to stare at her. I wished I had a camera to take a picture of her. To capture the moment.

To freeze-frame the happiness that swelled inside of me when I was with her.

~~~

As I pulled into the driveway, I was surprised to see that Mom's red SUV was in its usual spot. For the first time, she'd actually be home while Emma and I were working on our dialogue.

As soon as I opened the door, Mom was bustling out of the kitchen to greet me.

"Hey, honey, how—"

She stopped speaking when she saw Emma, smiling slowly. I could tell she was trying to figure out whether or not she'd met her before. "Oh, hello."

I dropped my bags next to the door. "Mom, this is Emma Pearson. Emma, this is my mom."

"Nice to meet you," Mom said. She was smiling, but I could see the skeptical look in her eyes. She was annoyed. "Charlotte, can I talk to you in the kitchen for a second?"

"Yeah, sure," I said. "Emma, I'll meet you in my bedroom."

As she disappeared into the other room, I followed Mom into the kitchen.

"How long has she been coming over here?" Mom spit out. "You know how I feel about you bringing random people over. Especially some girl I've never met before."

"She's not some random girl," I said. "Emma's in my Theater class. We have to do this skit together on Wednesday."

She glared at me. "You should have told me," she said. "I just don't like you bringing strange girls home when I'm not here."

"I know, Mom," I replied. "Sorry."

Just as I turned away to grab a few sodas from the fridge, she said, "She doesn't need to be in the bedroom. I'd prefer if you two practiced in the living room."

"What? You're kidding me, right?"

"Do I look like I'm kidding?" No. She didn't. She was shooting daggers at me with her eyes.

Furious, I snatched the sodas off the refrigerator shelf and stormed out of the kitchen. Who did she think she was?

And what did she think Emma and I were doing that I couldn't practice in my room? Could she read me like Preston did?

The thought of it made me so sick to my stomach that, as much as I wanted to spend time with Emma, I had to end our practice early.

~~~

Tuesday was our final get together before our performance on Wednesday. After having watched a couple other pairs go during class, we were feeling pretty confident. Others didn't seem to have memorized their lines as well as we had, and some definitely hadn't gotten along.

As soon as we walked into her room for our last practice, we began delivering our lines, and practiced without stopping for over an hour. I could tell she was just as nervous as I was about our upcoming skit in front of the entire class.

"Look, I wanted to let you know that Kenny asked if I would be his girlfriend," Emma said when we'd finally decided to take our break.

"What?" My head snapped up. "Really?"

"I told him I wouldn't say yes unless it was okay with you. I mean, you are his best friend and all. I feel like I should ask your permission."

It's not okay, I wanted to scream. I suddenly felt nauseous. "Go for it," I mumbled. "It's not my call. It's yours."

She averted her eyes away from mine. "Okay. Are you sure?"

No. "Yes." I hesitated before asking, "Are you?"

"I mean, there's somebody else I like, but Kenny's a nice guy." She shrugged. I was confused.

"But, if there's someone else you like—"

"It couldn't happen in a million years," she interrupted.

"Oh." I didn't want to probe further. I didn't want to know about all the guys she was crushing on. It hurt.

We grew silent.

It wasn't until I felt her hand on my thigh that my attention snapped back to her. My mouth went dry.

"Charlie, I want to let you know..." she trailed off. Her green eyes burned into mine.

I had to force myself to speak. My heart was running a marathon. "W-what?"

"You're a really good friend."

She leaned forward. Hugged me. I felt myself melt into her. What had I expected her to say? That she liked me?

Just because I had feelings for her didn't mean she felt the same. Just because I wasn't normal didn't mean everyone else wasn't.

Suddenly, Emma pulled away. Stood. "Maybe you should go. I think we've practiced enough."

I studied the side of her face, trying desperately to find any answer it may provide. There was nothing. She didn't look back over. With a sigh, I grabbed my belongings. "See you, then." I said, opening her bedroom door.

"Wait," I heard her say. I turned, hopeful.

"Don't forget your lines overnight," she said after a moment, mouth twitching into a weak smile.

I couldn't get over the feeling that she wanted to say something else.

~~~

When I got home, I was immediately drawn to my computer.

Her name didn't appear at the top of my buddy list. I sifted through my friends, thinking maybe I dragged her somewhere else. But it wasn't anywhere. She wasn't on.

As I curled up in bed, a charge was surging throughout my body. I was pretty sure I could feel my brain battling emotions with my heart. What did I want?

What did *she* want?

<u>Eleven</u>

My stomach was doing somersaults inside of me throughout the entire day. I'd taken Theater to get over my stage fright, and yet somehow it felt oddly enhanced.

By the time I made it to class, I felt like I had the shakes. I took my usual seat next to Emma and cowered in my sweatshirt as I waited for class to begin. She looked like she was feeling about the same. Her face was paler than I'd ever seen it.

"I hope I don't forget my lines," I said. I shoved my hair out of my eyes, stomping my feet to try to get my nerves to stop twitching.

"I hope I don't throw up," she replied. My eyes skimmed over her body. I felt bad for not dressing up. She was actually wearing a nice black turtleneck and a pair of khaki slacks. I, on the other hand, was wearing a grubby Hollister sweatshirt and some jeans with holes in the knees. What was I thinking? I was underdressed. It made me more nervous, if possible.

Woodbridge called attendance before the entire class flooded out to the auditorium. There were three groups scheduled to go including Emma and me.

"Who wants to go first?" Woodbridge asked.

"Do you want to get it out of the way?" Emma asked. I nodded. "Yes please."

"We'll go first, Ms. Woodbridge." Emma raised her hand tentatively. Woodbridge acknowledged us with a smile, motioning us to the stage.

Before we rose from our seats in the auditorium, Emma reached over and took my hand to give it a squeeze. "We'll do fine," she told me, holding onto my hand for a moment before dropping it. For some reason, I suddenly felt the same way.

The two of us took the stage and drew our chairs up side-by-side like we'd been practicing. We started by introducing ourselves and the name of our skit, *Who's on First* by Abbott and Costello. Although I tried to keep my voice steady, I couldn't help but stutter.

We started off a bit awkwardly. I stumbled through quite a few of my lines. Emma kept having to stop and think. But by the time we were halfway through, we were flowing as though the two of us were practicing in my room by ourselves. Our classmates were even laughing. When we finished, we were both feeling pretty good. Rising, Emma did a small curtsy for everyone. I bowed dramatically.

"I think we did alright," Emma whispered to me once we were back in our seats and the other pair had taken the stage. They looked about the same way we felt when we were about to start our own dialogue.

I nodded, eyes flickering towards her. She wasn't so pale anymore. Her face was even somewhat flushed. Probably from the feeling of being in the spotlight. Smiling, I leaned back in my seat and spent the rest of the class picking at the threaded holes in my jeans, glad that our hard work finally paid off.

~~~

Emma met me on the field after soccer practice. As we walked to the car, we argued about our grade. She thought we got an "A", but I voted for a "B" since I stuttered so much.

She shrugged, nudging me with her shoulder as we walked. "The stuttering was a cute touch," she said, kicking at a few rocks that scattered the gravel parking lot.

"No it wasn't." I laughed, tilting my head to the side as I shifted my Adidas bag on my shoulder. "Besides, I didn't even dress up. You did."

"It wasn't a requirement, though," she pointed out. "I actually just wore this because I forgot to do laundry and didn't have much else."

I looked over at her, reaching up to tug my hair out of its ponytail. I wanted to tell her that she looked gorgeous no matter what she was wearing, but I didn't.

"Kenny told you about his Halloween party, right?" Stupid question. Of course he did. They were dating.

"Yeah," she said. "Are you going?"

Kenny would kill me if I didn't go to his party. "Yeah, of course."

The two of us grew quiet once again. We trudged quietly across the gravel, Emma kicking at rocks and me dodging the ones that shot out to the side of her.

"I'm going to miss hanging out so much," I said finally when we reached my car. I tossed my bags inside.

Emma jumped into the passenger seat and slamming the car door as I did the same. "Why can't we still hang out so much? I mean, I am dating your best friend."

I turned the ignition of my car and it roared to life. As I made my way through the school parking lot's natural maze of vehicles, I felt myself going slower than usual.

"We can, I guess. If you want to," I replied, shooting out of the school drive to make it onto the main road before the light changed.

"Of course I do. Want to do something tonight? We can celebrate the end of our skit," she grinned at me, but I didn't return it. I actually kind of wished our skit would have taken more time. I enjoyed spending my evenings with her. "I don't think my dad is home," she added.

"Okay," I said, "but can I change first, and then head over?"

I was glad when she agreed. Practice was especially rough. I felt completely disgusting. And, for whatever reason, I felt the impulse to look nice for Emma.

~~~

Mom wasn't at the Psycho-Dome.

"Hey, Charlotte!" she called from her bedroom. I walked in to see her lying in bed with a blanket over her body, Wednesday at her ankles.

"Hey, Mom," I said.

"How did your little project go today?" She called it a project. I don't think she really even remembered what class it was for.

"It went well," I told her. "I was pretty nervous."

She chuckled. "I can imagine. I was never able to get up on the stage at my high school, even though a few of my friends tried to get me to try out for the school play a couple of times."

Wow, maybe she did remember. Impressive.

"So, I was thinking. Do you want to go out to dinner tonight? I have the entire night off for once." Until her little beeper went off and she had to book it to the Psycho-Dome, that was.

"I would love to, Mom," I began, frowning, "but I told Emma I'd hang out with her. I was getting ready to head over there now." I felt terrible. It was rare that she and I got to do anything together, but I had already told Emma we could do something.

"Oh, alright. Well, another time then," she said. "Her parents are going to be there, right?"

"Yeah, of course." I had to turn my face away from her, not wanting her to see through my lie.

I dashed off to my room to change. I struggled to do something with my hair, but it fell in the same straight, boring manner it usually did no matter what I tried to do. And my face, despite whatever different make-up technique I attempted, looked exactly the same. Giving up, I told Mom bye and put Old Reliable back into action to head to Emma's.

When I pulled into her driveway, I sighed with relief when I saw that her father still wasn't home. Emma really wasn't lying when she said he wouldn't be there. After all, she did tell me that he sometimes liked to work overtime for a few extra bucks.

Trevor was there, though. He answered the door in his Pikachu pajamas and shouted for Emma before disappearing back into their living room to resume watching what sounded like Cartoon Network.

I stepped into their house and shut the door quietly behind me as Emma emerged from their kitchen, brandishing a smile. "Geez, did you take long enough?" She motioned for me to follow her to her room.

I shrugged. "My mom was home. You know how it is, they ask a million questions." I immediately cringed at my own words. *Wrong thing to say, Charlotte.* Thank goodness Emma either didn't hear or just didn't acknowledge it. "I just had to change," I added.

"You mean, you didn't want to wear your cute little soccer outfit?" she said with a grin. I felt a blush creep into my cheeks as I sat down on her bed, fingers seeking a frayed spot on her white down comforter to play with.

"What do you want to do?" she questioned as she sat down next to me. "That seems kind of weird, huh?" she added with a chuckle. "I mean, we usually just practice."

I returned a weak laugh. "Anything," I told her, not really able to contribute, because I really didn't care what we did. I was just happy to spend time with her.

"Well, we could watch a movie," she said, motioning to her seemingly endless DVD collection. "Or play a game, or something."

I shrugged. "I dunno," I said. "A movie is good, I guess." A movie would be less awkward. There would be other people's voices to fill the void that seemed to spread between us when we were together.

"Okay," she hopped off the bed, crouching onto her knees in front of her DVD case. "What do you want to see, then? Comedy, romance, drama, more comedy." She listed a few genres. "Sorry, I don't have anything horror. I don't usually like the gory stuff," she turned to me, making a disgusted face that caused my stomach to flutter. *How can she do that to me?*

"Anything," I said. "You pick."

"Alright." Her finger floated across the movies to try to pick one. "How about 50 First Dates? I love this movie."

"I've never seen it," I told her.

"Well, you'll like it," she said. I watched as she pulled the disc from the box and slipped it into her DVD player. On the menu screen, I noticed that the movie starred Drew Barrymore and Adam Sandler. I liked Drew Barrymore.

As the movie started, she kicked off her shoes and jumped onto the bed to lie on her stomach. Moving two pillows to the foot of her bed, she rested her head on one and threw a blanket over her body. I stayed sitting at the edge of the bed, hesitant.

"You can lay here, too," she told me, pushing her other pillow a bit more towards me in an attempt to reinforce her statement.

I pondered her proposal for a moment before removing my shoes and climbing onto her bed to lie on my stomach beside her. I found myself trying to put space between the two of us, and for that reason I was nearly hanging halfway off her full-sized bed. I crossed my arms on the pillow in front of me and rested my chin on my hands.

I glanced over to Emma. Her hair splayed all over the place, the blonde making a stark contrast with the bright white of the pillow's fabric. Up close, her freckles seemed to stand out more than ever, as did the vibrant hue of her eyes.

"What?" she asked, making me realize that I'd been staring.

"Oh, nothing," I said, feeling as though my cheeks had to be burning the brightest shade of crimson possible. "I just." I tried to think of the right words, which is hard when you can't really think at all. "I think you're really cute."

A small smile etched across her features. "Me too," she said, before quickly adding, "I mean, I think you're pretty, too."

"Yeah, pretty weird," I joked.

She shook her head against the pillow, eyes flickering to the television screen briefly before falling back on me. "I don't think you're weird," she told me, taking the edge of her blanket and throwing it over my back.

The two of us turned our attention to the movie. I tried my hardest to concentrate on the plot, but I couldn't seem to with the knowledge that Emma was only a couple of inches away. I felt myself going out of my way not to touch her. Every time she shifted, I moved a little bit as well.

After a few moments, I managed to focus my energy on the movie. It was actually pretty cute. Adam Sandler was trying desperately to get the attention of a girl who had only a day-long memory. *That must suck*, I thought, *falling in love with a girl who can't even remember your name the next day, much less that she fell in love with you, too.*

After about half an hour, Emma slid out of the bed to stand. "I'm going to go get something to drink. Do you want anything?"

"Just some water is fine."

I watched her disappear from her room. Her hair was messy from being against the pillow. It made me smirk.

I glanced around her room while she was gone, taking note of the many pictures that dotted her desk and wall. Most were of Emma and her mother. They looked alike. Their hair was the same bright shade of blonde, eyes the same color. A few other pictures featured the family at Disney World, the Grand Canyon, or sprawled across the beach with huge smiles on their faces. The entire family looked so happy when Mrs. Pearson was alive.

I looked down. Something partially shoved under the bed caught my attention.

I reached down, pulling it out. It was the book she'd been reading. *Keeping You A Secret.* I flipped it over and studied the back, drawing a shaky breath.

It was about two girls falling in love.

The door creaked. Heart pounding, I shoved the book back under the bed and acted like I'd been staring at the photographs the entire time.

Emma handed me a glass of water and set her own on the floor next to her side of the bed.

I took a sip of my water and placed it on the floor just like she did. As she shimmied back under the blanket, she seemed closer than before. I could feel the fabric of her sweater touching mine. I bit my lip, trying to dispel the feeling that washed over my body. It was like an electric shock was sent through my nervous system every time she was close.

"I'm glad I have you to relate to," she said. I looked at her, feeling my face blanch. Oh, God. She'd seen me looking at her book. "It's nice to have someone understand what it's like to lose a parent."

I'd stopped breathing and hadn't even noticed. Struggling to recover my composure, I said, "It's not the same, though. Your mom was taken. My dad chose to leave."

"Yeah, I guess you're right." Her gaze looked faraway. "It does make it easier to live in this shithole, though."

"Connecticut's not that bad," I said.

"I like it fine," she said, resting her head to the side again to look into my face. "I'm actually kind of glad that we moved here. If I hadn't, I wouldn't have met you."

As soon as the words escaped her mouth I felt as though a lump had worked its way into my throat. I didn't say anything, and instead turned my attention back to the movie.

She shifted. Her elbow grazed my shoulder. I felt as though my nerves had gotten the best of me. My entire body was quivering. I willed it to stop so hard that my spine hurt, but it didn't.

"Are you cold or something?" she asked, tossing the blanket onto my body a bit more. "I have more blankets."

"N-no," I stuttered, bunching up my pillow to relax my chin against the soft fabric. "I mean, yes, a little," I lied.

She started to get up, but I reached out to grab her wrist. "No, it's okay. Don't go." I told her. Confused, she settled back into the bed.

We both turned our eyes back to the television screen. I didn't even bother trying to follow anymore. My attention span was about as long as a goldfish's, my head completely overwhelmed with thoughts other than what the movie was presenting.

Emma shifted next to me again. In the next moment, I felt her hand grazing mine. I tried desperately to focus on the hazy objects that moved across the screen. It was impossible. Her fingers played over my palm. My entire body was on fire. I didn't know what to do in the least. I was too nervous to make any sort of movement. Paralyzed.

I was finally able to tug my eyes towards her. She was looking back at me. When my eyes met hers a small smile played at the corner of her lips. I could feel her fingers tracing over the soft skin of my wrist, dancing against my limp fingers.

"Emma," I said. I wondered if she could hear my heartbeat. It drummed mercilessly against my ribcage, filling my ears with the most unbearable pounding imaginable.

I'm not sure who moved first, but before I realized what was happening, my lips were touching hers and we were kissing tentatively. Her mouth was soft and delicate as it moved against mine. I could faintly taste the cigarette that lingered on her breath, but didn't care. My heart was racing, electricity surging through my body.

I knew it was wrong. She was my best friend's girlfriend.

I didn't care.

Twelve

I didn't want to stop. I wanted to stay in the moment, to keep our lips together. But we couldn't.

We broke away slowly. I opened my eyes. Hers were still shut. My breath was caught in my throat.

Emma's eyes flickered open. They were filled with so much intensity that it was impossible for me to read what she was feeling. She withdrew her hand from mine. She opened her mouth as if she wanted to say something, but nothing came out. I felt the same way. I wanted to take her hands and kiss her again. I wanted to do anything to bring us back to that moment. Instead, I scrambled to my feet.

"I think I should go," I said. I slipped my shoes onto my feet and nearly knocked over my glass of water in the process.

Emma shoved herself onto her knees, ripping the blanket from her back and tossing it to the floor.

Wait," she begged.

"I-- I…" I stuttered, trying to think through everything that was happening. This was wrong on so many levels. "I can't stay. I've got to go."

Before she could offer another word, I was bolting from her room and out the front door into my vehicle. Part of me was yearning to stay, but the winning side was telling me to go. I kicked my Probe into reverse, my mind spinning as I made my way home. Everything was a blur. I couldn't even remember making the right turns or even acknowledging stop signs.

All I could do was rewind the kiss in my mind. Her hand caressing my palm, her lips touching mine. The entire thing was like a dream to me. Everything felt so right, which was the scary part. What we'd done was, by all standards, wrong.

"Hey, honey," Mom called from the kitchen when she heard the front door slam. "I made lasagna for dinner. Just took it out of the oven."

"I'm not hungry," I said, making a move for my room. It wasn't fast enough. She burst from the kitchen.

"What's wrong?" she asked. I swallowed hard, hoping she couldn't read me, praying she couldn't catch the scene that was on constant replay in my mind. "You're really pale."

"I just don't feel that great right now." I shook my head. "I think I'm just going to go to bed."

"Oh, okay," she said, looking worried. "Well, let me know if I can get you anything."

You can't possibly get me what I need, I thought as I quietly shut the door to my room.

Instead of changing into my pajamas, I sat down in my computer chair to log onto the internet. *Shes a Dilemma* appeared on the top of my buddy list.

I waited for a moment, wondering if I should maybe message her and say something. But what could I possibly say? Sorry we kissed and I left?

Shes a Dilemma: R u there?

Should I respond? It was obvious that I was there, considering I had just signed on. I shouldn't be a bitch. I *couldn't*. I was drawn to her like a moth to a flame. I felt my heart beating in my chest like I'd just played an entire soccer match.

CNHHATTRICK: Yes.

Shes a Dilemma: My dad just caught Trevor watching porn on tv. He's in huge trouble. Haha.

I felt a sigh of relief escape my mouth. She wasn't going to talk about it, which was good, because I didn't think I even knew how to approach what happened.

CNHHATTRICK: That's funny.

I wanted to tell her I liked her. I wanted to tell her I liked kissing her. I couldn't.

Shes a Dilemma: Have you thought about the party yet?
CNHHATTRICK: What about it?

Shes a Dilemma: What ur going 2 be?
CNHHATTRICK: No
Shes a Dilemma: Me either.
Shes a Dilemma: Hey, I've gotta go. Kenny's coming over 4 a little bit.

Kenny. Her boyfriend.

My best friend.

Shes a Dilemma: I'll talk 2 u later, Charlie.
Shes a Dilemma has logged off.

I hesitated at the computer, wishing she would sign back on. Wishing I could rewind time. Letting the kiss replay a thousand times in my mind.

~~~

I floated through the next day of school as though my entire life was one long dream. I felt different, somehow. New. It was amazing, but at the same time, scary.

Except whenever I saw Kenny. It was as if the betrayal was dormant until he came around. Then it would flare up, vicious and buzzing and endlessly screaming in my head, *Traitor! Traitor!*

By the time I reached Theater, I was more nervous and jittery than the day of our presentation. Taking my usual seat next to Emma, I pulled my notebooks from my bag to set on my desk. She was doodling in her notebook. I looked over to see the sketches were weird interpretation of everyday animals.

Picking up my own pen, I reached onto her desk to sketch a pair of long fangs on the grinning raccoon she just drew.

"Hey!" she said, raising her eyes to glare at me. "He was supposed to be nice."

I shrugged, putting on my most mischievous smile as I brought my pen to my mouth, blowing at the tip as though it was a smoking gun. "Well, now he's a vampire raccoon."

I twirled my pen in my fingers again before reaching once more over to her notebook.

"I don't think so." She grabbed my hand in a defensive movement. As soon as she realized what she was doing, she pulled her hand back to her side as though she'd just touched a hot burner. I did the same, swallowing hard as I dropped my pen on my desk and straightened up in my chair.

For the rest of the class, every movement was completely awkward. We went out of our way not to touch each other, not to look at each other. Instead of talking about it, we'd come to deny it.

And I was quickly finding out that denial was like a tumor, spreading and creeping its way into life until it consumed everything.

~~~

Our entire ride home was awkward. We both made small talk and joked about stupid things. It only seemed to make us more on edge.

"Kenny wants to have matching costumes," Emma said.

I winced. I had completely forgotten about his Halloween party.

I turned to look at her as I weaved my way in and out of lanes to avoid traffic. "What do you mean?"

"Like, a couple thing, I guess," she said.

"Oh," was all I could think to reply with. The couple thing. The Kenny and Emma thing.

There was a lull in our conversation, where tension and sadness seemed to work into the silence between us like a thick cloud.

To my relief, Emma finally broke through the hush. "What are you going to be?"

I exhaled a breath that I hadn't even realized I was holding. I was dreading the idea of having to salvage a costume. "I don't know," I answered. My old Little Red Riding Hood costume was probably still shoved into the corner of my closet.

Just like me, I thought as I bit my lip and pulled into her driveway.

"Let me know if you need any help," she said, smiling. Forced. She grabbed her bag from the backseat of the car and tossed it by her ankles. But just as she started to open the door, she turned back towards me. Reached across the center console of my car. Pulled gently at my hair.

I felt a sharp intake of breath as the tips of her fingers lingered at my cheeks for what seemed like an eternity. When she finally pulled away, I noticed her cheeks were burning a bright shade of red.

"You, um," she paused, holding up a blade of grass between her fingers, "you had this in your hair." Placing it in one of my cup holders, she kicked open the door and jumped out of the car.

I watched her walk towards her front porch. She turned to look back at me, but the expression on her face seemed pained.

I wondered if she knew that I felt the same way.

~~~

"It's time for our new assignment," Mr. Travers, my Photography teacher, announced as soon as class began on Friday, smiling brightly towards us as he paced the front of the classroom. "I absolutely loved your first works, so I hope you'll do just as well on this one."

Our first project had been to photograph any living thing. For me, this was completely easy. Mr. Travers had provided us all with Nikon D50's, so I didn't even have to buy a camera. Kenny and I had taken Wednesday to the park again, where I'd used an entire roll of film photographing her as she romped through the multi-colored autumn leaves. The final project had been completely gorgeous, something I wanted to get framed: Wednesday had rolled in a pile of dead leaves, and was looking towards me with a red one stuck to the side of her muzzle.

"For this project, I'd like you all to do something in black and white." He turned on the overhead projector and showed us a slideshow of portraits by Dorothea Lange, who captured the heart of the Great Depression with her photography.

He began handing out a sheet of paper which held the requirements for the project, which wasn't too much. Basically, we just needed to take the photograph with black and white film and have it developed.

I spent the rest of the class chatting with Veronica Gregory, a volleyball player who had been my friend since freshman year. She was pretty: blonde hair, blue eyes. Way tall.

"I'm going to take a picture of Malfoy," she told me.

"Malfoy?" I pictured Veronica sneaking through bushes to take a picture of Tom Felton.

She laughed. "My snake."

"You have a snake?" I raised an eyebrow. She was so girly. It seemed weird that she'd have such a gross pet.

"Yeah. He's just a little corn snake, though. I had to beg my parents for him," she grinned, pulling a picture out of her binder to show me. I made a face.

"What are you going to photograph?" Veronica asked.

"I don't know." I said. But I was lying. I did know. I knew exactly what I wanted to photograph, if she'd let me.

~~~

My Little Red Riding Hood costume was so old that the cape was faded and fringing. I worked the sewing needle through the fabric, trying in vain to fix the holes that mice had chewed over the years. Suddenly, my phone buzzed across the carpet. Emma's name popped up on the caller ID. I grabbed it.

Flipping my cell open, I answered, "Hey."

"Hey," she said. Her familiar voice filled the static on the other end.

"Have you decided on your costume for tomorrow night?" she asked.

I looked down at the mess in front of me. "Yeah. How about you?"

"Yup. So, what are you going to be?"

"I figured I'd be a beach girl or something. You?" I smirked.

"Oh, you know. Soccer player." We both laughed.

I felt a throbbing in my heart. A yearning. I wished that we could be more than friends. I wished that I was Kenny. I wished that she was mine, and I was hers.

I wished that I could recapture that kiss and know that it wouldn't have to end. That it wasn't wrong.

That it was ours.

<u>Thirteen</u>

James R. Ivory High usually had one of the worst teams in the division, but not this year. They were putting up a good fight. By the second half, we were only ahead by a goal.

I wasn't playing well. Maybe it was because I'd been so stressed out. Or maybe the absence of Emma was keeping me from pushing myself. Either way, Coach drew me out of the game about ten minutes in.

After she called a time out in the second period, she shoved me back into the game. I played as hard as I could. I even had a few shots on the goal, but I just couldn't seem to score. In the last five minutes, I was able to send the ball flying in front of the net for Sarah to knock into the corner. An assist was something, at least.

We ended up winning the game 2-0. While we were all glad, we weren't as excited as we were about beating Birchwood. Afterwards, Coach gave us a brief congratulatory speech before sending us on our way.

And as I trekked back towards the parking lot, I felt myself scanning the bleachers. I was hoping for a flash of green to catch my eye. Even if Kenny was with her. I just wanted to see her.

As much as I had wanted her to be, she wasn't there.

~~~

We were so close. I could feel her breath on my cheek, her energy searing my skin. My eyes held hers. I knew what she was going to say.

"I choose you," she said.

I smiled. She tilted her head, letting her lips graze my cheek. But just when our lips were about to touch, just as we were about to finally kiss, an incessant noise came from nowhere.

She pulled away. In a flash, she was gone, and I was pulled back to reality.

Wednesday stood next to the couch, whining loudly. Her tail thumped against the coffee table.

I blinked, reaching up to rub the sleep out of my eyes. I was still wearing my cleats, my shin guards. I must've fallen asleep.

"What is it, girl?" I asked.

Wednesday dashed towards the front door. She clubbed at it with a paw, barking. She wanted to go out. A jog would probably be good for me. Help clear the mind.

Sighing, I clambered up and grabbed her leash, hooking it to her collar. As soon as I opened the front door, she was off like a shot.

As we ran, I let my mind wander. To Dad. To Kenny. To Emma.

Emma.

Before I even realized where I was heading, I'd crossed the major road separating our neighborhood and was jogging down her block. I stopped in front of her house, chest heaving as I rubbed the sweat off my forehead with the back of my hand.

Wednesday strained against the leash, exploring some bushes on the edge of the property.

Her dad's truck wasn't in the drive. Before I could even move, the door was pulled open and Emma was looking at me curiously from the porch.

"What in the world are you doing?" she asked. Wednesday barked.

"Hi," I said with a nervous smile. "I was, uh, in the neighborhood. Walking Wednesday."

"All the way over here?" She chuckled, beckoning me inside with a hand. "Come in and at least get some water or something."

Tugging Wednesday along with me, I stepped inside. Her house was completely silent. "My dad and brother are out at Lowes or something," she said, making a face. Must've read my mind. "Boy stuff."

I followed her into the kitchen where she handed me a glass of water. I swallowed nearly the entire thing in one gulp without even realizing I had been that thirsty in the first place. Wednesday sniffed at the floor, no doubt wondering about the strange new surroundings.

Emma raised her eyebrow at me. "So, did you have a game this morning?"

"Yeah," I said, setting the glass down on the counter to let my chest heave for a moment. I glanced down at my uniform. "Is it that obvious?"

She shrugged. "A little." She grinned. I felt myself smiling back at her. We stayed that way for a minute before finally turning away.

"So, what are you doing here?" she asked finally, walking from the kitchen towards her living room. I followed.

"I told you. Just taking the dog for a walk," I replied.

"Sure. All the way over here," she said, resting against the counter.

I had to change the subject. "Do you need a ride to Kenny's tonight?" I asked.

"No, actually." She took a deep breath. "That's actually something I wanted to talk to you about. I'm probably just going to ride home with Kenny from now on."

"What?" It wasn't enough for Kenny to just have her, but to take away the one thing that we did together? I felt like I'd been slapped in the face. But I had no right to be annoyed. She was his girlfriend. It was her decision.

"It's alright," I said, picking at a thread on my sock in an attempt to not meet her eyes. "I don't mind. I mean, he is your boyfriend." I snapped.

"Look, I'm okay with it if you're gay," she blurted. I looked up, surprised. Her cheeks were a bright shade of red. "But I'm not. I have a boyfriend."

"What are you talking about? You're the one that kissed me." I instantly felt defensive. Who did she think she was? "And I'm not gay," I added.

I just had a crush on her. That was normal, right?

After another moment of unbearable stillness, she held my eyes with hers. "Maybe we're misinterpreting things, then," she said. "Maybe we're just really close friends."

I nodded, but didn't believe her. The words that left her mouth said one thing, while the look in her eyes said something completely different.

~~~

When I finally got home, all I could do was think about the situation with Emma. I knew for a fact that I was attracted to her, there was no denying that. But did that really make me gay?

I thought back to all the childhood crushes I'd had, most of which were on girls, now that I came to think of it. The only crushes I had on boys were because I thought that's what little girls my age were supposed to do. They were forced.

And there was the look Cory gave me the first day she was introduced to our team. The questions about whether or not Emma was my girlfriend. The way she practically accused me of being gay when I didn't believe it.

I felt my heart racing. I would see a girl walk down the hallway and think, *Wow, she's cute.* I always thought other girls felt the same way when they looked at each other. Maybe Cory saw something in me that I couldn't. After all, gay people were supposed to have some sort of radar or something, or so I'd heard.

Am I? I thought to myself. *Am I... a lesbian?* All I knew was that I wanted to be with Emma more than anything in the world.

I didn't know if I was ready for a label just yet.

~~~

I was running late.

I swung my repaired red cloak over my neck and bolted from the door. Everyone would be there already. Kenny would be pissed I wasn't among the first.

I could hear the party from two blocks away. Kenny was blasting hip-hop music. It took me a moment, but I found a parking spot on the street and made my way towards his front yard.

The entire senior class had to be there. Two girls were already retching into the bushes next to the porch. Gross.

I had to shove my way past a couple of drunken guys to get into his house. It was a good thing his parents agreed to let him have the party, or he would've been in trouble. The place was already looking pretty nasty. A ton of people were standing around his living room, sipping their beer or mixed drinks and chatting with friends.

Making my way into the kitchen, I immediately spotted Kenny. He was at the other end of a beer pong table chugging the contents of a cup. I didn't recognize the other players.

I broke into a grin when I saw him. He was the Cowardly Lion from the Wizard of Oz. I laughed. So fitting.

"Finally!" Kenny exclaimed, returning my smile. "Want to play?"

"No thanks," I shook my head. I was about to step towards him when I was tackled.

"Charlie!"

I writhed out of Emma's firm grip. Faked a smile. She was pretty much the cutest Dorothy I'd ever seen.

"Nice costume," I said.

"Same to you," she told me. There was something behind her voice. Longing? Regret?

Before we could say anything else, Kenny threw his arm around Emma's shoulder. "Hey, babe," he said, kissing her on the cheek. "Want to play on my team?"

"Sure." Her eyes met mine. Was she trying to send me some sort of message? Say something? I didn't know.

"Have fun," I said.

I stood back to watch them. Kissing. Flirting. Teasing. Playing. They looked so happy.

Emma's frequent glances towards me told me otherwise.

My eyes never left her as I ran through my head what the equation would look like if I subtracted Kenny and added me.

"Hey, Charlie. Can I talk to you for a minute?"

I nearly spilled my beer as Emma's familiar voice interrupted my thoughts and shocked me back to reality.

"Sure," I said, confused. "What about?"

She was swaying gently before my eyes. Drunk. I could tell. Nevertheless, I let her take my hand and steer me into the bathroom.

"Look, Emma, what is it—"

"I was wrong," she interrupted. She gazed at me, her eyes wide and expressive.

"About what?" I asked, even though I already knew. My nerves twitched underneath my skin with the realization that she was only inches away. A tilt of the head and I could capture her lips with my own. I refrained.

"Us. Kenny. All of it." She looked down, then back up. Was she closer than before? "I—I do have feelings for you, Charlie."

My breath stopped along with time, space. I felt frozen.

Emma moved first. Her arm snaked around my waist, pulling me closer. She leaned in. I could smell alcohol on her breath, but didn't care. As she pressed her lips against mine, all I could think about was how long I'd waited for this. She tasted like rum and cigarettes, desire and need.

I stumbled. She shoved me up against the bathroom door to salvage our balance, kiss never faltering.

Everything I'd been feeling towards her seemed to catapult throughout my entire body. My heart was beating so fast I was afraid it was going to burst from my chest. I felt her hands slide from my back to my face, her thumbs caressing my cheeks as her lips moved in time with mine.

It took a few moments for my conscience to catch up to the heart pounding in my chest and the blood racing through my veins. What was I doing? This was wrong. So wrong.

I shoved her away.

"Stop," I said. "I can't do this, Emma."

"What? Why not?" She looked confused. Hurt.

I wanted nothing more than to take her back into my arms and kiss her again. "You're with Kenny," I replied. "It's wrong."

"But I want to be with you—"

I felt my heart stop. Did I hear her right? I wanted to be with her. More than anything. "I want to be with you, too."

"But I can't."

A knock on the door interrupted us.

"Yo, Emma, are you in there?"

Kenny. I immediately straightened myself up. Scraped my fingers through my hair in the mirror. Emma shot me a glance before swinging the door open.

"What are you doing in there, too, Charlotte?" He stared past Emma towards me, confused.

I had to think fast. "I, uh, well—" Fail.

"She was helping me with my outfit," Emma blurted, green eyes meeting mine. Save. I forced a smile and nodded.

His faltering smile made me think for a moment that he knew what we were up to. That he could read the guilt on our faces. Sense the taste of each other on our lips.

After a second, he burst into laughter. "Girls," he said with a roll of his shoulders. "They're all a mystery." Reaching forward, he took Emma by the hand, pulled her forward, and kissed her. "C'mon, Em. Let's go play another round."

She turned her head to meet my eyes while Kenny dragged her off.

As soon as she was out of my sight, I couldn't get out of his house quick enough.

Fourteen

I wasn't looking forward to soccer practice on Monday. It was colder outside than it had been, and the frigid air seemed to easily penetrate my track pants and sweater. When I stepped out of the locker room and onto the field, however, I immediately took notice of Emma seated in the bleachers. I jogged towards her. She looked up from her Biology textbook when she saw me approaching.

"What are you doing?" I asked. "Where's Kenny?"

"He had an appointment after school so I said I'd just ride home with you. Is that okay?" She offered me a small smile.

I felt nervous. Awkward. "Sure," I said. "But aren't you cold? It's freezing out here. You should go inside."

"No, I'm okay," she said. Her hands were shaking as she held her book. "I want to watch."

I delved into my bag to pull out the hooded sweatshirt I wore to school. "Here, put this on, then."

"Aw, is your girlfriend cold?" Cory taunted when I jogged back over to the team.

"Shut up," I said. Kicked at a soccer ball near my feet.

"You mean, you're not going to insist she's not your girlfriend this time?" She smirked, crossing her arms. At the moment, I was glad all the other girls were engaged in their own conversations or were too far away to hear.

"Shut up, Cory," I said again, plopping down on the grass to begin stretching.

Sarah, who strode over to sit next to me, took in my peeved expression and looked towards Cory.

"What's going on?" she asked, kicking her legs out to either side of her.

"Nothing," I replied. I twisted my body to the side to stretch my back.

"I was just asking Charlotte if her girlfriend was cold, that's all." Cory shrugged, juggling a soccer ball at her feet.

"Who, Emma?" Sarah twisted herself around to look at Emma, who was completely engulfed in reading her textbook. She turned back to Cory, chuckling. "They're not lesbos. Emma's dating a guy, anyways. Go away, dyke."

She reached out to grab a nearby soccer ball and chucked it towards Cory, hitting the soccer ball she was previously juggling mid-air and sending the two bouncing across the field. Cory gave her the middle finger and stalked off to the goalpost to begin her own stretches.

"She's disgusting," Sarah said, shaking her head. "I don't know how anyone can be like that."

Swallowing, I glanced towards Emma, watching her look up from her book at the same time to wave to me. I didn't wave back.

~~~

By the time practice was over, it was nearly dark. I hated how the days got shorter as winter approached. It made me feel as though I had no time to do anything after practice. Taking a deep breath, I walked over to Emma. She had my sweatshirt wrapped around her arms.

"Finished?" she asked. She threw her bag over her shoulder.

"Yeah," I said, swiveling to see Cory eyeballing us from across the field. "Let's go."

I began walking quickly, making sure I was a few feet in front of Emma until we reached the parking lot and were completely clear of Cory's gaze.

"Why are you walking so fast?" Emma jogged to catch up to me. Feeling bad, I slowed my stride to walk next to her.

"That girl won't leave me alone," I said, frowning. She looked like she was freezing. I wanted to put my arms around her, warm her up. I knew better.

"Who? Sarah?" Emma folded my sweatshirt against her body. Her hands were drawn up inside of her own sleeves.

"No. Cory. Corinne," I said before realizing she probably didn't know anyone's name on my team besides Sarah. "You know, the goalie."

I swung around to the driver's side and hopped in, tossing my bag in the back before revving up the engine to blast the heat.

"What's she doing?" Emma finally asked.

I felt myself blush as I rubbed my hands together, waiting for the heat to start working. "She keeps calling you my girlfriend."

"Oh." Emma squirmed in her seat. "You told her I was dating Kenny though, right?"

"Sarah did."

I pulled out of the parking lot as my car started to warm up. When I was finally cruising on the main road, Emma reached over to touch my hand. I felt my heart jump.

"Charlie, we need to talk."

I felt myself swallow a tennis ball. "I know," I said.

"Pull over in this parking lot."

I blinked towards where she indicated. The parking lot for one of the old department stores that had recently gone out of business. Taking a breath, I turned the wheel and steered Old Reliable into the vacant lot.

"I'm sorry about the other night," Emma said. "I-I guess I drank too much."

I shrugged. "It's okay."

"It's not okay." She shook her head. "Look, Charlie." I felt her hand, gentle, on my arm. "I like you."

"I like you, too."

"It's different with you than with Kenny." She turned away from me to look through the window. "I don't know why. It's like I feel something with you." When she twisted her gaze back to meet mine, I could see the tears brimming in her eyes. "I want to be with you."

I felt my pulse quicken. Everything within me was telling me to wipe her tears away, so I did. I let the back of my hand linger against her cheek. I couldn't say anything, though. This was Emma's soapbox.

"But I can't." She exhaled. She moved her hand from her arm to intertwine our fingers. "It's not right, you know? I don't want to be this. I don't want to be gay."

"I understand," I said with a nod. I didn't.

"Maybe we should hide this." There was a flicker of hope in her eyes. "We don't have to tell anyone."

I didn't want to hide. But, nevertheless, I nodded.

When she leaned forward and kissed me, I knew that I would do anything to keep those soft lips against mine.

~~~

"Halloween is tomorrow night," Mom said when I finally walked through the front door after dropping Emma off at her house. I stopped in the doorway to look at her awkwardly.

"Nice observation," I told her.

She shook her head, smiling at me as she walked into the kitchen. I followed her, immediately noticing about fifteen bags of assorted candies on the counter. "I'm not going to be home, so I was kind of hoping you could hand all this out."

Striding to the counter, I ripped a bag open to pull out a Snickers bar. "Sure," I said, unwrapping the candy and popping it into my mouth.

"And by handing out candy, I don't mean eat it all." She grabbed the wrapper out of my hand and threw it away.

I started opening all the bags and pouring the contents inside a few Halloween decorated bowls she obviously purchased while she was getting the candy. "Do you mind if Emma comes over and we'll hand it out together?"

She turned. "I'd rather you not have people over when I'm not home at night." She said coolly.

"But you let Kenny hang out all the time."

"That's different."

I dropped a now empty bag of Snickers, crossing my arms as I scrunched my eyebrows at her. "How is that different?"

She let out an exasperated sigh. "That's because I know him, Charlotte."

I didn't understand. Why was she being such a jerk about it? It was just Emma. "But you know Emma, too, Mom."

"Look, the answer is no. Unless Kenny is here with you. Besides, don't you two get together and watch movies every Halloween?"

She was being such a bitch. What did she think Emma was going to do, steal all of our expensive stuff? The most expensive thing we probably owned was our secondhand refrigerator, and I would have to commend Emma if she loaded that onto her back and trekked through the door. "Fine," I said. "Kenny will be here, too."

He always seemed to be in the middle.

~~~

I was still annoyed by the time we'd finished eating dinner. I stalked off to my room. Who was she to tell me who I could hang out with?

And why didn't she trust Emma?

Flipping my cell open, I held down the number for Kenny's speed dial and pulled the phone away from my ear while it rang.

"Yo!" Kenny hollered into the phone.

"Hey, Kenny," I said. "I was wondering if you and Emma wanted to watch movies at my house tomorrow."

I could sense him grinning into the phone. "Sure," he answered. "I would never break tradition." He paused, and then said, "I have a question for you, though."

The change in his voice startled me. Suddenly, he was serious. Quiet. Had he found out about Emma and me? I swallowed. "Yeah?"

"Has Emma seemed a little distant to you?"

My mind flashed back to the time in ninth grade when a guy was harassing me on the bus. Kenny had taken it upon himself to protect me and gotten a black eye in the process.

He was my best friend.

He had defended me, and I was neglecting his trust. But even still, I couldn't tell the truth. Even while it dangled on the tip of my tongue, a lie spilled out.

"No. I think she's just stressed out about school. I don't think it has anything to do with you," I said.

There was a moment of stillness. "Okay. Thanks. That's good to hear. I was just hoping it wasn't me," he replied. "See you tomorrow, pal."

When I closed the phone, my heart was pounding.

I had to be the worst friend ever.

~~~

All through school the next day, I was looking forward to handing out candy. Only because I knew Emma would be there. Walking through student-packed hallways, I heard a lot of freshmen commenting about what they were wearing and how they were going to go trick-or-treating to get as much candy as they could. *Not if you come to my house,* I thought, rolling my eyes as I heard a couple of guys talking about how they were going to hit as many neighborhoods as they could, one of which being mine. I absolutely hated it when people my age went trick-or-treating. Halloween was a kid's activity. It wasn't for over-aged, rambunctious teenagers.

Emma and I received a grade for our dialogue from Ms. Woodbridge towards the end of class. "A-." She'd written a few things about my stuttering and Emma's missed lines, but overall, most of the things she'd put down were really positive. One thing definitely stuck out: "You two seem like you worked well together."

"I told you we'd get an A," Emma said.

"But I said we'd get a B," I pointed out. "This is an A-, so it was in between what we both said."

Emma shrugged, pushing her elbow out to nudge my side. I returned the gesture. We got into a small pushing war all the way to the locker room.

"Look, she said we work well together, too," I told her, showing her the part at the bottom before handing her the entire paper. "I don't necessarily agree with that."

She chuckled, looking at the sheet for a moment before shoving it into a folder in her bag. "I don't agree with that, either."

I glanced around. And, seeing no one nearby, leaned forward to plant a kiss on the corner of her lips.

~~~

"Hey, Charlotte." Kenny smacked the side of my head with a stack of DVD's as soon as I opened the front door to my house. His other hand was wrapped around Emma's, who was being dragged behind him like a doll. "I've got a ton of crap-tastic movies for tonight."

"Great." I rolled my eyes. Emma caught my gaze and smiled, to which I promptly responded with a blush. "What'd you get?" I asked as soon as she looked away.

He grinned, tossing the movies one-by-one onto the couch as he read them. "I've got Dead Alive, House of the Dead, and The Evil Dead."

"They sound horrendous," I grumbled.

Emma nodded, adding, "I'm pretty sure anything with 'Dead' in the title is automatically awful."

"That's not true," Kenny said, shaking his head. "Dawn of the Dead. The new one. That was pretty awesome." He let go of Emma's hand and tousled her hair. "You just need to spread your cinematic horizons to horror flicks, babe. Then you'll understand completely." He winked at her. I suppressed my gag reflex.

Emma looked irritated. "Hey, Charlie, how about I help you get the candy ready while Kenny gets the movie started?"

"But, the candy's al—"

"Let's go."

She grabbed my arm and steered me off to the kitchen before I could protest. When we finally rounded the corner, she shoved me up against the counter and kissed me. When she pulled away, a devious smirk flashed across her lips. "God, I couldn't wait to do that."

As much as I wanted her to kiss me again, I whispered, "Emma, we can't. Kenny's here."

"I don't care," she replied. But just as she leaned forward again, Kenny rounded the corner. The two of us flew apart like we'd been shocked.

"Movie's ready," Kenny said. He smiled at us, completely oblivious. My heart was still racing as I let out a sigh of relief, not even aware that I'd been holding my breath. "I chose House of the Dead. Sounded like a winner."

Emma gave him a weak smile. I could tell she was shaken up. "Great. Good. Sounds awesome. Let's go watch, Charlie."

And as we settled down to watch the movie with her bundled up in his arms, even her longing glances couldn't ease the hurt that pulled at my heartstrings.

~~~

The days seemed to pass more quickly as the weather grew steadily colder. Practice became nearly unbearable. But even on the days when Kenny couldn't give Emma a ride home, she still insisted on sitting outside to watch. I began to bring an extra sweater, or sometimes a blanket, to keep her warm while she waited.

After my game on Saturday, the three of us stopped at Tony's, a small restaurant close to home. I watched Kenny and Emma laugh and joke from across the table, feeling an ache burn through my chest.

It wasn't until our pizza was set down in front of us that the two seemed to notice I was there.

"You played awesome today, Charlie." She smiled, letting the tips of her fingers brush my hand as she reached for a slice of pizza. I felt my breath catch in my throat. "You're so much better than everyone on the team."

"No, I'm not," I said, giving her a little kick with the side of my cleat under the table. "Rebecca's way better. She's got a scholarship from five different schools."

I took a bite of my pizza and looked through the window adjacent to our booth. The sky outside had grown grey and cloudy, threatening to rain. At least it had held off until after the game.

"Well, that doesn't matter," she said, kicking me back as Kenny reached across her to scoop up half the pizza with his bare hands. "I think you're the best."

I grinned at her, giggling as she bit her pizza and the cheese refused to separate. She made a face, pulling her head back to elongate the strand to nearly a foot. I reached over and pulled it apart for her. She frowned.

"I was trying to set a record," she mumbled between chews. She kept a straight face for a moment which made me think she was actually serious until she started laughing. I loved her laugh. I reached underneath the table where her hand met mine in a gentle squeeze.

"Oh, yeah? Watch this," Kenny said. He jerked his head back and sent cheese flying across the table. Sauce splattered onto the window.

Emma, startled, pulled her hand away.

Why did he always have to ruin everything?

~~~

As soon as I got home from work that night, my phone began to ring. My heart leapt of the thought of it being Emma, but I was surprised to find it was a number I wasn't familiar with. Confused, I flipped open my phone and answered, "Hello?"

"Hey, Charlotte?" I heard from the other end. I recognized the voice immediately.

"Preston!" I broke into a grin as I dropped down into my computer chair. "What's up?"

"Nothing, really. I just found your number in my phone and figured I'd call you to see how you were."

"I'm good," I answered, and then asked, "And you?"

"Pretty good," he replied.

I played with a pen on my desk, suddenly feeling awkward. I didn't really know what to talk about. "How's lacrosse?"

"It's good, actually. I just hate how cold it's getting."

"I hear you. Soccer's been pretty miserable."

He laughed. There was a small pause. I sighed, rolling my pen in my fingers.

"So, how are the girls?" he finally asked.

I felt myself blushing furiously. I was glad we were on the phone and not face to face. "The girl is good," I replied, dropping my pen.

"Good. What's the girl's name?"

"Emma," I said. I rose from my computer chair to retreat to my bed, collapsing onto my stomach.

"The girl from the movies?"

"Yeah." I felt my cheeks burning red.

"Oh." He grew quiet. I could tell he was thinking. "Isn't she with that other guy, though?"

I swallowed, turning my head to the side to stare at the blank white canvas of my wall. "No," I lied. "She's with me."

For a moment, my heart elated with the thought of the statement being true. But it wasn't. Emma wasn't with me. She wasn't mine.

I could wish on every star in the sky and she'd still be with Kenny.

<u>Fifteen</u>

"So, what's up with you and Emma?" Kenny asked. I was watching him play the most interesting game of Halo I'd ever seen. Not.

"What do you mean?" I felt my heart start to beat faster. I looked away.

"You two are just spending a lot of time together," he said. My eyes were pulled back to him as he jerked his remote around. I watched his character crumple to its knees in the middle of a field.

"We're friends," I said, kicking my feet up onto his futon. "I mean, that's what friends do, right?" Did he know? Had he seen us? I held my breath.

He turned to look at me while his character re-spawned onto the television screen.

"I just want to make sure you're not replacing me," he said. "What do you two do, anyways? Does Emma ever talk about me?"

I let myself breathe, relieved. "Well, yeah, sometimes." I tilted my head back and listened to the sounds of gunfire and explosions on the game.

He grew quiet as he started chasing down another player, finger pumping rapidly on the trigger as he moved in for the kill. His hands were dancing across the remote like he was playing an instrument. I vaguely wondered how anyone could get so into a game.

"So, how old are these people you're playing with?" I asked, desperately wanting to change the subject. "Thirteen? Fourteen?"

"I don't know." His character died again. He slammed his remote angrily onto the futon. "So, what does Emma say about me?"

How much she'd rather be with me, I thought, tasting the words on my tongue.

I didn't dare say them.

~~~

"That's not how you kick a soccer ball." I cringed as I watched Emma send my ball spinning into Mom's hydrangea bush.

I scooped the ball out of the battered bush and juggled it for a moment before passing it back to her. It fell lifelessly at her feet. She stared at it before kicking it into my knee.

"I suck," she whined.

"No, you don't. You just don't know what you're doing."

"Teach me how to play?" She poked at the ball delicately with her foot.

I reached over and pulled it towards me with the bottom of my foot. "I can't teach you in just one day," I replied.

"Well," she said, "teach me just a little bit, then."

Her eyes were pleading. How could I say no to that face? Defeated, I passed the ball back to her.

"Don't kick it with your toe," I instructed. "You have no control over it like that. Use the inside of your foot."

She rolled her eyes at me. "Since when is this an exact science?"

I stepped backwards. "Pass it to me."

Emma kicked it with her toe again. I crossed my arms, glaring at her from across the yard. "I thought you wanted me to teach you?"

"Okay, okay," she said. "Kick it at me again, then."

Demonstrating with the inside of my foot, I passed it softly towards her.

What I got back, however, was anything but gentle. I didn't even have time to think before the ball struck the side of my face. Hard. I was stunned. I felt my mouth hanging partially open, but couldn't seem to close it.

"Oh my god," I heard Emma blurt. She rushed over.

"It's okay." I pressed my fingers to my upper lip. When I pulled it away, my fingers were stained red. My nose was bleeding. I tilted my head forward to watch some blood drip onto the grass.

"Oh god, I'm so sorry." I felt Emma's arm snake around my shoulder. I tried desperately to swipe the blood away with my sleeve. Despite my efforts, it continued flowing. Emma tugged me into the house and shoved me down at the kitchen table. Grabbing a handful of napkins, she pulled a chair up next to me and held them under my nose.

"I can't believe I did that to you," she said, one hand caressing the side of my face. "It's not broken, is it?"

"No," I said, taking the napkins and pulling them away to look at how red they'd turned. "Just bleeding, I think." I winced as her finger came near my eye. I was going to have a nice shiner, for sure.

I could tell she was pretty upset. I wiped the last bit of blood from my nose and set the napkins on the table, wrapping my arms around her. "It's alright," I told her, giving her shoulders a small squeeze. "It happens."

I got up to walk into the bathroom, washing the blood off my face. As I looked into the mirror, I could already tell I was getting a black eye. Sighing, I returned to the kitchen where Emma was seated forlornly in the same position.

"Don't sulk," I told her, plopping back down in my seat to press my forehead against hers. "I don't care."

"I care," she said, pulling away a bit to look me in the eyes. I watched her gaze travel to the bruise that was forming at the corner of my right eye. "Does it hurt?"

"A little," I admitted. She leaned towards me and kissed the corner of my eye so softly I could hardly feel it.

"Better?"

I nodded, but then grinned and pointed to my lips. "It hurts here, too."

She smirked, kissing my mouth. "Now?"

"It hurts more than that."

She leaned in once more, wrapping her arms around my shoulders as she pulled me closer. My stomach did a flip.

"Do me one favor?" I asked when she finally pulled away.

"What's that?"

"Don't attempt any more soccer. At least while I'm in range."

~~~

"What in the world happened to your eye?" Mom asked when she came home that night. I was sitting at the kitchen table struggling to read my boring History textbook. Why did the government have so many branches? What was it, some kind of tree?

"Soccer accident," I said with a snort, giving up my attempt to distinguish the legislative and judicial branches. Instead, I began flipping through the pages to look at the pictures.

She walked slowly over towards me and slipped her fingers underneath my chin, tilting my head up the slightest bit to get a good look at my eye. "Geez, Charlotte. This happened at the game yesterday?"

I shook my head, shrinking away when she attempted to touch the developing bruise. Because she was a nurse, she felt like she needed to touch every wound I ever acquired. "No," I told her, "Emma and I were playing in the backyard."

She retreated to the sink only to return with a wet dish towel which she tried to press against my eye. I pulled away, scowling at her.

"Can you cut that out?" I mumbled.

"It'll help the swelling go down," she said, grabbing the side of my head to pull me closer. I winced as she held the damp cloth to my eye. "You've been spending a lot of time with Emma. Isn't she dating Kenny?"

"Yeah, I guess so," I replied, fiddling with the corner of one of the pages in my History book. The two of us were silent for a long time while she held the cloth to my face. When she finally pulled away, I was relieved.

"Whatever happened to that boy you went on that date with?" she asked as she rinsed out the cloth and set it on the counter.

I shrugged, turning away from her. I was a horrible fibber, and I didn't want her to see my face. If she couldn't see my eyes, maybe she wouldn't notice my guilt. "He has a girlfriend at Capital," I lied, sucking in a deep breath.

She was quiet for a while, as if pondering the answer I'd given her. "Oh, I see," she said, almost more to herself. "Well, I'm pretty tired, so I'm going to go to bed. Are you going to be up late?"

"Probably not too much later," I replied, staring blankly at the pages in front of me.

"Tell Emma she needs to play nicer next time, or play with Kenny more," she added in a sarcastic tone before leaving the kitchen. I winced and pulled out my cell phone to text Emma: *My mom said you need to play nice.*

She texted me back within a matter of minutes, the contents of the text message making me laugh out loud.

Tell your mom I said she has a hot daughter.

I closed my eyes and swallowed. I had to tell Mom something, that was for sure, but it definitely wasn't that.

And I had no clue how I was going to do it.

~~~

The next day, I met Emma at her house after Kenny dropped her off after school. She'd told me that they didn't have plans, but I knew that she had lied to him about having to do something else. She was lying to him on a daily basis.

For me.

It was colder outside, but the frigid air didn't stop the two of us from walking, hand-in-hand, through her neighborhood park. I'd made sure to bring my camera and stopped frequently to take pictures of random animals.

When we were pretty far down the winding trails, I finally released her hand and backed up a few steps to begin taking shots of her. She laughed, jogging off into the grass to begin striking some poses.

I snapped furiously as I followed her, grinning at how beautifully photogenic she was. After about thirty frames, she sat down on the grass and rolled slowly onto her back, turning her head to look towards me. "I didn't know you were a photographer," she pointed out.

I plopped down onto my knees, setting my camera next to me. "I'm not. It's only for a project in Photography. Do you mind if I use one of your pictures?"

She shook her head. "No. Go ahead."

"Good, because I was going to use one whether you said yes or not," I joked, lying down next to her to stretch my arm across her shoulders. I pressed my lips to her neck gently before nuzzling my face into her cheek.

"I'm sorry about your face," she mumbled. I pulled away. Stared into her eyes. So green.

"It's okay. Really," I said, tightening my grip around her shoulders. "Besides, I got a lot of compliments on the new look today."

She chuckled, leaning forward to kiss me to the point where I almost forgot what we were talking about. "It does look pretty sexy," she said with a wide grin. Leaning forward, she pulled her crumpled pack of Marlboro Lights out of her back pocket.

"Glad you think so." I hesitated, watching her slide a cigarette between her lips and light it. "That's so unhealthy, Em. I wish you wouldn't smoke."

Her eyes met mine, a half-hearted smile tugged at the corner of her mouth as she exhaled smoke. "I know. Me too."

"How'd you get into it, anyway?"

"My mom." She looked away, a shadow crossing over half of her face. "After the accident, I found a pack of her cigarettes in the kitchen." She took a long drag on the cigarette before continuing. "It just reminds me of her, you know? It's a comfort."

I nodded. I wanted to say that I didn't understand, but that would be a lie. When I'd opened Dad's letter, the scent of his aftershave had washed over me like a tsunami. It brought me back to times long before the divorce. Back to days before he left.

She turned to wrap her arms around me and we stayed there, silent, until the sound of approaching voices forced us apart. With a sigh, we peeled our hands away to resume the appearance of two normal girls just being friends instead of two girls in love with each other.

<u>Sixteen</u>

Our first snow of the season was on November 15th, and it was just barely enough so that we were granted a snow day. I broke into a dance when I turned on the television and saw the magic words: *Hidden Springs High, Closed.*

Grabbing my cell phone, I immediately called Emma.

"Hello?" She sounded half asleep. I wasn't surprised.

"Hey," I said, unable to hide the excited pitch in my voice. "Why are you still asleep?"

"I dunno," she grumbled. I could hear her shifting around. "I'm sleepy."

"School is cancelled for today." I watched the schools flash by at the bottom of the TV screen. "Is your dad home?"

"Hold on." More shifting. "No," she finally said. "Trevor probably is, though, if school is cancelled."

"Can I come over?" I asked.

"Right now? It's so early, Charlie."

"So? C'mon, Em. It's our first snow day."

"Oh, alright," she mumbled. "Whatever."

"Okay. See you," I said, hanging up the phone. I slid into a pair of jeans, a heavy coat, and snatched a scarf off the floor of my bedroom before bolting outside. I was glad Mom wasn't home. Otherwise, I'd have a lot of explaining to do. She'd kill me for driving Old Reliable in the snow.

By the time I reached Emma's, it was nearly half past seven. I hopped out of my car and stomped through the untouched snow to her front door.

I rapped my fist on the door, then stood back to wait. No answer. I knocked again.

Nothing.

I twisted the doorknob. It was unlocked.

"Hey, Em?" I called as I slid quietly into her parlor. The house was silent except for the gentle ticking of a clock and the squeaking of the floor underneath my snow-covered sneakers. I took my coat off and hung it on the rack with the others.

I crept down the hallway and into her room, knowing exactly what I'd find.

She was stretched out across her bed, asleep. Her body was turned away from me, blonde hair a mess across the pillow. Grinning, I carefully shut her door and kicked my shoes off as I snuck over. Pulling the covers back, I clambered awkwardly into the bed. She jumped, rolling over to open her eyes. A sleepy smile slid across her lips.

"Charlie," she mumbled, shutting her eyes again and smiling. "What are you doing here?"

"I told you I was coming over, remember?" I asked. I tugged the covers up to my shoulders and snaked an arm around her waist, pulling her close.

She nodded, taking the hand that was at her stomach and clutching it as she snuggled into my body.

"Emma, c'mon. Let's go outside," I begged.

"Five more minutes."

I wanted to get up. To find some excuse for not being so intimate. Electrical surges were coursing through my body, making it nearly impossible to concentrate on anything.

My hand seemed to break away from hers of its own accord, roaming tentatively across her flat stomach. My fingers traced across the thin fabric of her t-shirt and up the center of her ribcage, coming to an abrupt halt only when I realized she wasn't wearing a bra.

I took a shaky breath, feeling Emma squirm slightly in my arms. She rolled over to face me, eyes flickering partially open. I yanked my hand away, suddenly aware of what was happening.

She didn't say anything. Instead, I felt her hand gently touch my stomach. I shivered, closing my eyes. Her breath was shallow as she began to move against me.

"Emma," I said, suddenly breaking away and nearly falling off the bed. "We can't."

"Can't?" Her eyes flew open. "Can't what, Charlie?"

"This." I regained my composure, standing up and straightening my shirt. "We're not ready. *I'm* not ready."

And I wasn't. Maybe she was ready to take that step, but for me, it was more like a plunge. Like standing on the edge of a canyon, waiting for the moment I knew I had no choice but to free fall into whatever lay below.

~~~

"This is awesome," Emma said when I'd finished packing the last bit of snow onto the igloo that we'd been working on for hours. Well, that I'd been working on. She wasn't much help. I watched her kneel down and crawl through the awkwardly shaped hole that was meant to be the entrance.

I felt a pang of guilt sear my gut as I took a step back and admired my handiwork. Kenny and I built an igloo every year on the first day of snow. I hadn't even bothered to pick up my phone and call him.

Shrugging it off, I smoothed the side of the igloo with my hand and made my way into the cramped inside.

"What do you think?" I asked Emma, grinning as I stretched my arms out. I couldn't even extend them all the way.

"I love it. This is so cool." She leaned forward and kissed my cheek. Despite the cold, I felt my face burning. "We hardly ever had snow in North Carolina. And definitely not enough to do this, that's for sure."

I smiled. "It's alright, I guess." I wanted to lean back, but was scared the walls would collapse. I had to admit, Kenny was a connoisseur of snow igloos. His were a lot better than what I scraped together.

The thought of it made my mind reel as I studied Emma's smiling face. He had so much more to offer her. He was a guy, so their relationship was automatically accepted. They could get married. Have children. He could provide for her in a way that I never would be able to.

Kenny could build her a fortress of snow.

All I could manage was a shitty igloo that couldn't even take the weight of a back leaning against the side.

I hadn't even realized I was crying until she said, "Charlie, what's wrong?"

Shaking my head, I swiped at my tears on my cheeks. "We shouldn't do this anymore. It's wrong." I met her eyes. For the first time, I could see the worry behind them. Her strength, her carelessness, it was all a front. She was scared.

So was I.

"I know it's wrong," she said, her voice hesitant. She expelled a breath, and with it a tear slid from the corner of her eye. "I feel bad for Kenny, but—"

"But what? Then we shouldn't do this. He's my best friend, Emma. And your boyfriend. Can you imagine what would happen if he were to—"

"But I love you."

Unlike the rest of her words, it slid from her mouth so smooth that it was like molasses dripping from her lips. My voice caught. I couldn't speak.

"Charlie, say something," she pleaded. She reached forward, touched a hand to my neck. "Please, say something."

"I love you too," I finally managed to choke out.

I leaned forward, capturing her lips with my own. She fell over backwards, striking the wall of the igloo and causing it to collapse around us.

We laughed towards the sky as our worries crumbled with the snow.

~~~

When I finally got home that night, I signed onto the internet. Emma was already on.

CNHHATTRICK: U there?

She didn't reply. I decided to surf MySpace when the sound on the computer let me know that she had messaged me back.

Shes a Dilemma: Hey, sorry

CNHHATTRICK: R u ok?

Shes a Dilemma: Kenny and I got into a fight.

Had he found out? I clenched my teeth as I typed back.

CNHHATTRICK: What happened?

Shes a Dilemma: He's pissed off that I didn't call him all day. Apparently he tried to call me like 10 times.

CNHHATTRICK: Why is he mad at that?

Shes a Dilemma: I guess he was worried that something happened. I don't know. He's just being a good boyfriend.

A good boyfriend. Why did she need that when she had me? I blew it off.

CNHHATRICK: So what did u tell him?

Shes a Dilemma: I lied. I told him that I slept all day.

Of course she lied.

The two of us were getting really good at it. Lying to Kenny. Lying to Mom.

Lying to ourselves.

~~~

"This place is crowded today," Kenny grumbled as we pushed our way through Tony's to find a booth. People were everywhere. Glancing around, I spotted a sign that advertised today being a charity event. No wonder.

When we finally found a place to sit, the three of us crumpled into our seats. When an older waitress came over to get our order, I could sense her eyes burning a hole in Kenny's shirt.

G_ F_CK Y__RS_LF. Would you like to buy a vowel?

"I can't believe you wore that to school," I told him when the waitress finally left.

Emma swiveled her head from looking through the window. "I don't get it."

"Are you kidding me?" I said, staring at her face in disbelief.

"Oh." She broke into a grin. "I get it now."

Kenny and I exchanged a look before bursting into laughter. Emma's cheeks burned a bright red as she glanced between the two of us.

"Oh, shut up," she said. I reached under the table and gave her knee a squeeze.

The waitress came back over, staring at us with reproach as she slid our drinks in front of us. When she left, I could've sworn I heard her click her tongue against her teeth in distaste. Whatever.

"So, are you going to Philadelphia for Thanksgiving?" Kenny asked me as he sipped his soda.

I nodded, sighing heavily. "Unfortunately," I told him. Mom and I spent every Thanksgiving she wasn't stuck working with my grandparents in Philadelphia.

"You're going to Hartford, right babe?" Kenny turned his attention to Emma, who was looking through the window once again.

"Emma." I nudged her arm gently to grab her attention. "Are you okay?"

She nodded, forcing a smile. "Yeah. I think I just need a cigarette. I'll be right back."

Kenny and I watched as she slid from the booth and disappeared through the front door into the parking lot.

"I've been trying to get her to quit for weeks," Kenny said, pulling my attention back to him. "I feel like I'm kissing a tobacco plant."

"Yeah," I replied before realizing what I'd said. "I mean, it's really not healthy."

I turned to look through the window at Emma, who was scuffing her sneakers against the curb as she puffed on her cigarette. I didn't so much mind the taste, really. I just loved the way her lips felt against mine.

Emma returned just as the waitress arrived with our pizza. Her thigh brushed against mine, making me take a deep, shaky breath. I grabbed a slice of pepperoni, grateful for the distraction.

Kenny bit into his piece. "So, you have a game this weekend, right Charlotte?"

"Two, actually," I said in between bites. "We play Hagerstown on Saturday and Coolidge on Sunday."

"Jesus," Emma chimed in. "Two games? That's kind of ridiculous. You don't usually have two games a weekend."

I shrugged. "Well, they're our last two games before Playoffs. If we win both of them, that is. If we win, we go head-to-head with Birchwood on Tuesday night. After that, I'm finished for the semester."

"We should go to both," Kenny said to Emma as he shook his shaggy hair out of his face. He tilted his head to the side and smiled at her.

Jealousy simmered underneath my skin. My hand slid over her knee.

"Of course we will," Emma said. I could feel her eyes burning into the side of my face. "I wouldn't miss one of Charlie's games for the world."

All I could think about was how much I wanted to kiss her.

Emma's hand slid down to her knee. Our fingers intertwined. A perfect fit.

"Can I get you all anything else?" The waitress popped unexpectedly around the corner. Emma and I jerked our hands away, but I could feel the woman's eyes trained on the two of us in an expression of disgust. My cheeks blushed furiously.

"No thanks," Kenny said, glancing to the two of us in confusion. He forced a smile.

The waitress nodded, giving Emma and me another long look before turning on her heel to walk off.

"Damn, what's her problem?" Kenny asked when she was finally out of earshot.

I nibbled my bottom lip, looking towards Emma. When she turned her eyes to meet mine, I didn't have to guess if her heart was beating as fast as mine. I knew.

__Seventeen__

I had come to the conclusion that our team officially sucked. Sure, we had easily defeated Hagerstown and Coolidge, but we were like fish out of water against Birchwood. It didn't help how rough they were playing. They were worse than ever before.

The sun had set, but the Hidden Springs' field was illuminated by the overhead lights. As I dashed across the grass, my eyes flew up to search the bleachers for Emma. It was useless. I couldn't find her in the dark.

"Charlotte! Over here!" I looked up to see Sarah screaming at me from the other side of a line of defenders. I juggled the ball between my legs before knocking it behind me to Rebecca. She made a move that didn't last long. A Birchwood defender sent the ball flying to one of their midfielders.

"I had a wide open shot," Sarah grumbled as the two of us jogged back towards our end of the field.

"You may have had a good shot, but there was no way I was going to get it past the defenders," I said, shaking my head. I shoved my bangs out of my eyes and wiped the sweat off my forehead with the back of my hand.

Sarah shook her head. "Did you just see that?" she asked, pointing down the field. "Their right wing just shoved Hannah. Did their coach tip the ref or something?"

"Must have," I said. Actually, I was pretty convinced about it after all the foul play I'd seen without a single card.

I glanced to my right to note the girl that had been marking me the entire game. She was way taller, and tough as nails. She looked towards me and sneered, then edged a little bit closer. I glared before turning my attention to our side of the field, where Cory had just saved a shot on the goal and was dropkicking the ball.

While I didn't particularly like Cory, I had to admit she was one hell of a goalkeeper. Maybe even better than Brittany. The ball landed around midfield where Lauren, one of our second stringers, received it and took flight down the side of the field. Sarah, Rebecca, and I bolted off with her, covering our respective areas.

I glanced around. I'd left the Birchwood girl in the dust. I had an open field in front of me.

"Lauren!" I yelled. I was determined. Birchwood was up 3-0 with ten minutes left in the game. It was looking grim, but I knew I could win it for us. I had to.

Just as one of their players reached Lauren's side, she sent the ball hurtling across the field to land a few feet away from me. I surged forward. Suddenly, out of nowhere, the girl who was marking me appeared.

We battled neck and neck down the field. I kicked and dribbled the ball in every which direction in an attempt to keep her from taking it from me. I looked to pass it to Rebecca and Sarah, but both of them were engaged in a dance of their own with another player.

I was exhausted, but I poured my energy into the run. I acted as though I was going to pass the ball and then swerved off to the right towards the center of the field, right in front of the goal. Clear shot. I took it.

It soared just past the goalkeeper's fingertips and hit the back of the net. In an instant, I was engulfed by cheering teammates.

The goal must've added some fuel to our team's fire. When the game started again, everyone seemed more determined than before. It wasn't long before we were fighting once more in front of Birchwood's net.

Sarah took a shot. Too far to the left. It missed. The Birchwood goalie laughed and I made sure to flip her off when the referee wasn't looking.

One of their midfielders went to take the corner kick. She'd been handling them all game, and I knew exactly where she would aim the ball. She would go for their strongest player. I began to stalk their center forward.

It paid off. Just like I'd calculated, she curved the ball towards the forward. I was quick to jump in front of the bewildered player and steal the pass, not wasting any time, sprinting past every defender for 50 yards and then finally shooting the ball which went straight past their stunned goalie.

Once again, I was pummeled by my teammates.

"C'mon, guys," I said to Rebecca and Sarah. "Two goals left. We beat them the first game. We can do it again. Grizzly Goal, let's go."

We high-fived. We could do this. We knew it. The Grizzly Goal was an intense move we'd developed as a team. We would cluster up and pass the ball so quickly and frequently that Birchwood wouldn't know what hit them.

After a brief scuffle near our goal, we took off. Our technique was working. The three of us were grinning as we flew by their line of defense.

Rebecca was the one to take the shot. It flew towards the corner of the net. It looked like it was going in. It had to. We were going to score—

Their goalie's fist struck the ball and sent it spinning in my direction.

Without thinking, I reeled back and slammed my forehead against the ball so hard that I think my brain collided with my skull.

I hadn't even realized the ball had hit the corner of the net until Sarah tackled me.

"Hat trick! You got a hat trick!" she was screaming. I shook my head, breaking into a grin. I had scored!

I immediately raised my head towards the stands. Had Emma seen that? I hoped so. God, I hoped so. I searched for her as I jogged back to my starting position, vaguely aware of Coach Reynolds going nuts on the sidelines.

We were a force to be reckoned with. The Hidden Springs team was damned and determined to win: we approached the task of a final goal with a renewed vigor and intensity. Everyone was ecstatic about the idea of actually winning the championship match against Birchwood.

Birchwood must have been disheartened by giving up three goals in less than six minutes, because now they seemed slower. Or maybe we were just faster. We were outrunning and outplaying them with every second that ticked by.

Sarah passed me the ball and I took off. Birchwood must've been expecting it, because they were all over me. The defender who had been marking me the entire game seemed to become desperate with hands and elbows.

But she wasn't going to take me down. I had a ferocity. A fire. I was going to win this game for Hidden Springs. I was going to show Emma what I could really do.

At least, I thought so.

Just as I jerked my left leg back to take a shot on the goal, I felt the bottom of the defender's cleat slam into the side of my knee. The ball went spinning off in another direction.

I hit the ground hard.

A whistle cut through the air.

"Fuck," I whimpered. The pain was searing throughout my body. I turned my head to see the referee arguing with the other girl and forced myself into a sitting position.

"It was an accident!" I heard her claim. Her face was red with anger as she waved her hands in some desperate attempt to prove a point.

"I saw the entire thing," Rebecca countered. "That was completely deliberate. She wasn't even aiming for the ball."

I glanced down at my knee. The rough ridges on the bottom of her cleats had done a piece of work. Blood was soaking into my sock and running down the inside of my shin guards. A chunk of skin had been taken clean off. I winced, rolling over to try to hobble to my feet, balancing myself on my right leg.

Sarah was at my side in the next instant, an arm around my shoulder. "Charlotte, are you okay?"

I nodded weakly, although I was well aware of the tears streaming down my face. I took a shaky breath, trying to dispel them. *Don't let that bitch see you cry,* I thought.

Coach emerged through the crowd of gathered girls. "Oh, Christ," I heard her say when she saw my knee.

As Sarah and Coach helped me limp from the field, I caught a glimpse of the referee giving the defender a red card. Well, however much the Birchwood coach had tipped him obviously wasn't enough. I couldn't hide a smile as I fell into the grass on the sidelines. Coach knelt at my side.

"Do you think it's broken?" she asked. Her hand gently touched my lower thigh as she examined the damage. I sat myself up on my elbows, staring at my bloody leg.

"I don't know." I shook my head. "I don't think so."

She grabbed a towel from Regina's hands and wrapped it around my knee. I winced at the connection, biting my lip hard as I watched the girls blur together on the field. The game resumed without me.

Coach gently pulled the towel away and picked up a nearby water bottle, pouring the contents onto my knee. I felt my body writhe in pain, hot tears staining my cheeks once more.

The Birchwood side erupted in cheers. They had scored.

"It's okay, honey," Coach said, placing a hand on my shoulder in an attempt to comfort me. I tried hard to concentrate on the game. Our players seemed to have lost all the determination as quickly as they had gotten it.

Emma and Kenny appeared at my side. For some reason, I was more relieved to have them both there. I leaned back against the grass, using the palm of my hand to try to wipe the tears away.

"We've got her," Kenny said. I watched Coach step away as he took over holding the towel against my leg. Emma crouched down at my shoulder.

"How bad is it?" she asked Kenny. He pulled the towel away and made a face.

"Pretty bad." He frowned. "That stupid bitch pretty much skinned the side of her leg." They were talking about me like I wasn't even there.

I felt Emma's hand run through my hair and leaned into her touch, closing my eyes.

"You okay?" she asked. I nodded.

The whistle blew for the end of the game. My teammates hadn't managed to score. Birchwood had won. We had lost the Fall Playoffs.

The team flooded off the field, seething about the foul players.

Emma drew her hand away from me and sat quietly. The girls came over one by one to check on me. Sarah lingered at my side like a fly that I couldn't seem to swat away.

"I can't believe that bitch," Sarah said loudly, scuffing her foot against the ground. "She deserved more than a red card. She deserved to be decked across her fugly face."

I chuckled, sitting up and wincing when Kenny unknowingly increased the pressure on my knee. Emma's hand flew to my shoulder at the sight of my discomfort, but then withdrew once again.

"Hey, Hayes." Cory shoved through a few girls to kneel next to me. "Amazing game. You'd have won it for us for sure if it wasn't for that dumb girl. How are you feeling?"

"Pretty pissed." I forced a smile and glanced down at my sock. It was covered in blood. Disgusting.

Cory shook her head. "Do you need to go to the hospital?"

I looked to Kenny. He shrugged.

"I don't think she does." He peered closer to inspect the damage. "I mean, there's not really much they can do. She'll just have to keep it wrapped."

"My mom's a nurse," I pointed out, wiping at some dried blood on my thigh. "She'll know what to do."

Cory nodded, and, looking at Emma, said, "Take care of her."

Did Emma blush?

"Do you have ace wrap at home?" Coach asked me when she had finished talking to the team. I nodded.

"Wrap it up good and put some ice on it as soon as you get home. Did you drive?"

I nodded again.

Coach Reynolds turned her gaze to Kenny and Emma. "Would either one of you be able to drive her home?"

"I can," Emma spoke up before Kenny had a chance to. "Or, actually," she said, frowning, "I can't drive stick."

"You can take my truck," Kenny offered. "I'll follow you in her car."

"Okay," Emma agreed.

Coach put a hand on my shoulder, smiling in her most reassuring way. "I'm going to go over and have a little chat with the Birchwood coach. I'll give you a call tonight to see how you're doing, okay?"

"Thanks," I told her. I felt Emma put her arms around my upper waist and pull, helping me to my feet. I staggered awkwardly onto my good foot.

Kenny grabbed my bag and slung it over his shoulder. Each of them took one of my arms and helped me hobble towards the parking lot.

"I'll meet you at Charlotte's house," Kenny told Emma when we'd reached the truck before disappearing through the jungle of cars to find Old Reliable.

As soon as he was out of view, Emma wrapped her arms around me and hugged me so tight I felt the breath being squeezed out of my lungs.

"I'm okay," I said.

Without speaking, she opened the passenger door and helped me clamber into the seat. I lifted my leg with my arms and placed it onto the dashboard to keep it elevated, tilting my seat back.

Emma leaned in and planted a kiss on my cheek. I couldn't help the smile that tugged at the corner of my lips. It quickly disappeared when I saw the snapshot series of Kenny and Emma kissing. It was taped to his dashboard, there for the world to see.

I couldn't take my eyes off it the entire way home.

A knock on the window broke me out of my stupor. We were home.

"I'll go get the bandages. Where are they?" Kenny shouted through the glass.

"Don't worry about it," Emma said, coming around the side to help me hobble out. "I've got her. Go home."

"But I can help." Kenny looked offended. Hurt. Nevertheless, he took his keys and handed my bag to Emma. "Well, call me when you get home." He kissed Emma. I cringed. "Feel better, Char'," he told me, doing one last inspection of my leg and giving me a squeeze on the shoulder before hopping into his truck.

I balanced on Emma as we staggered into my house and straight to my room. Wednesday followed, whining.

"Here, lay down." Emma helped me lean back onto my bed. I let my upper body collapse, lower legs hanging off the side of the bed.

Emma kneeled, removing each one of my cleats to toss to the floor before slowly peeling my socks and shin guards off. She was so cautious with my leg I could hardly feel her hands against my skin.

I looked down, watching as she examined my bloody mess of a knee. "This looks like shit," she told me, looking up to meet my eyes. I laughed.

"Thanks for that," I said. She disappeared for a minute before returning with two wet washcloths. She began wiping off the blood that had run down my leg beneath my shin guards, and gently dabbed at my knee. I winced, biting my lip hard as I felt my body jerk every time she touched it.

"I'm sorry," she said quietly.

"No, don't be." I met her gaze, offered a reassuring smile.

"Where's your Ace?" She set the washcloth on my bedside table. It was bright red.

"My mom's room. I think she keeps it in the chest at the end of her bed."

She was gone for a while. When she finally returned, her expression was grim. There was no bandage in her hand.

Something was wrong.

"Was it not there?" I asked.

"No." She shook her head. "It, uh, wasn't there."

"Well, it might be in the bathroom then, she usually—"

"Charlie," Emma interrupted. She took a step forward. That's when I noticed she was holding something else. "You said that letter from your Dad was the only one you'd ever gotten, right?"

"Well, yeah." I was confused. What did this have to do with anything? I felt my heart start to beat faster in my chest, the throb in my knee becoming distant, unimportant.

She lowered her eyes, as if she couldn't bear to look me in the face. As soon as she stretched her hand forward to drop what she was holding into my lap, I knew why.

It was a stack of letters from Dad.

Eighteen

My head rested against the cold glass of the passenger side window, gaze locked on the blurred scenery as it flew by. The rhythmic pattern of rain striking Mom's SUV combined with the quiet static of the radio caused my eyes to droop sleepily. Only an hour into this trip and I was already wishing it was over. With a sigh, I found the lever to lower my seat back, cocking my left leg awkwardly to the side to avoid any impact to my injured knee.

"You falling asleep, Charlotte?" Mom asked from the driver's seat. My eyes blinked slowly open. I tilted my head to look at her. Her gaze was locked on the road ahead through the gently swaying windshield wipers, both hands gripping the steering wheel.

I knew she was excited to see her family. She'd been talking nonstop about the trip all week. Still, that didn't mean *I* had to be stoked about it. And I definitely wasn't excited now, after learning she'd been hiding letters from me for years.

I grunted. Maybe if I pretended I was asleep, she wouldn't talk to me. I didn't want to speak to her. If I opened my mouth, I was afraid what might come out.

How could you?

What kind of mother are you to hide things from your own daughter?

I pulled my Adidas sweatshirt off to stuff under my head as a makeshift pillow, feeling tears sting the corner of my eyes as I remembered the weight of the letters in my hand. The way I felt, like a ten pound weight had been tied to my heart, as I ripped open the first aged yellow envelope to read the contents.

Mom smiled. "We'll be there soon," she said, reaching over to pat my knee. I winced, jerking away. She sympathetically retracted her hand.

"Whatever," I said.

She shrugged, fiddling with the radio to try to find a station that didn't consist of static or gospel. "What's the matter with you? Maybe we should have brought Wednesday to keep you company."

"Wednesday hates Petey, you know that." Petey was my grandmother's cocker spaniel, who was as grouchy as he was old. Wednesday despised him. I didn't blame her. Therefore, I made the decision to leave her at home and have Kenny care for her for the few days we were gone.

Mom grew silent. Crossing my fingers that it would stay that way, I turned to look through the window. Winter was taking its toll on the landscape and everything looked like a barren wasteland. The rain only added to the dreariness. I reached up to the window and drew a tree into the condensation that had developed on the glass.

"Don't do that," Mom scolded, shooting me a playful glare as she switched lanes to maneuver around a huge 18-wheeler.

I pulled my hand away, letting my head fall back against my sweatshirt. My eyes had just drifted shut when my phone began to vibrate in the cup holder. With a sigh, I grabbed the lever of the seat and brought it back into a nearly vertical position. I didn't know who I was trying to kid. Sleep was apparently not going to work for me on this trip. I was going to have to suffer through all of it.

Picking up my phone, I flipped it open to read the text message. It was from Emma, who was already with her relatives. She'd left early in the morning with her dad and Trevor. *How are you? Have you talked to your mom yet?*

My fingers flew over the phone. *No.*

"Who's that?" Mom asked, glancing briefly over before returning her eyes to the road.

"Emma," I replied, unable to hide the anger that sifted into my voice. I settled back into my seat and pulled my sweatshirt into my lap to rest my hands on it. My phone vibrated again.

You really should.

"You two sure do hang out a lot." Mom started toying with the radio again.

"Yup."

"She must be a really nice girl," she said.

"Yup."

"I'm so glad she's dating Kenny. She's good for him," Mom added. Her voice sounded strange. What did she mean by that?

I bit my tongue.

She must've finally realized I didn't want to talk because she didn't say anything else.

I opened my mouth. I wanted to ask why she hid those letters from me. Why she felt she had to protect me from Dad. For so many years, I'd been going along with the charade, thinking I had the worst Dad on the planet for not even sending me so much as a birthday card. But he'd sent me one every year. I just didn't get them. And so many letters that I would have loved to respond to.

And, oh, God. I'd sent him that horrible, horrible letter.

I was so angry. I felt my pulse quicken and pursed my lips.

I wanted to ask, but maybe I didn't want to know.

~~~

"We're here!" Mom announced, and I snapped awake to realize that at some point, I had lowered my seat back down and subsequently drooled all over the headrest. I quickly wiped at the corner of my mouth, blinking the sleep out of my eyes as I glanced around at the familiar surroundings of my grandparents' neighborhood.

I saw Grandma and Grandpa appear on the front porch. My mother was out of the car in an instant and racing up the drive to hug them. Throwing my sweatshirt back on, I pushed open the passenger door and scrambled out of my seat to slowly hobble after her.

"Oh, Charlotte, honey!" Grandma tackled me in a hug and planted a huge kiss on my forehead. I felt my ribcage slowly giving. I was pretty sure I was about to suffocate to death before she finally let me go.

"Long time no see," I said lamely, offering a broad smile. It really had been a long time, a little over a year. They both looked exactly the same, though: Grandma, with her carefully dyed brown hair in an attempt to fight the grey, and Grandpa, with his bright white head of hair and cheerful smile. Despite the discomfort of having to spend Thanksgiving with relatives, I really had missed them.

"You've gotten so big." Grandpa stepped forward and hugged me much more gently than Grandma did.

"I'm pretty sure the only thing that's grown since I saw you last is my hair," I joked, returning the hug as I balanced myself on the porch railing.

"Your sister will be here a bit later tonight," Grandma told Mom. Aunt Angie was Mom's only sibling, and the two weren't on the best terms. They hadn't gotten along ever since my parents' divorce. Because of it, I hardly ever saw my aunt and uncle, which was just fine with me because my cousin, Aidan, was a complete jerk.

I turned back to the car to grab our bags. Grandpa followed, taking Mom's suitcase out of my arms and lightening the load.

"Been fighting in the war?" he asked, raising an eyebrow as I awkwardly slammed the trunk shut.

"What?" I balanced my suitcase and bag in my arms as we made our way into the house. The two of us dropped everything by the door.

"You're limping something good." He directed his gaze to my left leg as we headed into the kitchen where Mom and Grandma were chatting animatedly.

"Soccer."

Nodding, he searched through the refrigerator before handing me a Sprite. "Sports can be dangerous."

Not as dangerous as family, I thought. I took the soda and popped the top. "Thanks."

"How is school?" He pulled out one of his bottles of club soda to take a swig as he leaned against their aged yellow refrigerator. "Straight A's?"

I laughed. "Yeah, not so much." Even though I usually got good grades, I'd never been a straight 'A' student in my life, and he knew it. "But, I'm doing pretty well. English is killing me, though. My teacher is horrid."

"You know what I did when I had a bad teacher in high school? I found out where they lived, and me and the guys tee-pee'd their house and put rotten eggs in their mailbox."

I nearly choked on my soda. "Are you kidding me?"

He shook his head. "Nope. Revenge can be sweet."

"I don't think I'm going to tee-pee Mrs. Norris's house."

Mom turned to eyeball me curiously, gaze sweeping back and forth between Grandpa and me. "Don't give my daughter any bad ideas, dad. I don't want her getting all rebellious in her senior year."

"Senior?" He mocked a face of surprise. "I thought you were a freshman."

"Shut up," I grumbled. "You did not."

Grandpa walked into the living room to turn on the television and immediately flipped to the ESPN Sports channel. I took a seat on the couch across from him, drawing my right leg up underneath me and moving my left leg to the side. I tilted my head back against the armrest, listening to Mom and Grandma still chatting in the kitchen.

I wanted to ask Grandpa if he'd heard from Dad at all. But just as I opened my mouth to say something, Aunt Angie came bustling through the front door.

"Janelle." Aunt Angie acknowledged Mom with a small smile when she and Grandma walked out of the kitchen.

Mom's face blanched. I wasn't sure of the history of the animosity between the two, I only knew that it had something to do with Aunt Angie siding with Dad during the divorce. Uncle John, who I actually liked, glanced over towards me and offered a friendly grin. I returned it.

Mom drew her lips into a tight smile. "Hello, Angie," she said, walking over to give her a rather awkward hug. "John," she added, embracing Uncle John as well. "Good to see you both."

"Charlotte." Aunt Angie strode over to give me a hug where I was sitting on the couch. "My, you've gotten big. I haven't seen you since, well, you know." Since the divorce. She didn't have to tell me, I knew.

My grandparents hugged each of them, making a fuss over how handsome Aidan had gotten. Personally, I didn't see it. He looked like a complete prick, but that was probably because I thought he was one. My opinion didn't matter. He was completely brilliant in my relatives' eyes. He was twenty, and somehow managed to get into Yale University. I supposed it was a good thing they didn't consider personality on college applications, because otherwise he wouldn't have had a chance in hell.

"Well," Grandma broke the silence that had enveloped us, "Janelle and I were just in the kitchen discussing our plans for tomorrow if you'd like to join us, Angie."

"So, Charlotte," Uncle John began once they had disappeared, "still playing soccer?"

"Yeah."

"You're a senior now, right? Have you picked a college?"

I shook my head, picking at the frayed edge of the couch cushion. "Not quite yet," I said, "I've applied to a few, though."

"I remember when I applied," Aidan cut into the conversation, running a hand through his short brown hair as he sneered at me. "It was so hard to pick between Yale, Harvard, and Duke."

He was such a jerk. I turned away, ignoring him.

I desperately wanted to get back to a life that didn't involve awkward holidays with relatives. Even though I didn't particularly want to be alone with Mom, I knew that I'd at least have Emma.

~~~

Mom and I spent the night in the guest room. I didn't sleep at all. I was already wide awake by the time she rolled over and stretched.

"Who were you texting for so long last night?" she asked.

"No one," I grumbled.

Her eyes scrutinized my face. I turned away.

"What's your problem these past few days?" she asked.

Grandma poked her head into our room. "You two awake? Oh, good. We have breakfast ready downstairs."

Relieved, I shot out of bed. But it was like leaving one battle zone to enter another.

"Jeez, did you sleep in enough?" Aidan commented from the breakfast table as soon as I walked in. I smoothed my hair with my hand, trying to get rid of my serious bed-head. He was already dressed in khakis, a button down shirt, and a sweater vest. I hated how he tried to be the typical Ivy League student.

I rolled my eyes, taking a seat next to him to set my phone down in front of me and pour a glass of orange juice from a pitcher on the table. I could feel him staring at me. I squirmed uncomfortably.

Mom sat down across from me. I avoided her gaze and absently chewed at a piece of toast.

"What colleges did you apply to?" Aidan asked.

"Local ones," I said. I watched a small bird land on the edge of the birdbath outside the window.

"Are you eighteen yet?"

I sighed. "No. Not until May." Maybe he was done speaking to me. No such luck.

"Do you talk to your dad at all?"

I felt my face grow hot. "No," I said.

"Oh. Why not?"

*Oh, I don't know. Maybe because Mom has been hiding all of
his letters from me for five years so I never even knew he was trying
to contact me?*

I bit my lip. "None of your business."

I turned my attention back to the bird, which had submerged its
tiny head and was splashing water all over the place. I wished I were
that bird. I wouldn't have to worry about annoying relatives, lying
parents. I wouldn't have to hide who I was.

I had to get away.

My hand shot forward to grab my phone, but instead I met bare
wood. I looked around in confusion. Maybe I'd accidentally pushed
it somewhere else.

"What the hell?" I said.

"Charlotte," Grandma looked appalled. "Language."

"What's wrong?" Aidan asked.

"I thought I brought my phone down here," I said, searching the
pockets of my sweatpants. Not there.

He rolled his broad shoulders in a shrug before rising and
leaving the table with Aunt Angie. I continued to search the table
before returning to the guest room to scour every possible crevice for
my phone. *How in the world did I lose it?* I thought to myself. *I had
it with me.*

I couldn't find it anywhere.

~~~~

I sat on the couch and set the television on a marathon of America's
Next Top Model while everyone was in the kitchen preparing the
Thanksgiving feast. The solitude was nice.

Until Aidan slumped into the couch next to me.

"I love this show," he said. I turned towards him. He smirked,
making me realize just how much I would've loved to wipe that
cocky look off his face. "These girls are so hot."

Typical guy. I shrugged.

"That brunette, man." He pointed to the one having a one-on-
one interview with the camera and snapped his fingers. "I'd tap that.
What about you? Blonde or brunette?"

"What are you talking about?" I asked.

"I was just asking if you liked blondes or brunettes better. So?
Which is it?"

"Blondes, I guess."

He nodded. I watched him stuff his hands into his pockets from the corner of my eye. "So," he began, "is this Emma chick a blonde?"

I felt my heart skip a beat as I turned my eyes to look into his arrogant face. "W-what?" I stammered. I didn't remember mentioning Emma to him at all. I felt my expression alter from confusion to anger as he pulled my phone from his pocket, waggling it in front of him.

I instantly flew across the couch and wrestled it out of his hands.

"What the fuck, Aidan?" I heard myself scream. "How dare you! You went through my phone, didn't you?"

He shrugged. Anger bubbled in my throat. I wanted to punch him in the face. My fists clenched at my sides.

"Oh Emma, I love you, I wish I was with you instead of my fucked up family," he mocked in a fake female voice. I set my jaw, swallowing hard.

"You're an asshole," I managed to spit out after a moment. "I can't believe you."

He flashed his teeth in a huge grin. "Whatever. Does your mom know?"

I didn't respond, and instead tried to light him on fire with my eyes. At that moment, I really wished I was Carrie. Pig blood and all.

"She doesn't know?" He burst into laughter, feigning a look of surprise. "Your mom doesn't know that her little girl is a *lesbo*? Wow."

What did he mean by that?

I pushed myself off the couch, wanting so bad to just pummel the life out of him. Instead, I limped up the stairs and disappeared into the guest room, collapsing face first onto the bed.

My heart was running a marathon. Acid boiled in my veins.

Aidan was going to tell Mom.

I covered my face with my hands and suppressed a scream.

~~~

"Are you alright, Charlotte?"

Mom's voice cut into my thoughts. Her hand pressed against my forehead and snapped me out of my stupor.

I pulled away and sat up. Sure, I felt ill. But it wasn't because I was sick. "I'm fine," I lied.

"Dinner's ready. Come eat."

I followed her downstairs. A dead girl walking.

Everyone was already at the table. Silverware clanked against plates as everyone took huge helpings of everything. There were green beans, mashed potatoes, olives, stuffing, squash casserole, bread, cranberries. A huge turkey sat in the middle of the table.

None of it looked appetizing.

I sat down, feeling Aidan's eyes on me from across the table. I avoided them like the plague.

Somehow, my plate managed to fill up. I prodded at everything with my fork, knowing I wouldn't be eating anything.

"Hey, Charlotte," Aidan called from across the table. "Can you pass the green beans?"

I looked at the bowl of green beans which seemed much closer to Aunt Angie than me.

"I've got it," Aunt Angie said, picking up the dish and handing to Aidan.

"Thanks, Mom," Aidan said. "Oh, hey, Charlotte. Didn't you have something to tell everyone? You know, what we were talking about earlier?"

I let my fork fall to my plate with a loud clatter, my eyes shooting daggers into his. I could feel the heat rushing into my face as everyone at the table turned towards me.

"What?" I hoped he could sense the venom in my voice.

"Yeah, I thought you had an announcement." He shoved some potatoes into his mouth, smirking the entire time.

So this was it. All eyes were on me.

Behold, the gay girl.

My mind shifted in every direction, trying to think of something to tell them other than what Aidan was implying. This couldn't be it. This didn't have to be how they found out.

"You have something to tell us?" Mom asked. Confused, she set her utensils down next to her plate.

"I think I've decided to take that scholarship to UConn next year," I blurted.

"Oh, wow!" Mom exclaimed, reaching over to give my arm a squeeze. "Did you get the letters back from Fairfield and Wesleyan yet, though?"

My skin pulsed. "Not yet."

I could sense Aidan staring. I clutched the edge of the table so hard my knuckles turned white, struggling to keep myself from throwing my plate in his face.

"You should have applied to PennState. That's where Daniel went, right? Isn't that where he met—" Aunt Angie stared.

"What?" Mom cut in. She must have realized her mouth was hanging open because she quickly shut it. "Angie, now is not the time."

Aunt Angie shrugged. "Charlotte just reminds me so much of Daniel, that's all."

I felt my face blanch.

"Excuse me?" Mom's eyes flashed with anger.

Uncle John was glaring at Aunt Angie. "So, how about that game tonight?"

I thanked him with my eyes. Even though the conversation changed, the animosity remained. It filled the room like smoke, clinging to my skin, prodding at my mind.

I wanted more than anything to be away from my so-called family and where I truly belonged: back in Hidden Springs with Wednesday, with Kenny. With Emma.

~~~

When Mom and I were both finally in the car and pulling out of the driveway, I could sense the relief between the two of us.

"That was a hell of a visit," Mom said.

"Yeah." I pulled out my iPod and began shuffling through songs. Being alone with her made anger flare in the corner of my mind.

"What was going on with you and Aidan?" she asked.

"Nothing," I said. "He's a jackass."

"I didn't know you decided to go to UConn."

"Yeah. I guess I decided this week." I shrugged, turning to look out the window. Goodbye, Pennsylvania. And good riddance. Mom focused her attention on the road.

I was mad at her, sure, but I couldn't let her find out about me that way. I had to be the one to tell her. The thought of it made a lump rise in my throat.

She had lied to me. But I was lying to her.

And a lot of other people, too.

~~~

When Mom finally pulled into our driveway three hours later, I was surprised, but excited, to see Kenny's truck parked out front. I literally bolted (simultaneously realizing my leg felt better) to the front door, where he greeted me with my overly exuberant husky at his side.

Before he had a chance to say anything, I wrestled him into a tight hug.

"Whoa. Hey." He laughed. "Good to see you, too."

I let go to bend down and wrap my arms around Wednesday, tugging her in close and burying my face into her neck. It was good to be home.

"I'm guessing your Thanksgiving sucked?" Kenny asked.

I looked up, forcing a smile.

"I guess you could say that."

Nineteen

"Wow, your cousin is an asshole," Emma said once I'd told her everything that happened over Thanksgiving. I could hear her pencil scratching against paper as she struggled to finish a Government assignment that was due in the morning.

"Yeah." I flipped aimlessly through the magazine spread out in front of me and looked up at her from the floor. Her hair looked soft, gleaming in the dim light of her desk lamp. I wanted to run my fingers through it.

"So are you really planning on going to UConn?" Emma swiveled in her chair to meet my gaze. I snapped out of my stupor.

"I just needed something quick to say," I said. "But, I guess. I have a scholarship."

We grew quiet until the sound of her book slamming shut made me jump. She rose before settling down on the carpet in front of me, so close that her nose was only millimeters from my own. I felt my breath catch.

I reached one hand forward, tentatively running my fingers through her soft hair, watching as it cascaded like a waterfall against her smooth forehead. She smiled.

"I wish I could tell my mom." I pulled my hand away. "I don't know how she'd react."

"I know my dad would have a fit," Emma whispered. She leaned forward to kiss the tip of my nose. I closed my eyes, savoring the moment.

"Charlie, I think I'm gay."

I took a deep breath. Opened my eyes. Emma was searching my face, as though I alone held the answers she sought. "What?"

"Look at me," she said. Sorrow tinged her voice. "I'm sneaking around behind my boyfriend's back with his best friend who's a girl. How can I not be gay?"

"I—I don't know," I answered. I knew that I was. That she was. But I'd already learned that saying it out loud didn't lead to acceptance. "Maybe I'm a phase," I offered.

She reached forward, brushing the backs of her knuckles across my cheek. "What in the world would ever make you think that? I love you." She drew her fingers up underneath my chin and pulled me forward, pressing her soft, inviting lips against my own. When we pulled away, I found her piercing eyes trained on mine. In them, I saw a mixture of emotions: love, happiness, worry.

"How long do you think we'll have to hide this, Charlie?" she asked.

I shook my head, dropping my eyes as I felt her fingers lace into mine. "I don't know," I said. "I guess until we think we're ready to let people know."

She sighed, dropping her chin onto her still hand. I ran my fingers across her palm, leaning my forehead against hers. I closed my eyes.

"The world's not ready for us," Emma joked. Only it wasn't so much of a joke. It was the truth. A truth I didn't understand. We had to sneak around while other people could just love outright.

We had to hide from our friends, our parents. Ourselves.

~~~

One day the next week, as I was waiting for Emma to make a quick run to her locker after Theater class, Sarah approached me.

"Hey, Charlotte." She stopped beside me and peered around. "Where's Emma?"

I turned to look down the hallway, expecting her to emerge from around the corner. Not yet. "At her locker. Why?"

She shifted her bag on her shoulder, running a hand through her dirty blonde hair. "I was just wondering if the two of you wanted to see a movie on Friday. Bryan and a few of his buddies want to go see this movie, and I don't want to be the only girl there," she said.

"Sure, I'll go. I'll have to ask Emma, though."

"Okay. Awesome. Just give me a call later and let me know, okay? Oh, by the way, Preston will be there." She gave me a wink before turning on her heel and disappearing through the front doors of the building.

Preston. I hadn't talked to him since he called. I smiled.

As I turned the corner to the hallway Emma's locker was on, I saw her. Her back was turned. It looked like she was digging around in her bag for something.

I glanced around to see if there was anyone else in the area. Empty. Grinning, I crept up behind her and threw my arms around her shoulders.

She nearly dropped her bag. Her muscles tightened under my grip. She whirled, the anger in her eyes melting into relief when she saw me.

"My God, Charlie." She giggled. "You scared me."

I grinned, pushing her hair over her shoulder to kiss her neck. I felt her hand on my chest, pushing me away.

"Sorry." I frowned. "Sarah just invited us to the movies on Friday."

She narrowed her eyes. "What?"

"Sarah wanted to know if we would go to the movies with her on Friday," I repeated.

"Dude, that'd be awesome," Kenny's voice came from behind us.

I whirled. I hadn't even realized he was there. Had he seen anything? I faked a smile, feeling the heat rising in my cheeks.

"Tell her we'd love to," he said. He wrapped his arms around Emma and squeezed her.

A fire was burning in the pit of my stomach. Who was he to invite himself? Oh, sure, he *was* her boyfriend and all. But still.

Emma looked equally pissed. I watched her eyes glaze over as she smiled at him. She obviously hadn't wanted him to go, either.

My mind traveled back to what she'd said the other night about being gay. I couldn't help but notice how much happier she was to see me.

It wasn't a phase.

~~~

"Does Emma seem like she's acting weird to you?" Kenny asked through a mouthful of his chicken sandwich. We'd decided to get a quick dinner at the local Wendy's, one of Hidden Springs' few fast food restaurants.

I dipped some fries into ketchup before shoveling them into my mouth, chewing slowly as I watched a family place an order with the cashier. "No. She seems fine. Why do you keep thinking that?" I asked. I took a sip of my soda. It tasted flat.

"She just seems distant," he said.

"Don't know," I lied.

A thoughtful frown flitted across his lips. "I feel like something's wrong," he said.

I didn't reply. Instead, I sought out the family, who had chosen a booth on the far side of the restaurant. A small boy, apparently unsatisfied with his own toy, was trying in vain to snag what his older sister had gotten.

"Davey, no," I heard his father scold.

I watched him shove a transformers figurine into his son's hand. Davey threw it to the ground, bursting into tears as he tried desperately to reach across the table to snag his sister's Bratz doll.

"That's a girl's toy, Davey." The man seemed oblivious to his son's tears as he reached down to pick up the toy and shove it back into the little boy's arms. "Boys don't play with dolls."

I narrowed my eyes. I felt for the little boy as he tossed his toy to the side once again. The father turned to glance towards me and I quickly looked away, frowning. *Why can't you just let him play with the toy?* I thought. *Why can't Davey be who he wants?*

Why couldn't Emma and I?

~~~

"Is that her?"

Preston pointed to Emma's back as the group of us stepped into the movie theater. Grinning, I whispered, "Yeah."

We watched as Kenny slipped his hand into Emma's, lacing their fingers together. I could feel the change in Preston's disposition as he stared at them. "Wait, but—"

Turning, I placed my index finger against my lips in a hushing gesture.

"Playing the part of the home-wrecker." Preston smiled. "Appalling, yet commendable. Very nice, Brangelina."

I offered a weak smile. Home-wrecker? That was a label I didn't want.

But it was one I deserved.

"She's cute, though. Totally worth it, if it all works out," he whispered.

If it all worked out? What did *that* mean?

I watched Kenny kiss Emma right in front of the ticket booth. Her eyes flickered to meet mine, a gentle blush appearing in her cheeks.

"They're so cute," I heard Sarah say. She nuzzled closer to Bryan.

I looked away.

When we finished getting our tickets and walked into the designated theater, I made sure I would be sitting next to Emma. Maybe it wasn't the smartest idea, but I desperately wanted to be close to her.

Her eyes met mine and she smiled. My organs melted. I couldn't hold back a smile of my own.

As the movie started, I tried to get into it, to disappear into the struggles of fictional characters instead of what was going on in my own life. But I couldn't.

I could only watch them out of the corner of my eye. He was kissing her. Touching her. Nuzzling her. It was disgusting.

It was what I should have been doing.

I had finally forced myself to watch the movie and was slowly becoming interested when I felt Emma's hand graze over my knee.

I glanced towards her, but her eyes were locked on the screen, just like everyone else's. Even Kenny's.

I looked away, tried to concentrate. It was impossible. Her fingers were moving gently over my leg. The pressure was so light, and yet it felt like it was bringing my blood to a boil beneath my skin. My breath grew shallow as her hand traced down my thigh.

Kenny could easily see us. All he had to do was look to the left. It was dark, but the lighting was definitely good enough.

I couldn't take it. I leapt to my feet and flew from the theater, down the hall. When I finally reached the bathroom, I let myself breathe.

Leaning against the sink, I glanced into the mirror. I looked flushed, frazzled. Just how I felt. I sucked in air and closed my eyes.

The door creaked open.

"Charlie?"

I opened my eyes, looked up. Emma slipped in, shutting the door gently behind her.

"Are you okay?"

"Fine," I lied, forcing a smile. "Fine."

She stepped forward, placing her hand on my cheek and sliding it around to the back of my neck. It was warm. I leaned into it, sighing.

"I'm so sorry," she said. "I know it's hard."

Hard was an understatement. More like painful. Like a knife searing through my gut every time I saw them together.

Before I knew what was happening, I was leaning into her. Feeling her body, soft and welcoming, mold into my own. I tilted my head and captured her lips with my own.

She relaxed into me. I wrapped my arms around her waist, feeling myself grow desperate as I pulled her closer. Everything melted away. I didn't care where we were, who we were with.

We were lost in the moment, and yet we found ourselves in each other.

The door to the restroom burst open. The two of us broke away like a couple of guilty children.

I drew a sharp breath and held it when I saw Sarah. She was staring at the two of us with one hand still holding the door, mouth ajar in shock.

"What the hell?"

I watched her expression change from bewilderment to anger. Color flooded into her cheeks. "I—I came to check on you, Charlotte. And…" she trailed off. Shook her head. "Wow. Are you serious?"

I swiped the back of my hand over my mouth. My chest heaved. I glanced to Emma. She wouldn't even look at Sarah; instead, she focused on her shuffling feet.

"I can't fucking believe this. I stood up for you, Charlotte," she said. "I've been telling that girl you weren't a dyke. But, no. You are one."

"I…" I bit my lip. "It's not like that, Sarah."

She ignored me. "And you." She jabbed a finger at Emma. "You're supposed to be with Kenny. What would he think, I wonder? This is disgusting." She whirled on her heel. "You're both disgusting!"

The door slammed behind her, leaving Emma and me to stand in an awkward hush.

I felt as though my heart was going to beat out of my chest. I averted my eyes to keep from looking at Emma. "We should go."

"Yeah," she said. Her voice was cold. Venomous. "You should."

I felt my eyes widen. Tears threatened to spill down my cheeks. More than anything, I wanted to cry. To let go. I held it inside. "It's not my fault, Emma."

"Then whose fault is it? My life's about to be ruined, Charlotte!" She was screaming now. Anger and pain filtered into her voice. I winced, stepped back.

"And what about mine?" I choked on a sob. "You're the one who followed me in here. Your life isn't the only one at stake, you know. It's not all about you."

"Well, sorry I ruined your fucking life. I've got to go. You should leave," Emma said.

Before I could say anything else, she was gone.

I couldn't make it to my car fast enough. As soon as I slipped into the driver's seat, I slammed my clammy palms down on the soft rubber of the steering wheel and let my forehead fall forward onto the back of my hands.

My mind replayed Emma's harsh words. The way Sarah looked at us, spoke to us. The disgust in her eyes, the poison laced into her usually friendly voice.

I was about to lose everything. But I had lost Emma, too.

Oh, God. What had I done?

<u>Twenty</u>

When I walked into my house, I tried to be discrete. Wednesday busted me.

She raced from Mom's bedroom, whimpering as she danced around my feet, her tail wagging animatedly. I tried desperately to hush her. I didn't want to face Mom.

"Charlotte," Mom called from her bedroom, "is that you?"

Too late.

"Yeah, it's me," I said. I rose to hang a quick left into the kitchen just as she appeared in the doorway of her bedroom. I tossed my keys onto the counter, quickly wiping at my eyes as the sound of footsteps grew closer.

I opened the refrigerator and made a show out of looking for something to eat just as she strode in.

"How was the movie?" she asked.

I grabbed a Coke, took a deep breath, and stood. "Fine," I lied.

She turned towards me. I could feel her eyes searching my face. I averted my gaze.

"Are you alright?" she asked.

"Yeah, I'm fine. Really." I left the kitchen and slipped down the hallway into my bedroom. Maybe she would leave it at that. No such luck. Why did she have to pull the motherly thing now? She stopped in the doorway.

"What's the matter?" she asked. "Did something happen tonight?"

I shook my head and plopped down on the edge of my mattress, setting my Coke on the bedside table. "No," I said, watching Wednesday lope into my room with a dripping mouth.

She frowned, letting her hand trace down the wall as she walked over to take a seat next to me. Putting an arm around my shoulders, she gave me a gentle hug. I found myself leaning into her.

"Is it Emma?" she asked after a moment. "Did you two have a fight?"

I started to shake my head, but then decided not to lie. I was already doing enough of that. And Mom was only trying to help, after all. I nodded, clenching my fist as I felt my eyes start to water up once again. Her last words, *Sorry I ruined your fucking life*, the way hurt and anger radiated from her eyes. The truth was that she hadn't ruined my life at all. She'd embellished it to a point where I didn't even recognize the girl I had become. I was so happy. So alive.

"Yeah." I swiped self-consciously at my eyes. "We did."

She set her jaw. "The two of you will make up," she told me in a sympathetic tone, placing her hand on my knee to give it a soft squeeze. "You're close, fights will happen. Don't let it get to you."

She didn't know how close we were. She didn't know how much I stood to lose if the fight meant the end of us. How much I stood to lose even if we were still together.

It was a double-edged sword.

I looked towards Wednesday, who had climbed onto my bed and was now stretched across my blue comforter. Her tail was thumping against the fabric even while her eyes were closed. I found myself wondering how a being could be so happy all the time. What was her secret?

Then I remembered. She didn't have to worry about falling in love with someone you were never supposed to be with. She didn't have to worry about betraying her friend. About disappointing her mother. About her entire life being ruined just because she was different.

Mom drew me from my thoughts. "Charlotte," she began, removing her hand from my knee to rise into a standing position, "you can tell me anything. You know that, right?"

A smile glimmered on her lips. A smile filled with hope, love, comfort. Everything I saw when Emma looked at me. She didn't give me a chance to respond and simply turned on her heel to walk out of my room, shutting the door quietly behind her.

I realized I'd been holding my breath and let out a long sigh, leaning back on my mattress to turn my head and look into Wednesday's sleeping face. I should be able to tell her everything. She was my mother. I should be able to ask her why the letters under my bed had been hidden for so long. About what really happened between her and Aunt Angie.

But it wasn't that simple, and we both knew it.

~~~

As I stood idly behind the host stand at work, scenarios of what was to come seemed to be on constant reply in my mind.

The potential of losing Emma. People classifying me as nothing more than a lesbian. Calling me a dyke. A faggot. They all ran through my head, seared into my mind.

It amazed me how many words for hatred there were. And I was about to be called every one on a daily basis at school.

I didn't want to go through it alone. I wanted Emma at my side, to be there for me. An anchor. Someone to understand exactly what I was going through and experience it with me. Was that selfish? If Sarah outed us, at least I wouldn't have to go through the humiliations and taunts on my own.

From being on the soccer team with Cory, I knew just how people like me were treated. The other girls were constantly calling her names, whispering about her behind her back, asking her questions that were entirely too intimate and probing. I didn't want to be on the outside like she was, and that was exactly where I'd be when everyone found out about me. Charlotte the lezzi. Charlotte the dyke.

The ridicule would be the least of it, though. I would lose my best friend. My thoughts traveled back to the days when Kenny and I would ride our bikes up and down the street. Laugh and joke about how we would be friends forever.

I knew that Kenny wouldn't be my friend when he found out I was playing him.

I was so lost in my thoughts that I hardly realized when a couple walked through the front door and approached the stand. I stared blankly into space, not even acknowledging them with a hello.

"Uh," the older gentleman said after a moment of not even being recognized, "two, please?"

"Oh." I jerked my head up, snapping out my thoughts. "Sorry," I said.

I grabbed some menus and a couple rolls of silverware to lead them to a booth across the restaurant. When I returned, a small family had arrived and was waiting quietly at the host stand. I quickly sat them before returning to my chair.

"Dude, Charlotte." Libby, one of the servers, came storming into the lobby. I turned to her. Took in her angry expression. "What the hell are you doing?"

My eyes shifted over the restaurant for a moment before returning to Libby, confused. "What?" I squirmed in my chair.

"You just double sat me, and Kyle has three tables open." She tilted her head in the direction of her section. I rose, moving into the restaurant to check how I'd filled up her tables. The few other servers milled around the wait station at the opposite end of the building, bored.

"Oh, I'm sorry," I said, pushing my hair out of my face as I turned back to her. "I didn't mean to, I wasn't thinking."

She heaved an exasperated sigh, swiping at her apron with her hands. "Well, do you suppose you could start thinking? You did this last night, too. You know how to host. What's going on with you?"

I bit my lip, swallowing hard and resting my arm on the host stand. "I don't know. Sorry, Libby," I lied.

She rolled her eyes, trekking off down the short hallway and over to her section to greet the two tables.

I plopped down in my chair, leaning back and pulling my cell phone out of my back pocket. I couldn't keep this up. I wanted, needed, to know if at least one situation was under control. I hesitated for a moment before texting Emma.

I'm sorry.

She didn't reply.

~~~

"Hey. Why did you leave the movie early last night?"

I broke my concentration from repetitively wiping down the same spot on the host stand and turned to meet Kenny's gaze. Sarah must not have told him. I felt my face begin to burn.

"I, uh— well, I wasn't feeling too great." I looked down. Could he tell I was lying?

"Oh." Had he bought it? "Are you sure something didn't happen with Emma? She seemed pretty upset."

"Not that I know of." I was lying through my teeth. Not that it was anything new.

He took a seat on one of the benches in the waiting area, opening a box in his hand to offer me a chicken finger. I shook my head.

It was a minute before he said, "You okay? You don't look too well. Do we need a best friend one-on-one? Haven't had one of those in a while." He paused, took a breath. "I'm really sorry. I've been so caught up in Emma and haven't been a very good friend lately."

If only he knew. I offered a meek smile. "It's okay."

"It's not." He looked down, dropping his half-eaten chicken finger. "I really love her, you know."

His gaze locked with mine. I felt my eyes burning into him and tried to force my expression into what I hoped was friendly.

You're not the only one, I wanted to say. *And that's the problem.*

~~~

Mom wasn't home. I slid from the driver's seat, shivering as soon as my skin made contact with the freezing air. The bitter cold penetrated my thin blouse and slacks, chilling me to the bones.

I walked up the steps to my front porch and stopped in my tracks. A figure was curled up in one of our chairs. I could see the glow of a cigarette, a cloud of smoke colliding with the cold air as a breath was exhaled.

"Emma?" I took the last few steps and stopped in front of her.

She looked up, lowering her cigarette to her side as she forced a smile. Her lips were blue. "Hey."

I could see her body trembling, even beneath the layers of her coat and sweatshirt. "What are you doing here?" I asked. "I mean, how long have you been waiting?"

"Uh, I got here around nine."

I looked down at my watch. It was ten. "Jesus, Emma," I said. "How did you even get here?"

"I walked." She threw her cigarette to the ground, grinding her foot on top of it before staggering to her feet. I felt myself shivering, but not only from the cold. I searched her eyes for some sort of clue as to why she was here. Did she still want to be with me? Was she here to tell me it was over?

She threw her arms around my neck, pulling me into a tight embrace. I closed my eyes. Hugged her hard. Breathed in the familiar scent of vanilla and cigarettes.

"Charlie." She backed away, leaving her hands on my arms. "I'm so sorry."

"Me, too," I said. I settled back into her arms, closing my eyes. "I didn't mean any of it, Emma."

She kissed my cheek. Her lips were cold.

"Let's get inside," I said. "I'm freezing."

I broke away, fumbling with the keys to unlock the door and push it open. I was relieved when the warm air struck my body.

"So, why'd you walk over here?" I asked. Wednesday came thumping over, tail wagging. I opened the back door to let her into the yard.

She shrugged. "I wanted to see you."

"I would have come over, you know," I told her. "You didn't have to risk hypothermia by walking all the way over here and waiting for me to get off work."

"Yeah, I know." She pushed her hood off and ran a hand through her hair. "But I realized tonight that you've given me everything and I've given you nothing. It's not fair."

I took her coat and hung it up. "That's not true—"

"Yes, it is," she interrupted. "I'm going to break up with Kenny."

"What?" Excitement throbbed through my veins. "Are you serious?"

She shrugged. "I can't keep doing this, Charlie. It's not fair to you. It's not fair to us."

"He's going to be upset," I said, remembering how he'd told me he loved her.

She nodded, saying nothing.

We stood in silence for a long time, just taking everything in. I felt like I could taste the freedom of having her to myself. No Kenny. At the same time, I felt horrible. "Do you want to spend the night?" I heard myself ask.

"I don't have any of my stuff." She frowned.

"That's okay," I said. "You can just borrow some pajamas. We'll stop by your house on the way to school in the morning."

"Okay," she replied. "Let me just call my dad."

I drifted into the bathroom while she was on the phone, pausing to look at myself in the mirror. Why did I ask her to stay? She'd never actually spent the night before. Mom still didn't want her to stay here with me at night. Alone. But Mom wasn't home. I hoped she didn't think I expected anything from her. I didn't even think I was ready to take that step.

As Emma was taking her turn in the bathroom, I shoved some dirty clothes under my bed and grabbed a pair of old soccer shorts to put on. I was slipping a t-shirt over my head when Emma walked in.

"I'm sorry." She stepped back and turned her head away. I quickly yanked my shirt all the way on before turning to look at her.

"It's okay," I said. Her cheeks were bright red. "Really."

I turned the light off in my room and the two of us clambered into my bed, sliding under the covers.

"Are you sure this is okay?" she asked, glancing over at me.

"Yeah, it's fine. Mom probably won't even be home until late tomorrow morning. And she won't know." I paused, drew a breath. "What do you think tomorrow will be like? Do you think Sarah told anybody?"

"I mean, she didn't say anything after you left. She just didn't talk to me," she said. "But I don't really know."

We grew quiet, both of us staring at the ceiling, maybe trying to find an answer written somewhere across the white paint.

I turned my attention back to her, my eyes running over the bridge of her nose, her constellation of freckles, the way her hair splayed wildly across the pillow. I felt myself trembling.

"Will you set the alarm for me?"

She nodded, turning to the side to fidget with the buttons on my alarm clock. "I don't know how," she finally said. "Yours is confusing."

I reached over her to set my alarm and was about to retreat when I felt her hand slide up my wrist to gently grab my arm. My eyes locked with hers. They drifted over her face to the soft skin of her pale neck, the outline of her collarbone, the way my shirt seemed to hug her thin body.

I felt my breath catch in my throat and before I knew it, I was leaning down. Kissing her. A jolt of electricity seared my stomach as she slid her arms around my waist, pulling my body into hers.

Our kiss was hesitant, exploring. Slowly, it turned into something more: desire, need. Her hands slipped up my shirt and explored my back.

When her hand came around to brush against my breast, I felt a spark shoot through my nervous system. An explosion in my gut. It was too much. Too soon. I pulled away.

"I can't," I gasped, moving to the side to lie next to her. "I can't, I'm sorry."

She withdrew her hands, moving one to cup my cheek. "It's okay," she said.

"I mean, I've never been with anyone like this before."

"Me either," she told me. "It's okay. We can wait."

"You mean, you didn't with Kenny?"

She shook her head.

I smiled, leaning forward to plant a kiss on the corner of her mouth. She rolled away from me, tugging my arms around her stomach and nestling into me. I buried my face in her soft hair, listening to her breathing become slower as she drifted to sleep.

When morning came, I might not have my friends, my reputation, or any sense of reality. But at least I had her. And for now, that was all that mattered.

Twenty-one

I held my breath and pushed open the front doors of school, expecting insults to come flying my way. I waited for people to swivel their heads and give me a look of pure disgust, to whisper about me behind my back.

I had mentally prepared myself for whatever was to come.

But, to my surprise, nobody said anything. There was no staring, no hushed whispers, no laughter ringing in my direction. But maybe it was just the calm before the storm. Taking a deep breath, I looked to Emma. She seemed tense, like she expected the same.

"Well," I said, "see you in Theater."

She shifted her bag on her shoulder and offered me a small smile. "See you."

I walked into class. Took my usual seat between Seth and Kenny and pulled my supplies from my backpack. Glancing towards Kenny, I noticed that he was staring at the World War II notes scrawled across the chalkboard. He noticed me and smiled.

I felt a pang in my gut, remembering Emma was supposed to break up with him in a couple hours. How would he react?

"What's up, Hayes?" Seth's voice drew my eyes to him.

"Hey, Seth," I replied.

"So, have you started the paper yet?" He rapped his fingers against the wooden desk.

I shook my head. "No," I said. "I haven't, actually." Great. Another thing to worry about. I had completely forgotten that we had a paper due in less than a week.

"What are you going to write about?"

I shrugged. Out of my peripheral vision, I noticed Kenny had sprawled across his desk. I wanted to say something to him, be a good friend. Even though it was too late. His world was about to turn inside out and it was my fault.

Suddenly, Brittany Osborne appeared in front of my desk. She leaned against the empty chair in front of me, eyes running over my face. "Hey, Charlotte."

I felt a lump rise in my throat. I knew what was coming. Quivering, I adjusted my position to try to look less nervous than I actually was. Which, I quickly realized, was impossible.

"Hey," I said."

"So," she began, tilting her chin upwards, "I just wanted to tell you that I heard—"

I felt a convulsion run through my nervous system. This was it. I wouldn't deny it. I wouldn't make a show of what Sarah said as being false. This captain was going down with her ship.

"—that Reynolds wants the team to meet later this week."

I looked at her in confusion, releasing a breath that I hadn't even realized I was holding. I must have had a pretty awkward look on my face, because she repeated herself.

"I heard you," I said. "Thanks for letting me know."

"Yeah." She narrowed her eyes to scrutinize my face. "Are you alright? You're pretty pale."

Nodding, I broke her gaze to look down at my desk. "I'm fine," I replied. "I just missed out on breakfast this morning."

"Alright," she said. "Well, get something to eat, alright? You don't look good at all."

I sighed with relief as she turned to retreat back to her desk. *Maybe Sarah didn't tell everyone after all,* I thought.

I looked towards Kenny to say something, but couldn't muster the strength. I decided to keep quiet.

After all, trying to be the good guy when I'd caused the havoc in the first place was like the United States trying to apologize for dropping the bomb on Hiroshima.

~~~

Every time I saw someone looking at me in the hallway, it seemed as though they were seeing the side of me that I didn't want them to. If Sarah did tell anyone, though, no one was bothering to approach me about it.

As I was on my way to Theater after third period, I happened to notice Sarah idling at her locker, talking to Katie Dillon, a cheerleader that went to her church. I paused, holding my breath. Waited for the girl to leave. When she finally did, I approached Sarah.

"Hey, Sarah," I said, noticing how tense my voice sounded. "I just wanted to—"

"I didn't tell anyone, okay?" she snapped. "Not even Bryan. It's not anybody's business."

I felt my entire body sigh with relief. "Thanks."

Her eyes scanned my body. Judging me. "I don't accept it," she finally said. "You're so pretty, Charlotte. I don't understand why you chose to be like this."

"I didn't choose it." My voice rose a notch higher than what I intended. I felt my face flushing.

Sarah twisted her body to gaze off down the hallway before saying, "It's gross, Charlotte."

"It's not like that, Sarah. I love her."

She shook her head, turning her eyes to meet mine. "That's not love, Charlotte. It's just wrong," she replied. "And I'm sorry for you." She slammed her locker shut and walked off without so much as a glance over her shoulder.

Sorry for me? My entire body was on fire. My head pounded with every word she'd said. Gross. Wrong. I wanted to cry. *I didn't choose this,* I wanted to scream after her. *How could anybody choose this?*

~~~

People were everywhere. Emma and I had to literally push our way through the throngs of shoppers at the Hidden Springs Mall. Apparently everyone else in the city got the memo that Christmas shopping was to be done at the last possible minute.

"Is Sarah still not talking to you?" Emma asked as we trekked through the hordes of shoppers, scouting out the next store we wanted to visit.

I shook my head. "No. You never told me how it went with Kenny. Was he upset?"

"Well—"

She was interrupted by a couple of rowdy guys who walked by, headed in the opposite direction. One of them slammed their shoulder into Emma, not even bothering to move out of her way.

"Geez, excuse you!" she exclaimed, rolling her shoulder as she turned and shot him a glare. I looked back in time to see him pivot and flash his middle finger. Emma raised one back at him.

"People can be so rude." She whirled around and suddenly pointed to a nearby music store. "Hey, do you want to go in here?"

She didn't wait for an answer. Just walked in. I cringed at the swarmed aisles and made a beeline for the Oldies section. It seemed to be the least crowded.

As I was sifting through the multiple CD's in search of one Mom might like, a familiar voice turned my attention away.

"Charlotte? Hey!" I glanced towards the voice and saw Veronica.

"Oh, hey," I said, forcing a weak smile. "Are you Christmas shopping too?"

"Yeah," she replied with an exaggerated sigh. She held up the CD's in her hand for emphasis. Some weird bands I'd never even heard of. "Boyfriend. Are you doing the same?"

I swiveled my eyes back to the rows of CD's. "Trying to find something for my mom right now." I pulled out a Billie Holiday album. Maybe Mom would want this.

"Are you here by yourself?" Veronica asked.

I shook my head, looking towards Emma. She was standing in another aisle with headphones on, listening to something at one of the demo stations. Her head bobbed gently with the beat.

"Oh. " Veronica's gaze followed mine to linger on Emma for a moment. "Hey, isn't that the girl from your photographs?"

Emma's eyes caught mine from across the store and a grin sparked across her face. She waved with one hand, the other glued to a headphone. I felt myself smile. "Yeah. It is."

Veronica glanced at the digital watch on her arm. "Oh, shoot. I need to get going. I'm supposed to meet my mom somewhere in ten minutes. See you tomorrow."

I watched her leave, vaguely aware of Emma appearing at my side.

Emma swiveled her head in an awkward attempt to read my CD. "Whatcha got?"

I held it up in front of her so she could read it.

"My mom loved her." She trailed me to the cashier where I forfeited 15 dollars for the album. "She used to play her music really loud in the kitchen while she cooked."

Not really knowing what to say, I wrapped an arm around her waist and gave her a gentle squeeze. "I'm sorry you lost her."

"That's okay," she said. She stopped in the middle of the crowd and turned towards me, smiling.

She leaned forward. I closed my eyes, expecting her lips to touch mine. Waiting for that familiar spark. But it never came.

When my eyes blinked open, I found her staring at me. She looked worried, scared. "What's wrong?" I asked.

"Charlie, I have to tell you something." She drew a breath. Held it. "And you won't like it."

I swallowed hard.

"I didn't break up with Kenny."

~~~

There was a note in my locker. It was still wedged into one of the slots. I heard the paper rip as I yanked it out.

As I wandered into class, I slowly unfolded the note.

Meet me in the upstairs bathroom at 9:00, it read.

The handwriting was loopy, girly. There were little hearts above all the I's.

Emma. Maybe she'd decided to break up with Kenny, after all. I couldn't help but smile.

My mind trailed off as I stared at the clock, watching the minutes tick slowly by. Mrs. Lancaster lectured at the front of the class about the aftermath of the bombing of Hiroshima and Nagasaki.

8:59. My hand shot in the air.

Mrs. Lancaster stopped mid-sentence. "Yes, Ms. Hayes?"

"May I go to the restroom, please?"

She nodded towards the pass that she kept on her desk. Leaping from my chair, I grabbed it and darted from the room to make my way to the upstairs bathroom.

I was grinning as I opened the door, expecting to see Emma. Expecting good news.

Instead, I saw Cory. And froze.

"Hi," she said. A nervous smile quivered at the corner of her lips. "I—I guess you got my note."

I looked down at the carefully folded paper in my hand, letting everything sink in. The note hadn't been written by Emma at all. In fact, now that I thought about it, Emma always capitalized her R's. And her S's were lopsided.

"I wanted to wait until the meeting," Cory said, "but I figured that wouldn't be a good choice. Sarah doesn't seem to like me very much."

My eyes met Cory's. They were blue. I'd never noticed. Her blonde hair had grown out—no longer spiked, she'd combed it carefully to the side. A few stray pieces fell across her forehead.

She took a step forward, making me realize I was still holding the door open. I let it clang shut, sucking in air. This was weird. Why did she want to talk to me? It wasn't even like we were friends.

"I'm going to ask you a question," Cory said. "And I want you to be one hundred percent honest with me."

I nodded.

"Do you like girls?"

I hesitated before nodding again. It felt weird to admit it—but at the same time, I was relieved, even happy. Even though I wasn't really friends with Cory, it was easy to confide in her. She was like me.

Cory let out a breath, lips curling into a smile as she laughed. "Thank God. I had to know that I wasn't falling for a straight girl."

My heart stopped. "What?"

"I mean, you're not with that Emma girl, right? Isn't she with some guy?"

My mind flew to Emma. About how she'd told me in the music store that she hadn't broken up with him.

"He—he told me he's in love with me, Charlie" she'd said. *"I don't want to be the girl who breaks his heart."*

"But—" I'd reached towards her, taken her hand. *"I love you, Emma. Doesn't that mean anything?"*

"It means everything," she'd answered.

But apparently it hadn't meant enough to give me all of her.

"No," I finally said. "We're not."

She stepped forward. I felt her hands on my arms. I let it happen—I don't know why. Maybe I felt like I owed Cory a chance. She was willing to give me something Emma wasn't. Maybe Emma and I weren't meant to be.

Cory leaned forward. Her lips grazed mine, tentatively at first. Then she kissed me. Her lips were wet, warm. Inviting.

But I felt nothing. It was wrong. All wrong.

I stepped back. "I'm sorry," I said. "I can't."

I turned, raced from the bathroom. But not before I glimpsed the hurt and disappointment that flared in those blue eyes.

~~~

A week later, Armageddon struck during Lit.

"Hey, Charlotte." I heard a whisper to the right of me and swiveled my head to let my eyes fall on Collin Burroughs. He was a first-string football player who I'd never talked to before despite sitting next to him since the beginning of the semester. I was surprised he even knew my name. I tapped my pencil gently against the desk.

"Can I ask you a question?" he asked. A smirk slid across his face.

"Sure," I replied.

He glanced across the room before he looked back at me. "How do you, you know, do it?"

My pencil froze in my hand. "What are you talking about?" I whispered.

"You know." He waggled his eyebrows. "How do lesbians have sex, exactly?"

I felt my breath catch in my throat. My pencil slipped from my grasp to roll off the side of my desk and clatter to the floor. I bent over to grab it, turning my eyes away from Collin and ignoring his question. I guess he realized I wasn't going to reply because he laughed and looked back at his book.

A quiver ran through my body. Had Sarah finally told? That bitch. I was going to kill her. She promised she wouldn't. Or Cory? Maybe he was just kidding. A prank. Guys my age loved pranks.

As soon as the bell rang, I threw my belongings carelessly into my backpack and shot out of the room before Collin had a chance to approach me.

I wasn't headed to Theater, though. I realized it when I was halfway down the Math hall. Cory was at her locker, shoving her textbooks inside.

My fist slammed into the cold metal locker. She jumped. Her eyes snapped up to meet mine.

"It was none of your business, Cory," I nearly shouted. She stepped to the side, surprised, and nearly dropped her books.

"What are you talking about?" she asked. Her voice quavered.

"You told. About me." My skin twitched. I couldn't stop my hands from shaking.

"I didn't," she said. "I wouldn't."

"Like I'm supposed to believe that?" I was so angry. I could feel my face reddening. My fist clenched around the strap of my bag so that I wouldn't accidentally punch her.

Cory's face burned red. "Believe what you want. But I didn't do it. I can tell you who did, though."

That's because it was you, I thought. I gritted my teeth and said, "Okay, who?"

"Callaghan. I heard her talking to some people the other day during the meeting."

I felt my mind flash back to the night Sarah walked in on Emma and me. To the malice in her eyes, her voice. To a few days later, when she told me how disgusting I was.

But she'd said she wouldn't.

She lied.

I turned on my heel, desperate to seek vengeance, so blinded by my anger that I slammed into a bunch of people who laughed and said, "Watch where you're going, dyke."

And as I ran down the hallway, I barely heard Cory yell after me, "Don't hide it. Embrace it!"

I was nearly out of breath when I reached Sarah's locker. But, just as she came into view, I felt someone's hand fling in front of me and nearly knock me over.

Dazed, I shook my head and looked up.

It was Kenny.

His face was a furious shade of crimson. His eyes were red-rimmed, puffy. He'd been crying. Tears were still threatening to fall from the corners.

"Charlotte." He straightened up so that, even with his short stature, he was towering over me. "How could you do this to me?"

I shook my head, feeling my mouth fall open but no words come out. After all, I didn't even know what to say. What was there that I could possibly vocalize to the best friend I'd deceived, betrayed?

"What, nothing to say?" he said. His voice was laced with hurt. "So much to do behind my back, but nothing to say to my face? Some friend you are." He backed a step.

"I'm sorry," I spit out, knowing it was useless. What good was sorry going to do? Everything had been done.

Tears were streaking down his face now, disappearing into his goatee and falling onto the front of his t-shirt. In all the years I'd known him, I suddenly realized I had never seen Kenny cry.

And I was the one to make him do it. My mind reeled. I choked back a sob.

"I don't know why you're crying. You've got everything you want now, don't you? You've got her all to yourself, Rainbow Brite. Too good to even tell me about that, aren't you?"

"Kenny, I'm so sorry," I said again. Maybe if I told him a thousand times, a million, a billion, he'd realize that I was being sincere.

"I loved her, Charlotte," he replied, jabbing a finger into my chest. "And you know what? I loved you, too."

I stumbled back, collapsed into a locker. His words felt like a smack in the face. I watched as he walked away, but not before punching a locker so hard that it left a huge dent behind.

What had I done?

Twenty-two

I skipped class and hid in the last stall of the same bathroom I'd met Cory in the week before. When the bell finally rang, I grabbed my belongings and made my way as fast as I could downstairs to meet Emma as she walked out of Theater class.

"Where were you?" she said as soon as she saw me. "Why weren't you—what's wrong?"

I guessed she saw the tears that were still fresh on my cheeks. I shook my head, took her by the hand, and didn't stop walking until we'd reached my car where I burst into sobs.

"Everyone knows." I said. "Even Kenny."

"What?" Emma's eyes widened. "How? Who?"

"Sarah," I said.

"I'm going to kill her," Emma said. She threw her bag onto the ground and clenched her fists as she took a step towards the school.

I couldn't even imagine a girl as little as Emma trying to take on someone as muscular as Sarah. But, that wasn't the reason I'd stopped her. I would've loved to see Sarah get what she had coming to her.

I stopped her because I knew Kenny was still in the building.

"Let's just go home," I pleaded. "Please. We'll talk at your house."

I hadn't even realized that there were tears sliding down her face. I stopped rushing and instead gathered her into my arms, held her tight.

"Kenny," she sobbed.

"It'll be okay," I told her, even though I didn't believe it myself.

After a moment, she pulled away from me, her bright green eyes searching mine. "What do we do now, Charlie?"

I looked away.

It was the one question that was on my mind, too.

~~~

"Trevor, where's dad?" Emma called.

He was sprawled across the couch in their living room, his hands dancing across the Game Boy that he held firmly in his grip.

"Trevor, I asked you a question."

Once again, he blatantly ignored her.

"Trev!" Emma shouted. His head snapped up.

"What? Geez, I'm busy," Trevor grumbled. "Dangit! Now you've killed me, and I was all the way up to level 7." He threw his Gameboy dramatically against the couch cushion, exaggerating a sigh.

If only he knew that there would be bigger problems in life than not being able to reach level 8. Like not being able to reach the age of 18 because everyone in your school was currently plotting your demise.

Emma rolled her eyes, agitated. "Do you know where Dad is?" she repeated.

"No clue," he mumbled, fingers once more flying across the buttons of his Game Boy after he'd fished it out from underneath a pillow. "At work, I guess."

"He's useless," Emma muttered under her breath as she began walking towards her room. I tagged after her, watching her throw her bag to the floor and turn to lock the door behind us. She removed her coat and tossed it on a growing pile of clothes.

I had thought the tears were over, since she cried the entire way home in my car. But I was wrong. As soon as she sat down in bed, the floodgates opened and she began to cry. I strode over, sat next to her. She wrapped her arms around me and buried her face in my shoulder.

I hugged her back, feeling a few tears of my own leak from my eyes.

"The worst is over," I said.

"Yeah," she replied with a sniffle. "Until my dad finds out."

I hadn't thought about that. What if Kenny told Mom? Or somebody else, for that matter?

I felt the fear rising.

The two of us lay back, silent for a long time. I guess she was doing the same thing I was: imagining scenarios of what would happen when our parents found out. Mom wouldn't approve of me being gay. That's why she was so happy to believe that Emma and Kenny were dating.

I turned my head right at the moment Emma had picked hers up. Our lips met unexpectedly, but lingered, as though that's where they were meant to be all along.

I kissed her. I couldn't help it. I needed her, wanted her. Hands roamed, fingers tickled—before I knew it, we'd collapsed across her messy bed, lost in each other.

Her fingers slid underneath my shirt, lifted it off. I mimicked her.

I could sense the worry from the day dissipating with each move that we made, each step we took to get closer to one another.

The sound of a car door slamming outside made the two of us reel away from each other so quickly we nearly fell off the bed.

"Shit," Emma said. "Dad's home."

She grabbed blindly for her shirt and threw it over her head. I struggled to find my own clothing.

The front door slammed. "Emma, are you home?" I heard him call. Footsteps grew closer. Shit, my shirt was on backwards. I tried to steady my breathing.

"Yeah," she replied. Just as she swung open the door, I sat down on her bed. Halfway trying to look innocent, halfway trying to hide how messed up the sheets were.

"Just making sure you got home okay. Oh, hey Charlotte."

"Hey, Mr. Pearson," I said.

"I was going to order pizza for tonight. Charlotte, you want to stay and eat with us?"

"Uh, actually, I need to run," I rose, snatching my coat off a pile of dirty clothes on the floor. "Mom's expecting me. See you, Em'."

I slid by Mr. Pearson and dashed out of the house as quickly as I could, anxious to get away from the awkward situation. Yet, as I sat in the driver's seat of my car, I couldn't drive. My hands trembled on the steering wheel as I closed my eyes.

I could still feel the fireworks. Feel her hands. Touching, exploring.

It was then that I realized I would out myself to the entire world just to be able to finish what we'd started.

Twenty-three

Sushi was disgusting. As I watched Mom pop an eel roll into her mouth, I found myself wondering how a person could eat something so vile. Total gag.

I zoned out as I stared at the far wall, trying to imagine some way to tell Mom. Would I leave her evidence behind that made her realize? Would I just tell her?

And, better yet, what would happen?

I had to tell her before she found out something from someone else. I'd already seen the damage that route could reap.

I felt the thickness of guilt and regret in my throat again, as I did every time I found myself thinking about the subject.

"So, the other night we had this boy about your age come in. Shot in the neck." She shook her head. I snapped out of my thoughts and looked up. "It was gruesome."

I sighed, dropping the piece of chicken teriyaki back onto my plate. Double gag. "Okay, can we really talk about something different? I'm definitely trying to eat here." She'd been telling me gross hospital stories the entire meal. Couldn't she think of a more appropriate time?

Mom chuckled, shaking her head as she popped another roll into her mouth. "Well," she said in between chews, "I do kind of have some bad news."

"Yeah?" I fumbled with my chopsticks, trying to get them to work. I never could quite get a grasp on how they functioned.

She leaned back against her chair to take a quick sip of her water just as the waitress stopped by to check on us. I don't know how, but somehow Mom could understand her thick Japanese accent.

"I have to work on Christmas day this year," she finally told me when the girl left.

"Are you serious? You never have to work on Christmas."

She swirled a roll in her soy sauce and gazed down at the table. "I know, honey. I couldn't get the day off. They gave the priority to people with families. We're just so short staffed—"

"But you have a family!" I interrupted, feeling my face grow hot with anger. "I mean, what the hell? Just because it's just you and me doesn't mean we aren't a family."

"I know," she said. "It's alright though, Charlotte. We'll work it out. We can just have Christmas the day after or something."

I shoved my plate to the edge of the table. I didn't think it was alright. Just because we weren't whole anymore didn't mean we weren't a family.

~~~

For the second week in a row, Monday brought an intense feeling of dread. But nobody really said anything to me. Not even Collin.

I could hear the whispers, though. Behind my back in class. As people walked by my locker while I was getting books. But that didn't bother me as much as the way Kenny was treating me.

He didn't even sit next to me in History anymore. Instead, he sat as far across the classroom as he possibly could. I could hear him in the back. Joking. Whispering. I could feel his eyes burning into the back of my skull.

It was as bad as if anyone had said anything to my face.

But I had done the same thing to Kenny. Gone behind his back. Kept secrets. Lied.

I had no right to deny him the same privileges.

So, as hard as it was, I tried to ignore everything but Emma.

When I walked into Theater class, she was already in her usual seat listening to her iPod. I sat down at the desk next to her, forcing a small smile in greeting.

"What are you listening to?" I asked, trying to act like everything was normal. Even though it wasn't. But it had become sort of a game that we played at school. Maybe if we acted as though everything was alright, it truly would be.

"What?" She pulled her headphones off.

"I asked what you're listening to," I repeated.

She took out an earplug and offered it to me. I held it against my ear, listening. The music sounded like rap but had an almost techno jive that made me want to stand up and dance. I handed it back to her. "What is that?"

She shrugged. "I downloaded it last night. It's some band called—"

"Hey," Zach cut in. He took a seat next to me.

"Hey, Zach," I said.

"So, I had no idea you two were dating." A huge grin flashed across his tan face.

I froze, blushing. Emma just stared at him as she put her iPod into her backpack.

"I mean you are, aren't you?" Zach asked, confusion lacing his voice. "Or is it just a rumor?"

I watched Emma shrug towards me as if saying, *it's up to you.* Turning my attention back to Zach, I nodded slowly.

"Seriously?" He was grinning again. "That's awesome. You two are so cute together."

I was pretty sure my face was the brightest shade of red possible. "Uh, thanks," I replied, not quite sure of what else to say. It was the first nice thing that anybody had said to us about the entire ordeal.

"You two should join the GSA. I'm the president this year. We've only got about six members right now." He leaned casually across the desk with his arms stretched out in front of him.

I stared at him. "What's a GSA?" I finally asked, feeling like a complete idiot. I glanced towards Emma, but her expression read that she didn't know, either.

Zach started giggling, but stopped when he finally realized we weren't joking. "GSA," he repeated. "Gay-Straight Alliance. It's like a club where we discuss problems in the gay community. Anyone can join. Gay, straight, whatever."

Before Emma and I could say anything in response, Ms. Woodbridge began to call attendance.

"Think about it," he said. "It'd be awesome to have you two." I watched as he retreated back to his desk.

For the rest of the class, I juggled the idea of a Gay-Straight Alliance. It sounded like a great concept, but I didn't know if I was ready to join something like that.

After all, I had denied who I was. I had betrayed my best friend. I was the biggest joke in the school.

Who was I to call myself an ally?

~~~

"Hey, Charlie!"

I nearly fell down when Emma sent a snowball splattering across the front of my coat.

"Gotcha," she said. She tossed another snowball in her right hand. I bent over and began shoveling snow between my gloved hands.

Emma chucked her other snowball and ran. It hit my shoulder, crumbling on impact.

"That's it," I yelled. "You're dead!" I took off after her with my own armful of snow.

I hit her in the back with a snowball and she nearly toppled forward. She whirled, laughing, and began scraping snow off the ground to throw at me before taking flight again. I paused, spitting snow out of my mouth.

Even though she stopped me for a minute, it didn't take me long to catch up to her. I threw my arms around her waist and we both went tumbling down together in a mess of thrashing limbs and giggles.

"I forfeit, I forfeit!" she cried, finally collapsing limp into the snow with her arms outstretched. I rolled off her body, collapsing next to her. She twisted her body over and draped her arm across the front of my coat, pressing her frigid cheek against mine. Her breath came in heavy gasps.

"You know, you wouldn't be so out of breath if you quit smoking," I said. "It really messes up your lungs."

She sat up. Looked away. After a moment, she turned back to face me and grinned. "You're right."

"What?" I pushed myself up. I'd been pestering her for weeks about smoking and she'd just shrugged and lit another cigarette. But now she was agreeing with me?

She fished her pack of cigarettes out of her pocket and stood. I followed suit, shaking the snow off my coat.

"I don't think I need these anymore." She clutched the pack firmly in her hand, eyes trained on mine. "And you're the reason why."

I watched her pull her arm back and throw the pack of cigarettes as far as she could. They flew over my backyard fence, disappearing behind a bank of snow.

I grinned. Took her in my arms and kissed her. It would be the last time I tasted nicotine in her lips.

"I want to tell someone," Emma said when we broke away. "No, I want to tell everyone. I want to tell the world."

"So tell everyone," I replied.

She stretched her arms out, opened her mouth, and screamed, "I quit smoking!" Her shrill voice cut through the cold winter air, pierced the silence around us.

We were both laughing when another voice cut in.

"Cold turkey's the best way to quit. That's how I did it."

The familiar tone made my heart stop. Memories impaled my mind. But it couldn't be, could it? We both whirled. My smile faltered.

Dad was standing at the backyard gate.

Twenty-four

"I should go," I heard Emma say. I ignored her.

"Dad."

His lips spread in a hesitant smile. He rested his hands on the gate, glancing between Emma and me.

I stepped forward. Tears stung the corners of my eyes. I stared at him. At the short brown hair that had more grey than I ever remembered. At the five o'clock shadow that framed his face. At the deep brown eyes he'd passed on to me. I wanted to run to him, fall into his arms. I opened my mouth to tell him I was sorry for the letter I'd sent. But, instead, "What are you doing here?" barely escaped my lips.

"I was in the area. I really wanted to see you. I was kind of hoping I could take you out. You know, grab a bite. Talk."

I swallowed. Nodded. Then turned to look at Emma. Wide-eyed, she glanced back and forth between Dad and me. "I, uh… I'm just going to go," she said, thumbing over her shoulder towards the road.

"No," Dad said. "Why don't you come with us? After all, you just quit smoking. Let's celebrate." A grin flickered across his face.

I felt my feet start to move. Unable to stop myself even if I'd wanted to, I swung open the gate that separated us and threw my arms around Dad's waist. His arms closed around me, holding me tight.

"I missed you, Dad." He smelled the same. Like metal and aftershave. Like decade old memories.

It was like a dream, a mirage. He'd been gone for years, but now he was here. With me.

~~~

This was awkward. I couldn't think of anything to say.

Dad took a sip of his tea and smiled at me from across the table. I glanced at Emma. She looked like there were a million other places she would've rather been.

"You're so grown up," Dad said. "I can't believe I missed so much of your life. Did you pick a college yet?"

"Yeah." I stirred my straw in my Coke, avoiding his eyes. "UConn."

"Nice." He nodded. "I went to Penn State."

"I know," I said.

He looked to Emma. "It's Emma, right? Have you chosen?"

She shook her head. "Not yet."

"I have to get this out," Dad suddenly said. "I wasn't in town. At all. I wasn't even in the state, actually. Your Mom asked me to come."

I blinked. Glanced up. Did I hear him right? "What?" I said.

"She said you've been acting really off. I don't know. She hasn't let me see you in over five years and suddenly she wants me here." He held his palms out in front of him in a defensive position. "So what's up?"

He'd been trying to see me? I clenched my jaw. Did he know she'd hidden his letters to me? Did he know she'd slandered his name for the past five years? I wanted to tell him. I took a deep breath. I was about to vent when something completely unexpected came out of my mouth.

"I'm gay."

I blinked. Had I just said that? Heat rose into my cheeks, burned to the tip of my nose. Emma's head swiveled, her eyes widening in shock.

"Charlie…" Emma started.

"Have you told her?" Dad asked.

I stared straight into Dad's face. It was emotionless—empty. I wanted to read it, to know whether he approved or didn't. Why did he have to have his poker face on now?

I hesitated before saying, "No."

He nodded and looked down, as though he wanted to tell me something. He lifted his tea and took a sip. "Do you want me to tell her?" he finally asked.

I shook my head. "No. I have to be the one to do it."

He reached across the table. I felt his calloused fingertips brush against my forehead, pushing my bangs out of my eyes. He slid a finger under my chin and lifted it, forcing me to look him in the eyes.

"Charlotte," he said. "I'm going to tell you the one thing I've learned from being a parent. Even if I'm not much of one anymore. And that's that I have always and will always love you. No matter what." Pausing, he dropped his hand and smiled. "And your mother and I didn't agree on much, but I'm certain she feels the same."

I hoped he was right.

~~~

His truck wasn't there.

I pulled Old Reliable to a stop in front of the two-story brick house that was so familiar to me. The stoop that Kenny and I would sit on and chat for hours. The front yard, where we'd build igloos every year. His basement room, where we'd goof off, watch television, play games. The memories were vast. Never ending.

Much unlike our friendship.

I carefully eased myself from the warm confines of my car and into the frigid air, watching my breath appear in a cloud before my face. Wrapping my arms around the package I held, I trekked through the snow towards his front porch, wary of every car coming down the street. Who knew how he'd react if he saw me at his house.

Stepping around a few patches of ice on his stoop, I stopped at the front door and lowered the wrapped package next to the cloth mat. I had only written one thing: his name. Not who it was from. After all, if he knew it was from me, he might just throw it away.

I lingered for a while, my gaze trained on the darkness within the house, wondering whether or not I would ever be invited in again. If I'd ever slip my running shoes off at the front door. If I'd ever run down to Kenny's room.

~~~

Mom was home.

I slipped my coat off at the door and walked into the kitchen, taking a deep breath. It was now or never. I was going to tell her.

"Hey, Mom."

She was seated at the table, sipping a still steaming cup of hot chocolate. "Where have you been?" she asked.

"Kenny's," I said. I hesitated before adding, "And with Dad."

"I see." She took another sip of her hot chocolate before setting it down on the table. "So he actually came."

I nodded, feeling myself lose bravery with each passing second. Weakness seemed to overtake my body in waves. I leaned against the counter, staring at Wednesday, who was snoozing on Mom's feet. "Mom." Fighting the tears that I knew were coming, I said, "Why did you keep his letters from me?"

Her head snapped up. "What?"

"I found them." The tears were streaming down my cheeks now. Hitting the front of my shirt. I took a deep breath. "In your chest. Why, Mom?"

Her eyes glistened, face paling. "I—I don't know, Charlotte," she said. At least she wasn't denying it. "I thought I was protecting you."

"Protecting me from what? My father? Who you had to call on because you couldn't ask me yourself what was wrong with me?" I felt myself gasping for air. My head was spinning. My skin was tingling. My fingers closed around the edge of the counter and held fast.

"I was afraid he would hurt you the same way he hurt me." She was crying, too. "I didn't want you exposed to that."

"Exposed to what? Having two parents?"

"Your father cheated on me with a woman half my age," Mom blurted. Her hands flew to her mouth, as though she couldn't believe what had just escaped. She closed her eyes, a sob pulsing through her body.

It took me a moment to realize that my mouth was open. My mind flew back to my childhood—to a young blonde woman. How she'd only seemed to be over when Mom wasn't home. To fights between Mom and Aunt Angie. Aunt Angie had known. She'd tried to tell Mom.

"Mom…" my voice trailed off. I didn't know what to say.

"I didn't want you to know," Mom said. She shook her head, sniffing loudly. "I thought it was something I'd done. Or couldn't do. I didn't want you to carry that burden, too." She rose, sending a startled Wednesday skittering across the floor. In one quick motion, she was next to me, taking me into her arms. I let her.

"I'm so sorry, Charlotte," she said into my hair. I felt her tears wet on my cheek. "I'm so sorry."

Suddenly, I pictured Kenny and realized, in one paralyzing, heart-stopping instant, that everyone had been right all along: I was just like Dad.

~~~

I couldn't spend Christmas with Mom, but at least I had Emma.

As the two of us trudged through the snow to the park, with Wednesday dashing along ahead of us, I told her everything. I was lucky to have someone to talk to. I vaguely wondered who Kenny shared his secrets with now.

"Try not to think about it," Emma said. "After all, it's Christmas."

Christmas. It wasn't much of one. I thought back to the tree that Mom and I had failed to decorate. About how I wouldn't find what I really wanted in a neatly wrapped package underneath our pathetic tree.

But Emma was right. I owed her enough to not be emo on Christmas.

"Check out the pond," Emma suddenly blurted. "It's frozen over!"

She bolted across the deserted park. Wednesday charged after her, tongue dangling from her mouth. I followed.

"I don't know if that's such a good idea," I said as she took a tentative step onto the ice. I'd heard horror stories of people who had fallen through ice. It was dangerous.

"It's safe. It's frozen." Emma placed both feet onto the ice and slid towards the middle. "Come on!"

I hesitated before stepping onto the ice. She was right. It felt pretty secure. I acted like I was skating until I nearly fell over and quickly stopped. No wonder I'd never tried to ice skate.

She whirled. Took a few steps towards me. An ear-splitting crack filled the air.

And she was gone.

The ice had cracked. She'd fallen in. "Emma!" I shouted.

Hysterical laughter filled the air. I realized, as the panic slowly dissipated in my veins, that the pond was only a few feet deep. She was alright.

"It's s-s-so cold," Emma stuttered in between cackles. "Charlie, help me out."

I took a step forward. Another crack and I felt water fill my clothing. Great.

"Now how do we get out?" I asked. My teeth chattered uncontrollably.

"Just like this." Emma lifted her foot to try to step out onto the edge of the ice. It broke. She kept going. Eventually, we were able to make it to the shore where we scrambled into the snow and fell down next to each other.

"I'm freezing," Emma said. Her body shivered next to mine.

"Me, too." My clothes were soaked. I felt like I was carrying half my weight. I shouted for Wednesday and helped Emma to her feet.

When the two of us finally slammed through the front door of my house, we were laughing. We were freezing, but it didn't matter. Wednesday shook snow and water all over the floor, the walls. I didn't care. My clothes were nearly frozen solid.

My hands felt like they were burning. Emma and I raced to my room, tossing our shoes as we went. I was shaking so hard it was nearly impossible to get my coat off.

"I told you that was a bad idea," I said. My nerves jerked as I reached over to help her get her coat off. Her face was flushed.

"Well," she said, "how was I supposed to know the ice wouldn't hold your fat ass?"

"Oh, shut up." Our bodies trembled as I slid her coat off her shoulders.

She backed up. I could hear her teeth clicking together as she began shedding the rest of her clothes.

I began to feel my body warming as I peeled the wet layers of clothing from my body.

"I'm freezing." Emma laughed. I watched her t-shirt hit the sopping pile of clothes.

"It was your idea, genius. You're the one who…" I forgot what I was going to say when I looked up and saw her standing in front of me. She wore only her underwear.

My breath stopped. Suddenly, I wasn't cold anymore. The heat started in my toes and worked its way up my body. My muscles tensed.

"Charlie." She expelled a heavy breath. Stepped forward.

"Maybe we should get changed," I suggested. My heart struck my chest in a merciless rhythm.

"No," Emma said. Her fingertips seared into my skin as she wrapped her arms around me. She leaned forward, lips brushing against mine. "Not yet."

I wanted to kiss her, so I did. Our lips connected and a series of sparks flew through my body. I pressed my mouth hard against hers, my hand grasping for hers.

We pressed together, clinging to each other as if letting go would mean the demise of both of us. I ran my hands over her body, trying desperately to touch every inch, to map out every curve, every dip.

"Charlie," she gasped, pulling her lips away from mine and stalling her hands on my chest. "Are you—"

"Yes," I answered quickly, holding her emerald eyes with my own. "Yes. I love you."

"I love you, too," she said, and pressed her lips against mine once more.

~~~

There were no lit candles outlining the windowsill. No vanilla scented incense. No soft music playing in the background, like I imagined my first time would be. There was just darkness, and the only sounds were the two of us: our gasps, our moans, our giggles as we tried anxiously to discover one another. The truth was that we didn't quite know what we were doing. We were a mixture of fumbling hands and tangled limbs, of unsure whispers and awkward laughter.

It wasn't what I imagined it would be.

It was beautiful. No. Perfect.

Our breath came in heavy gasps as we clung to one another, silent. Eventually, she turned and pressed her forehead against mine.

"Em." I didn't have anything to say. I just wanted to hear her voice.

"Yeah?" She pushed her naked body against mine and tugged the blankets closer around us. "What is it, Charlie?"

"Merry Christmas," I said. Lame.

"Merry Christmas," Emma replied. Her lips brushed against mine, a whisper of a kiss.

As I watched her drift off to sleep, I tried to mold myself around her. I clung to her, afraid I might float away if I let go.

I had imagined that it would feel wrong. Like everyone said. But it didn't feel that way. There was nothing wrong about us at all.

It was so right.

Twenty-five

We were inseparable.

We spent every possible minute together. It was like we had discovered an entirely different side to our relationship. A new, unexplored world.

One night, Emma drove her dad's truck over to spend some time at my house. Most of the snow had melted away over the week, but I still couldn't drive my car safely. Mom's rules.

"Charlie!" I heard her call. The front door slammed. She'd become accustomed to just entering on her own. Mom didn't really care anymore. Kenny usually did the same thing.

Or, he used to.

"Hello, Emma." Mom reached the parlor at the same time as I did. She smiled, tossing a dirty rag over her shoulder. The house reeked of cleaner. "How's Kenny? I haven't seen him in a while."

"Oh, hey Ms. Hayes." Emma blushed. I offered an awkward smile. "He's fine. Just busy with college admissions and stuff."

"I was, uh, just watching TV." I motioned for Emma to follow. Mom raised an eyebrow at us, but said nothing. She turned on her heel and headed back into the kitchen.

I sank down onto the couch. Emma sat at the opposite end. I could feel her eyes on the side of my face as I watched television. "I didn't know your mom was here," she whispered.

"Sorry, I forgot to mention," I told her. I noticed she was wearing my Abercrombie sweatshirt. I'd been wondering where that went. "It's not like you haven't been here with her before," I said.

She shrugged. "It's no problem. I just didn't know."

"Hey, girls." Mom poked her head into the living room. "I'm going to be in my room if you need me."

"Alright, Mom," I swiveled on the couch and watched her vanish down the hallway. I turned back to Emma. She was eyeing me mischievously.

We must've been thinking the same thing, because as soon as we heard Mom's door slam we met in the middle of the couch, lips colliding forcefully. She managed to get the upper hand and eased me onto my back, grasping my arms to pin me down. I giggled.

Her fingers snaked underneath the front of my jeans. I squirmed away. "Emma," I said, "my mom is home."

"Yeah." She flashed me a grin, sliding her hand further down. I had to bite my lip to keep from making any noise. "And?"

She was doing things to me that made me have to turn my head to grab a couch pillow and shove it into my face. My breath caught in my throat. I tossed the pillow aside after a minute, making a grab for her wrist. "Emma, stop," I whimpered. I didn't want to stop, but I knew we couldn't be doing it. Mom could see.

We both heard Mom's bedroom door open and Emma flew across the couch so fast she nearly hit the floor. Breathing through my nostrils, I sat up and straightened out my clothes. The guilt was so thick between us that I was praying Mom couldn't sense it as she walked into the room.

"What are you girls up to?"

"N-nothing," I stammered all too quickly, glancing at Emma to see how red her face was. She turned away, looking towards the television.

"Why don't you call Kenny?" Mom strode all the way into the living room to collapse onto the love seat. "I'm sure he could use a break from his work."

"It's okay," Emma said. "He's really stressed over it. Thanks though."

I glanced down. Shit. My pants were unzipped. I grabbed the couch pillow off the floor to shove it over my lap, hoping Mom didn't notice.

"Alright, then." She turned her attention to the television. I guess she was going to stick around. Great.

"Uh, I should probably get going." Emma rose. "Maybe you're right, Ms. Hayes. I'll stop by at Kenny's and see if I can help him somehow."

"See you, Em." Our eyes met. She offered a half-hearted smile before grabbing my sweatshirt and disappearing from the living room. I heard the front door shut quietly behind her and the truck roar to life outside.

"She's such a sweet girl," Mom said as she watched Emma leave. "Kenny's a lucky guy."

I opened my mouth, almost wanting to tell her that she wasn't with Kenny. She was with me. But I didn't. I was too much of a chicken. "I'm gonna go take a shower," I said, and rose to hurry off before she could see the state I was in.

I was sneaking around behind her back, and I hated it. I resolved that I'd have to get the guts to tell her sometime soon. *She can't hate me, right? I mean, after all, she is my mother.*

Instead of going directly into the shower, I found myself sitting down in front of my computer to bring up the search engine. I hesitated before typing: gay, coming out, parents. Thousands of websites popped up in response. I sifted through them before selecting a web forum.

I became sick to my stomach as I glanced through the threads. One guy talked about how his parents kicked him out of the house. One girl's mom tried to kill her. Another girl had her entire college fund taken away. All of this for being gay. All of this for being different. *This is the price*, I realized. *I could be sacrificing the same thing. My home, Mom, college. Everything. Despite what dad had said, I still worried about her reaction*

I shut off the monitor and stumbled into my bathroom, my eyes fogged with tears. I blindly grasped the nozzle and turned it, cranking the heat up as I let water flood into the tub. I stripped and stumbled into a bath that nearly scorched my skin, but I sucked it up. Holding my breath, I let my head sink into the water, leaving myself underneath for a second too long until I came up gasping for breath. I was half tempted to just leave myself submerged until the water filled my lungs and consumed me.

But I didn't need water to feel like I was drowning.

~~~

"I want to see Times Square someday."

I glanced over to Emma, who was sprawled across my living room floor on her stomach. Her emerald eyes were locked on the television as she studied the animated crowd of people who all shouted with excitement. They took turns chatting with the reporters about their New Year's resolutions while waiting for the ball to drop. With only ten minutes until midnight, everyone was going crazy.

And even while I was comfortable with it just being Emma and me, I felt off. Kenny and I were always together on New Year's Eve.

Without him, it felt different. Incomplete.

"You've never been there?" I asked, finally ripping my attention away from the horde of happy people on the screen.

"No." She shrugged, turning to let her eyes settle on me. "You have?"

"Yeah."

"Well, you've lived up north for like, your entire life. I don't think I ever left North Carolina before I moved here." Emma scrambled to her feet to shuffle, yawning, over to the couch where I was sitting. She collapsed dramatically next to me, leaning her shoulder against mine. "How long do we have?" she mumbled. "I'm sleepy."

I glanced at the counter on the television. "8 minutes," I told her. I gave her hand a gentle squeeze and her eyes fluttered shut.

"What's your resolution?" she asked.

Tell my mom, I thought. "I guess to do better in school," I said. "You?"

She seemed contemplative. Quiet. "Get into a good college," she finally said.

I bit my lip, looking away towards the television and the throng of people dancing and partying in Times Square. I hadn't considered what would happen when the time would come to go away to college. Would we still be together if we went to separate schools?

I let my eyes settle on the television before asking, "Have you applied anywhere?"

Emma's lips contorted into a weak smile. "A few places."

My attention shifted to the huge sparkling ball that began lowering slowly. Emma pushed herself into a sitting position and the two of us began counting along with them.

5, 4, 3, 2...

I felt Emma's lips connect with mine as she launched across the couch and kissed me.

"Happy New Year," I said.

"Yeah, Happy New Year," Emma replied. I broke into a grin.

A new year. Soon, a new school, a new start.

A new me.

It was supposed to feel refreshing. Why did I feel so empty?

~~~

It was almost impossible to wake up for school.

After over a week of sleeping in, I'd broken out of the ability to shoot out of bed at 7 A.M. sharp. I had kind of been hoping it would be a snow day, but the sun had come out the day before and melted away the rest of the snow except for the disgusting brown remains piled up on the side of the road.

I didn't want to go back to school. At all.

The knot in my stomach seemed to grow as I made my way through the crowded halls to my classes. Emma was lucky. She'd gotten sick the day before.

I threw myself into my usual seat once I reached my Lit classroom, tossing my belongings to the floor. I felt eyes on me. *What are you looking at?* I wanted to scream, *I'm not any different!* Resting my arms across my desk, I let my head fall onto my makeshift pillow.

"No sleeping, Ms. Hayes," Mrs. Norris called from her desk. I scowled, opening my eyes and picking my head up. I wasn't sleeping. Class hadn't even started yet.

She began lecturing about some story in our textbook. It was difficult to stay awake, so I had to turn to scribbling in my notebook to place my focus somewhere. I tried to write Emma a note, but I just ended up doodling her name instead. With a sigh, I raised my hand.

"Yes, Ms. Hayes?" Norris paused her speech to let her eyes fall on me.

"May I go to the restroom, please?" I asked.

Her eyes ran over me for a minute, as though trying to decide whether I really had to go or just wanted to meet up with friends. "Yes, hurry," she finally said. "This is important."

I slid out of my desk to scurry from the classroom and meander down the hallway. I did have to go, but I'd take my time anyways just because I wasn't looking forward to getting back to class.

There was only one other person in the bathroom. I used an empty stall next to her. Just as I pushed the door open, a voice caught my attention.

"Hey."

Turning, I saw Katie Dillon. Sarah's friend. She paused as she emerged from the stall adjacent to mine.

"Uh, hey," I said. I'd only spoken to her once before. She'd asked to borrow a textbook in sophomore year.

"Shouldn't you be in the boy's bathroom?" Her face crinkled with disgust as she went out of her way to push against my shoulder on her way to the sink. I heard the tap squeak and the sound of water splash against the porcelain.

Feeling the blood retreat from my face, I focused hard on the back of Katie's head. I should have stayed silent. But I was over it. This was getting ridiculous. "No," I said. "I'm not a guy."

"You might as well be, lesbo." She twisted the water off and grabbed a few paper towels. "Or do you just come in here to try to find a quick fuck?"

My fists clenched at my sides. I quickly tried to restrain my anger. I couldn't get mad at someone so dense. It was what she wanted. It was a weakness she was looking for. "I just came here to use the restroom. Excuse me." I took a step towards the sink.

"I hope you know you're going to hell," she replied. I turned towards her again to see her toss her hair arrogantly over her shoulder. "God hates people like you."

"Shut up." I couldn't hold my anger back any longer. "Shut up. You don't know what you're talking about."

"I know you're a dyke," she quipped, exaggerating the last word. I stepped forward, my hands clenching and unclenching at my side. "And your little girlfriend. What's her name? Emily? Amy?"

I was so mad I couldn't even find it in me to move, much less to lift my arm and punch her across her superficial face. I was trying to find something to say when I sensed someone entering the bathroom. I twisted my head to see Sarah standing a few feet away. She glanced between the two of us.

"What's going on?" she asked.

"Just trying to explain to this dyke that the school bathroom isn't a dating service," Katie said with a sneer. I felt my teeth chomp down onto my bottom lip.

"Why don't you just fuck off and leave her alone?" Sarah replied. Anger flooded into her face.

"What, so you're on her side? You a lesbo too, Callaghan?"

"I said get out of here, bitch!" Sarah yelled so loud her voice echoed throughout the bathroom. She grabbed Katie by the shoulders and shoved her. The smaller girl hit the wall.

"Whatever. Fuck you," Katie muttered. She disappeared from the restroom.

Sarah whirled to face me, the rage dissipating from her face until an expression of concern remained. "You alright?" she asked.

"Yeah. Who wouldn't be?" I fought back tears.

Sarah shook her head. "I can't believe people like that."

I nibbled my lip. Looked away. "Thanks for standing up for me. I probably could have handled it, though."

"Yeah, you looked like you were handling it." Sarah laughed. I shrugged.

"How's Emma?" she asked.

"What do you care?" I looked up.

Sarah sighed, a frown etching across her lips. "Look, Charlotte, I'm sorry. I know I've been a bad friend, it's just—just, well, it takes some getting used to, you know?"

I shrugged, trying to imagine the shock she probably felt when she saw Emma and me kissing. "Yeah, I guess," I said. *You didn't have to tell the whole school, though,* I thought.

"I know you probably don't want to have anything to do with me," she began, "but I'd like to hang again. Maybe you and Emma can go out one night with Bryan and me sometime or something."

I tried to decipher whether or not she was serious. Her expression didn't falter. I weighed the options: Sarah had ruined my life at school. Yet, at the same time, I had pretty much ruined Kenny's and wished to the moon and back that he'd forgive me.

"Sure," I finally said, smiling. "I'd like that."

She grinned and threw her arms around me. "Let me know if that bitch messes with you again." She vanished into a stall.

I glanced at my watch. I'd been gone from class for nearly fifteen minutes. I knew Mrs. Norris was going to be pissed. She'd probably even hand me a detention.

Somehow, I didn't care.

<u>Twenty-six</u>

"Hey, how are you feeling?"

Emma was still sick the next day, so I visited her after school to see how she was. She was sprawled across her bed watching television. From the way her sheets were so messed up, she must not have gone very far.

"Alright." She rolled onto her side and smiled. "Tired of being sick."

I held out the thermos of soup that I stopped by my house to make before swinging over to her place. "I made you get well soup."

"Aw, really?" She sat up. Her hair was so messy it stuck out in nearly every direction. "What kind is it?" she asked.

I unscrewed the lid to look at the contents. "Uh, vegetable." I told her, handing it over.

"I didn't know you could make soup." Emma took the thermos from my hand. She sniffed it for a moment before taking a tentative sip. "It's still hot."

I smirked as I took a seat on her bed next to her.

"So, how has school been?" she asked. "Have I missed anything in Theater?"

"No, not really. Woodbridge assigned monologues, but that's it."

She nodded. "Great, more stuff to memorize."

I chuckled. I wasn't too excited about it, either. "I talked to Sarah, too," I said. I decided not to tell her about Katie and the bathroom incident.

"Oh, really?" There were dark half circles underneath her eyes.

"Yeah." I sprawled across her bed. "She wants to hang out sometime."

Emma grinned as she placed the soup on her nightstand and let her body fall next to mine. "Told you she'd come around."

"Whatever." I reached over to tickle her stomach. She squirmed away, bursting into laughter as she tried to push my hands away. She was so ticklish.

"Stop, stop!" She tried to fight me off as she giggled hysterically. "Charlie, please."

"Okay, alright." I pulled my hands away and leaned forward to kiss her.

"You're going to get sick." She pulled her lips away.

I laughed. "I'm already gonna get sick just by being around you, Em."

"Well, then. I'll have to make you soup, too." She sat up to grab the thermos off the nightstand and took a sip. "So, where'd you learn to make it, anyways?"

I sat up and crossed my arms over my chest, bursting into a grin. "Well, my mom taught me how to use a can opener when I was seven."

~~~

"How come you and Emma didn't go to the Winter Dance?" Seth asked me after History on Wednesday. I twisted the combination to my locker and tugged it open to begin exchanging my books.

"We didn't feel like it," I said. Lie. The real reason, if she was thinking the same as me, was because we were both too scared.

"Oh, I see." Seth lingered with me for a moment. "You didn't miss much, anyways, it was lame," he said. "Anyways, I've got to run. See you."

Just as Seth left, Emma came into view, navigating her way through a few rowdy students.

"Hey," I greeted, smiling. "Decided to get your lazy butt out of bed today?"

She nodded, coughing into her hand. "Yeah. Dad made me."

Just as I was about to reply, Cory appeared next to us seemingly out of nowhere. She was dressed in the baggy clothes she usually wore, blonde hair spiked into a faux hawk. "Hey, what's up?"

"Uh, hey Cory." I glanced at Emma. I hadn't told her about what happened with Cory. I crossed my fingers, praying she wouldn't say anything.

"Sorry, I didn't mean to intrude." She shoved her hands into her pockets as she looked between Emma and me. "I was just wondering if you two had thought about joining the GSA. Zach told me he talked to you about it, and, well, I just wanted to tell you it'd be great to have you both. We need members." She threw us an awkward smile.

"I don't know." I looked at Emma, who was zoned out staring at Cory's rainbow necklace. "Hey, earth to Emma." I kicked at her shoe and she jumped slightly, green eyes swiveling to meet mine.

"What? Huh?" Emma brushed her hair out of her eyes, sniffling gently.

A few guys from the hockey team walked by, gawking at us. A couple of them sneered, turning to each other to snicker and whisper behind their hands.

"Hey, check it out. A flock of dykes," one of them said with a chuckle. "Can we watch?"

Cory whirled. I only had a second to see the anger flash across her face. "Fuck you," she spat. "How about you go jerk each other off?"

The guys quickly shut up, turning their heads and vanishing down the hallway among a group of meandering students. Cory turned back to the two of us, a small smile tugging at the corner of her lips.

"So, anyways." She continued as if nothing happened. "Meetings are Tuesdays after school in the art classroom. I'll see you there if you decide to come."

She walked off, leaving Emma and me speechless. At the moment, I wasn't even thinking about the GSA. I was too amazed by how she handled the situation with the guy who joked on us. I wouldn't have been able to say anything. I admired her ability to stand up for herself.

I wondered if I'd ever be as comfortable in my own shoes.

~~~

Emma and I made plans to hang out after school. I dropped her off to swing by my house to take a shower before getting dressed to head back to her place.

"Where are you going?" Mom intercepted me as soon as I placed my hand on the doorknob.

"Emma's." I turned to see her leaning against the door frame to the kitchen. "Is that alright?"

"You're over there almost every night." She crossed her arms.

I shrugged, shifting my gaze back to the front door. "I'll be back soon," I told her. I hated how guilty she was making me feel, but I'd already told Emma I was coming over.

"Alright."

I slipped out onto the front porch before she could say anything more, tugging my coat tighter around my body as I trudged through the snow to Old Reliable. I wished I had at least thought to dry my hair.

When I reached Emma's, I was surprised to see her sitting on the front porch. I got out of my car and she immediately jumped up to walk towards me.

"What are you doing out here? It's freezing tonight," I said.

She shrugged, grinning. "I figured you might want to go get coffee instead of hanging out at my lame house."

"Okay," I said.

"There's this new place near Tony's, we can try it out if you want," I told her as we climbed into my car.

"Sure," she said. I could feel her eyes on me as I kicked Old Reliable into gear and began maneuvering through her familiar neighborhood. As I floored it onto the main road, I felt her knuckles cold against my cheek, making me shiver.

When I pulled into the shopping center, she withdrew her hand. I parked directly in front of the new coffee shop, turning my eyes up to look at the bright neon lettering above the door.

"Bad Ass Coffee? Really?" Emma laughed, pushing open the passenger door. "That's a ridiculous name."

I grinned. "I'm guessing their coffee is pretty bad ass, then."

Emma gave my hand a gentle squeeze and swung the door open for me. The two of us stepped inside, glancing around the new shop. It wasn't too busy. Only a couple of people sat in the sofas that lined the back wall. It was a cozy little joint. Eccentric artwork was hanging in random areas and quotes were scribbled across the colorful walls.

The girl behind the counter looked us over. "What can I get you two?"

Her hair was streaked vibrant shades of purple and red. Piercings dotted her pale face. There was a tattoo of two female symbols linked together on her wrist, but I knew before I saw it.

"Um, I'll just take a latte," I told her. "A small one."

Emma looked over the menu before ordering some sort of peppermint concoction. I watched the girl's eyes shift over her body, and, feeling the need to be possessive, slid one arm around Emma's waist. The girl broke into a smile.

As we waited for the coffee, Emma threw me an awkward glance. Her body was stiff against my touch, but I felt her muscles steadily begin to relax against me. Grinning, I leaned forward to give her a small kiss on the cheek. She blushed.

The two of us took our coffee over to a table at the back of the store and sat down across from each other. I nearly gagged on my latte and immediately dumped a few sugars in it. Emma sipped daintily at her drink. The scent of peppermint wafted across the table.

"So have you thought about joining the GSA at all?" Emma asked.

I shrugged, sipping my latte and tapping my toe against the floor. "I don't know." I frowned. Anytime the subject was brought up, my stomach seemed to do this uncomfortable turn.

"I might join."

"What? Really?" I was surprised. Emma seemed just as nervous as me about being affectionate in public, and yet she wanted to join the school GSA?

"Sure." She shrugged, holding her drink up to her mouth. "Why not? I mean, it would be cool to get to know other people like us."

I didn't say anything further, but instead thought about what she'd just said to me. *Like us.* It made us seem so much more different than everyone else.

But I guess we were.

~~~

When we finally left the coffee shop, the sky was completely black. I started to get into the car, but Emma's voice stopped me.

"Hey. How about you teach me to drive your car?"

I glanced up at her. I started to tell her no, but I couldn't.

"Sure." I forced a smile.

A grin broke across her face . She started to come over to the driver's side. "Wait," I blurted. "We should get into an empty parking lot or something. I don't want to hit anyone's car."

She threw me a pout. "You think I'm that bad a driver? Geez, Charlie."

"No, it's just—"

She chuckled, opening the passenger side door. "No, I'm just kidding. Let's go."

I knew of an empty parking lot just down the road where they were building a new shopping center. It was completely vacant. I came to a stop in the middle of the vast expanse of concrete, putting my car in neutral and popping the emergency brake. The two of us jumped out of the car to switch places. It was strange to be sitting in the passenger side of my own car.

"Alright, now, put your left foot on the clutch," I instructed.

"Okay." I watched her left leg move forward. "Now what?"

"Now, take the emergency brake off."

She did as I said, her hand grasping the emergency brake and pushing it slowly down. Her green eyes swiveled to meet mine.

"Put it into first, and accelerate while you take—"

As soon as she shoved my car into first gear, she slammed her foot onto the accelerator and removed her left foot from the clutch. The engine roared. Old Reliable stalled.

Emma's knuckles were white on the steering wheel. "Oops."

I whipped the seatbelt across my chest. "It's okay. Put your foot back on the clutch and turn it on."

She hesitantly turned the ignition and the car came back to life. I gave the Probe a gentle pat on the door, as if to say *I'm sorry.*

"So, clutch, accelerator, first gear," she mumbled to herself. The car roared again as she put her foot on the accelerator, leaping forward a few feet before stalling once again. Ouch. Whiplash.

"Damnit!" Her hand slammed onto the wheel. "This is so hard. There's just too much going on."

"You'll get the hang of it." I tried to sound reassuring, but I was feeling sorrier for myself than her.

Emma started the car again. It took a few more tries, but she finally jumped the car into first gear and managed to get rolling. She nearly squealed with delight. "Now what?"

"Now put your foot back on the clutch and pull the gear shift straight back into second," I told her. "Then accelerate."

She put the car into second and it sped forward when she hit the accelerator, leaping awkwardly into gear.

"Emma, watch out!" I shouted when she nearly took out a telephone pole. Her hand spun on the steering wheel and we missed it by inches. She was so surprised that she slammed on the brakes and the car stalled once again.

"Oh God." She shook her head. "This is so horrible. How do you do this? It's impossible."

"It's not impossible," I said, laughing. My nerves were in bundles. I pushed myself up against the back of the seat and sighed. "You know how to do CPR. You should be able to figure this out."

"Yeah, well—" she trailed off. Even though it was almost completely dark, I could sense the smile in her voice.

"Do you want to try again?" I asked.

I felt her hand touch my arm and slide down to find my hand. "I don't know," she said. She turned the ignition slightly, but only to the point where the heater turned back on.

"Emma, what are you doing?" I asked. Her body was twisted towards me, one hand linked with mine and the other snaking across the front of my coat.

"Stuff," she replied. She took one hand away to turn the headlights of the car off, and before I knew it she was scaling the console and into my lap. She pressed her lips hard against mine, and suddenly it didn't matter how awkward and cramped our position was.

~~~

My eyes flickered slowly open. I tilted my head groggily to the side. It didn't take me long to realize Emma and I were still in the backseat of my car where we'd ended up. We must've fallen asleep. My arms were still wrapped around her.

I shivered. The only thing covering us was one of the towels I kept in case of a wet practice. The car was still heated, at least. Sitting up, I glanced to the console to take a look at the time.

It was almost midnight.

"Shoot. Emma, wake up." I shook her shoulder. Her eyes flickered open, mouth spreading in a yawn.

"What?" she mumbled.

"Em, we fell asleep. It's nearly midnight. Wake up," I told her. She shot up next to me, eyes locking on the clock.

"Are you serious? Shit."

The two of us began scrambling to get our clothes back on, which was tough. My car was cramped. We ended up falling all over each other as we tried to get dressed.

"My mom's going to be pissed," I said.

Emma slid her t-shirt over her head before shimmying into her coat. "She's not working tonight?"

"No."

"Damnit."

In a matter of minutes we both managed to get into all of our clothes and climbed back into the front seats. *At least we're close to home*, I thought as I shot out of the empty parking lot. It didn't take me long to reach Emma's neighborhood. I sped down the quiet streets.

I pulled up next to her dad's truck. She kissed me on the cheek before jumping out of the car. As I flew out of her drive and towards home, I picked up my cell phone to see if she called.

She hadn't. That was weird. She was usually mad if I was coming home so late and would have at least left me a message. I was thinking that she could've have gotten called into work, but the presence of her car in the driveway nixed that idea.

I turned my car off next to hers and jumped out, throwing a confused glance to her SUV before making my way up to the front porch. The light in the kitchen was still on. The front door was unlocked, too.

"Mom?" I called. I heard paws thumping as Wednesday raced down the hallway to greet me. Ignoring her, I wandered into the kitchen to stop in the doorway.

Mom was seated at the table with her back to me.

"Hey, Mom, I'm sorry I was out so late." I nibbled my lip. I set my car keys on the counter. "Emma and I just—"

She turned in her chair to face me. She'd been crying. Her eyes were red and swollen. The tears had streaked mascara down her cheeks.

But it wasn't the fact that she'd been crying that made my heart stop in my chest. It was the piece of paper I saw clutched between her fingers. A note that Emma had written to me in class.

My heart stopped in my chest.

Twenty-seven

"Mom?" My voice sounded as wobbly as my legs felt.

"Why didn't you tell me?" she asked. Her eyes were searching my face. I could hear the tears in her voice. She was trying desperately to hold them back.

I hesitated, stepping forward slowly and forcing myself to look into her face. I didn't really know what to say, so I decided to stay quiet. My hand rested on the counter in an attempt to support my buckling knees. I felt weak. My stomach churned.

"I knew you two were pretty close, but—"

I opened my mouth to say something: an excuse, or maybe one of the well-knit lies I'd been thinking of in case this happened. But, instead, I blurted, "Mom, I'm gay."

She sighed. I watched as a few fresh tears slipped from her eyes to make a rivulet down her cheeks. I suddenly realized that I was crying, too.

"I know," she said, her voice nearly a whisper. "I know, Charlotte. I kind of suspected it. I was just kind of hoping I was wrong."

I didn't know what to do or say. My heart was pounding so hard against my chest I wouldn't have been surprised if it burst straight through my ribcage and ended up on the linoleum in front of me.

"I'm sorry," I told her. It was the only thing I could think to say.

"And what about Kenny?"

I took in a deep breath, switching my gaze to the linoleum floor. "We're not friends anymore."

She grew quiet, taking everything in. I wondered if she was thinking back to her own relationship with Dad. "Why couldn't you tell me, Charlotte? Am I that bad of a mother?" Her brown eyes were searching my face. I could read the hurt behind them.

"I wanted to," I said, trying my best to tell her with my eyes that I was being truthful. "I just couldn't, Mom."

Wednesday walked into the kitchen, her toenails clicking against the floor. She tried desperately to get our attention. I suppose she could sense the tension between us. We both ignored her.

"I just wish you had told me." She rose. She reached forward, took my hand. It was warm. "You have to understand it's hard for me. If this isn't a phase, if you are... what you say, you're giving up a lot." She inhaled deeply before continuing. "It means I'll never have grandchildren, or be able to come to your wedding—" She stopped herself, throwing her arms around me as she cried. "I don't want this for you, Charlotte."

She was clutching my hand so tightly that I thought my fingers were going to break. "Do you hate me?" I asked after a minute. It was the one question I'd wanted to ask. All I could think was, *Please don't let my own mother hate me.*

Mom pulled herself away from me, her damp eyes searching mine. "No, Charlotte. I could never hate you." She hugged me again. I felt the breath squeezed out of my lungs. "You're my daughter, Charlotte. I love you no matter who you are."

"And Emma?" I choked out. "Can I still see her?"

"Of course you can still see Emma," she said. "But not until Sunday. You're grounded."

"What?" I pulled away. "For what?"

"It's past twelve on a school night. Curfew is eleven, you know that. Now go to bed." She forced a smile. It didn't quite reach her eyes.

I started to turn away but decided at the last second to hug her once again. "I love you, Mom."

"I love you too," she said.

I broke away, calling Wednesday to come with me as I turned to wander down the hallway towards my room.

"Hey, Charlotte." Mom's voice stopped me.

"Yeah?"

I turned to see her walk into the hallway, her lips spreading into a small smile. "You're my daughter, no matter what. You can tell me anything. Your dad will always be there for you, too. I'm going to make sure he's in your life a lot more from now on."

Right then and there, I made a vow to always be honest with my mother.

I stepped into my room and collapsed onto my bed, my mind spinning with the night's events. I had expected to be rejected, or kicked out of my house, or worse. I felt horrible for thinking Mom could ever be like that.

As soon as I heard Mom's bedroom door shut, I picked up my cell phone to call Emma. It took a few rings for her to answer.

"Hello?" She sounded like she was asleep.

"Hey, Em'. It's me." I rolled over on my bed and stretched out across the mattress.

I heard her yawn. "What's up?"

"My mom found one of our notes," I said.

"What?" She immediately sounded more awake. "Seriously? Did she say anything?"

"Yeah," I said. "She knows."

Emma grew quiet, and for a moment I didn't hear anything but the gentle buzz of the phone line. "And what happened?"

"Nothing," I replied. "I mean, she just seemed kind of upset that I didn't tell her, but she wasn't angry or anything." Sighing, I added, "I should have just told her earlier."

"Wow," she said. "That's great, Charlie."

"Yeah. I am grounded, though."

"For what? Coming in so late?" she asked.

"Yeah." I chuckled. "Seems like no big deal right now, though."

"That sucks," Emma said. I could sense the smile in her voice. "You're lucky your mom was okay with it, though."

"You should tell your dad," I told her. "Then we wouldn't have to hide it from our parents anymore at all."

She grew quiet again. I heard her sigh. "I don't know about that," she said. "I mean, I've heard what he says about gay people, and you know how he gets."

"You never know," I said. "He'll probably accept it, too."

"Maybe. Look, I'm going to get back to sleep. I'm pretty tired."

"Oh, alright. Goodnight."

"'Night, Charlie." The line clicked and went dead.

I dropped my phone and lay on my bed. I felt different, somehow. Relieved. Free.

I wanted Emma to feel the same way.

~~~

All through school the next day I couldn't help but smile. I felt like a huge weight had been lifted from my shoulders. *I'm not going to be one of those tragic stories*, I thought to myself.

Throughout my classes, I found myself thinking of ways for Emma to tell her dad. Maybe it would be best if I was there, or maybe she could discretely leave him some sort of hint. I had been so worried for no reason. I hoped it would be the same for Emma.

After school, as Emma and I were trekking across the gravel parking lot towards my car, we were intercepted by Sarah.

"Hey, Charlotte, Emma, hold up." She was breathless as she jogged to catch up, her back pack bouncing against her side. She brushed her long hair behind her shoulder as she slowed down to walk next to us. "Do you two want to hang out with Bryan and me tonight?"

I turned to Emma. She shoved her hands into the pockets of her white coat as she looked back and forth between Sarah and me. She shrugged. "Sure," she said.

"What'd you have in mind?" I asked.

"Well, Bryan and I were talking about going ice skating. We haven't been yet this season," she replied.

"Yeah, we'll go," Emma told her before I could say anything. I pursed my lips.

Sarah broke into a grin. "Okay. You two want to meet us there around six?"

I kicked at a rock on the ground. "Yeah. Sure."

"Alright. See you then." Sarah turned to walk off in the direction of her car, leaving Emma and me in silence. I unconsciously began walking. Emma followed at my side.

"You alright, Charlie?" she asked.

I shifted my bag, shoving my hands into my pockets to fiddle with my keys. "I can't ice skate. You know that."

Emma gave me a soft nudge with her elbow. "Well, I'll teach you. It's not too hard, really. Have you ever roller skated?"

"When I was a kid," I said.

"Well, it's just like that. Only, it's on ice."

"Alright," I turned and kissed her on the cheek. "I'll trust you on this one."

~~~

Somehow, I managed to get past the fact that I had been grounded. I was really hoping Mom would say I couldn't go. It would have been an excuse. But she said yes.

By the time Emma and I got to the skating rink, my nerves were on fire.

"Hey!" Sarah greeted. She grinned, hugging both of us.

"Hey, guys," Bryan said. He thumbed towards the gate. "You ready?"

Ready? Hardly. I was about to make a fool out of myself. Sucking in a breath, I followed them to the skating rink.

It was outdoors, surrounded by a white picket fence. Luminaries spotted the rink, and spotlights were installed underneath the ice to light it. Cotton candy and apple cider wafted through the air. The place was already crowded, even for a Thursday night.

We had to pay at the gate. I automatically took care of Emma's fee.

"Why'd you do that?" Emma asked, cutting me a glare. "I could have paid for myself."

I looked at her, confused, and handed her the ticket. "I was just being nice," I said. "I didn't know you had a problem with it."

She forced a smile. "It's fine," she said. She took my hand and squeezed it.

"What's wrong with you?" I asked. "You've been in a bad mood all day."

Her green eyes averted to Sarah and Bryan, who were busy renting their ice skates. "Nothing. I'm just not having a good day. Sorry."

After that, it was obvious she was forcing herself to be nice. As we sat down on a bench to slip into our skates, she leaned up against me to whisper in my ear that she loved me. I offered her a weak smile in response. Despite the fact that she was trying to make up for acting distant all day, I couldn't help but think her attitude had something to do with me.

"You guys ready?" Sarah asked. I nodded slowly. I wasn't, but it was now or never. I lived in Connecticut. I should have accepted that I'd have to go ice skating one day.

As we stepped onto the ice, Emma took my hand in hers. I lifted my legs awkwardly, wincing as I felt the blades connect with the slippery surface. Gritting my teeth, I took a wobbly step forward.

"Just act like you're rollerblading," Emma said.

I slid forward. My feet went out from under me and I would have gone tumbling down if it hadn't been for Emma's waiting arms. She hauled me back to an upright position, laughing. I grinned back. This wasn't so bad.

I watched Sarah and Bryan go skating off across the ice like experts, hands linked.

Emma dropped my hand as she glided forward, swiveling in a circle and skating backwards. I gawked at her, my knees still wobbling as I stood in the same place, afraid to move.

"How do you know how to skate?" I asked.

"There are skating rinks in North Carolina." She laughed. "They're just indoors. Come on, Charlie. Give it a try."

I stared at all the people whizzing by me, skating as though it was no big deal. Hesitantly, I slid my feet forward and shuffled towards Emma. She grinned, stretching her hands towards me. I took them.

"See, it's not so bad," she said. She skated backwards, guiding me along.

I laughed and promptly lost my balance. I hit the ice, dragging Emma with me. People had to swerve around us, some laughing.

"Sorry," I said. She was laughing so hard she had to push herself off of me to hold her gut. After a moment, she scrambled to her feet and helped me up. I could feel myself blushing.

"It's okay. You suck, but it's okay." She struggled to stifle her giggles. "Let's try again."

I was eventually able to glide across the ice without falling. She held my hand as I skated next to her. I kept my legs straight, worried that if I bent them like her, I'd fall down. Sarah and Bryan joined us occasionally, but I was going so slow they didn't seem to want to stick around.

"So, I thought about you telling your dad soon," I began once we were skating more effortlessly, "and I think it would be best if you just sat him down and told him."

Emma sighed. "Look, Charlie, I don't think it's such a good idea to tell him right now."

"Why not?" I asked. "It could be just like with my mom. He loves you, Emma," I added.

She took a deep breath. "He's not like your mom, Charlie. He's different. He hates gay people, he doesn't understand—"

"But I'm so relieved," I interrupted. "I want you to feel the same way."

She let go of my hand to skate off the ice and sit down on a bench. I made my way over, nearly getting taken out by a little boy along the way. I sat down next to her.

"I just think it's a good idea." I placed a hand on her knee.

"Well, I don't." She sounded angry. I quickly pulled my hand away. "I don't understand why you think I should do it. Just because you're all out and proud now doesn't mean that I'm ready to be."

I gaped at her. "But you're the one who was talking about joining the GSA," I countered.

"That's different." She started to untie the laces on her ice skates. "I wanted to join so I'd have people to talk to about it. You know, that have been through the same thing and could maybe offer some advice."

I bit my lip. Her face was red, voice lingering on the verge of yelling. "I was just trying to help," I said.

"Well, stop! Stop trying to help me. I don't need help. I don't need your advice on telling my dad. I don't need you to pay for everything," she spat. "Damnit, Charlie, I'm your girlfriend, not your pet."

I watched her as she climbed to her feet, kicking the skates off and picking them up into her hands. "Where are you going?" I asked.

"I'm going to go sit in the car," she said. "I want to go home."

I watched as she stomped off to get her shoes and disappeared through the gate. Sarah and Bryan skated slowly over, skidding to a stop at the edge of the rink.

"Where's Emma going?" Bryan asked. "Is she alright?"

I began to untie my laces. "She doesn't feel well," I lied. "I'm going to take her home."

"Oh. Alright," Sarah said. "Well, I'll see you at school tomorrow."

The entire ride back to her house, Emma didn't speak to me. She didn't even bother to say goodnight. My eyes followed her as she walked up to her porch and disappeared into her house without so much as a glance over her shoulder.

I had already lost Kenny. Had I lost her, too?

~~~

I felt sick to my stomach at school the next day. I couldn't tell if I was actually sick or if it was because of the fight I'd had with Emma. Did she hate me? Were we over?

By the time I reached Theater, I'd pretty much chewed my nails to the quick.

Emma sat next to me the way she usually did, her iPod blasting music into her ears. I tried not to look at her, not knowing whether we were going to be civil with each other or if she was still angry. I nibbled my lip nervously, watching from the corner of my eye as she turned her iPod off and put it away.

"Hey," she said, her voice quiet. She looked worried.

"Hey," I replied. I fiddled with my pencil. "Look, Emma, I just want to say—"

"I'm sorry," she cut me off. "You were just looking out, I know. I overreacted."

"I shouldn't have made you feel like that, though. I mean, I think you should tell your dad, but I'm not trying to force you."

"I know," she said.

Before we had a chance to say anything more, Woodbridge began to call attendance and snapped our attention away from each other.

My eyes remained on Emma while class started. She looked sick. Paler than usual. I wondered what was on her mind.

~~~

We didn't talk much on the way home. I guess we were both afraid we'd argue again.

I dropped her off and headed home. Mom was at work, so I spent a little time with Wednesday before collapsing onto the couch to watch television. I wasn't able to pay attention. My thoughts circled around Emma and our argument. *Do I try to control her?* I wondered. *Am I a bad girlfriend?*

I must've fallen asleep, because a pounding on the front door startled me to the point where I nearly fell off the couch. I scrambled to my feet and wandered to the front door, confused. The pounding repeated.

I swung open the door.

Emma was standing in front of me. She was only dressed in my light Abercrombie sweatshirt and a pair of jeans and was shivering hard. I vaguely took notice that her dad's truck was nowhere in sight. She must have walked.

But it wasn't her underdressed state that caused a rush of cold dread to pulse through my veins. It was the tears running down her cheeks, the fear bold in her eyes.

It was the panic in her shaking voice when she finally mustered the strength to speak.

"I told my dad."

Twenty-eight

"Oh, my God," was the only thing that I could force from my mouth. I threw my arms around Emma just as she burst into tears. I couldn't do anything but hold her. After a few minutes, I steered her into my living room to make her sit on the couch.

"He threw the T.V. remote at me." She latched onto me, burrowing her face into my shoulder.

"Jesus, Emma." I felt tears spring to my own eyes. "What happened?"

She took a shaky breath, pulling her hands away from me to wipe at her cheeks with her palms. "I sat with him and told him I needed to talk to him. A-and I just told him." She paused, her eyes focused on her fidgeting hands. "And he freaked."

I immediately felt overtaken with guilt. If I wouldn't have tried to convince her to tell her dad, she probably wouldn't have been sitting next to me in the state she was in. If we hadn't gotten in that argument, this would never have happened.

"He told me to get out," she said.

I wrapped my arms around her, pulling her into me and kissing her forehead in some attempt to try to make her feel better even though I knew I couldn't.

She hesitated, leaning into my body before speaking again. "So, I came here." Her eyes caught mine and the pain behind them was almost more than I could bear. "I don't know what to do, Charlie." Her body was trembling. "Would your mom mind if I stayed here?"

"I doubt it," I said. "You can stay here as long as you need to."

We sat in silence for what seemed like forever. Tears continued to spring from Emma's eyes.

"Charlie?" she finally spoke up.

"Yeah?"

"What if he doesn't take me back?" Her eyes trained on my face. She was begging for an answer.

I wanted to be able to tell her that everything was going to be okay, that her dad would come around and still love her. "I don't know, Emma," I said, finding myself unable to lie.

The only thing I knew was that I was to blame for all of her heartache, and I hated it.

~~~

The good thing about it all was that Mom welcomed Emma with open arms. It made me glad that even if she didn't feel wanted at her house that she had someplace to go.

By Sunday, Emma's dad still hadn't made contact with her. I let her borrow my clothes over the weekend. It wasn't until later in the evening that she finally got the call. I had just gotten back from work, and the two of us were just lying in my room watching television when her phone started to vibrate across my mattress.

"It's him," she said. I picked myself up off the bed to look at her phone.

"Are you going to answer?" I reached over to touch her knee, trying to give her some courage.

She hesitated, her eyes meeting mine before she answered her phone. I instantly heard her dad's voice on the other line.

"Emma? Where have you been?"

She drew a deep breath before answering. "Charlotte's," she said.

There was nothing but silence on the other end for a long time. Whatever he said next I couldn't hear.

"Alright," she said. I watched as the tears began to fill her eyes. "I know, Dad. I'm sorry."

She paused again to let him speak. I gave her knee a gentle squeeze.

"What'd he say?" I asked after a minute, turning my gaze to look into her eyes. A few tears slid down her cheek.

"He's coming to get me," she replied, her voice nearly a whisper.

"What? And you're letting him? Are you sure?"

"Charlie." She sucked in air. "He's my dad. I want to go home. He said he's sorry. I just want to be normal again."

I nodded, quiet for a moment as I took this in. "Alright," I said. We rose.

"Mom," I yelled. "Emma's dad called. She's going home."

I watched Mom stagger out of her bed where she had been reading to rush to the doorway. "Are you sure, sweetie?" she asked Emma, who nodded slowly in response. Mom looked to me, but all I had to offer was a shrug.

"Call if anything happens, okay? You're welcome here any time."

"Thanks," Emma said. She let Mom wrap her arms around her and hugged her back.

A loud knock brought our attention to the front door. Emma pulled herself away from Mom to stride down the hallway. I followed.

She opened the door. Her dad stood before us, a nervous Trevor at his side.

"Come on, Emma." He tried to force a smile.

Emma stepped forward and followed Trevor out to the truck, turning only briefly to exchange a look with me and mouth, *I love you.*

I turned my gaze away to see her dad still standing before me, his usually gentle blue eyes burning into my own.

"How could you do this to my daughter?" he asked. I opened my mouth to say something, what exactly I didn't know, but before I could he turned on his heel to march off to his truck.

I stood in the open doorway, aware of my mom looking over my shoulder, of the truck backing out of our driveway, of the possibility that Emma's dad might never let us see each other again.

And all I could think was how he was right. *How could I have done this to her? How could I have done this to us?*

~~~

Emma wasn't in school the next day, which worried me. I texted her a few times during History and Photography, but there was no answer. I called her as soon as the bell rang for lunch.

"Hello?" Her voice filled my ear after a couple of rings. I felt relief seep through my body.

"Emma, where are you? Is everything alright?" I had a million questions, but I tried to keep it short.

"I'm alright. Dad made me stay home today. I'll tell you about it later, okay? But I have to go. I'm not supposed to be talking to you."

"Oh, okay. I love you." I sighed.

"Bye," she replied. The line clicked dead.

I felt sick. Nauseated. Her dad didn't want her to talk to me? Did that mean she wasn't allowed to see me, either?

Later, I told Cory everything that had happened, figuring she'd have some advice for me.

"I wonder why her dad made her stay home. Unless he just doesn't want her to see you," she said. It just made me feel sicker. It was exactly what I had been thinking.

"No." Cory shook her head. "You can't blame yourself for this. He would have found out eventually, Charlotte. It's part of coming out. My parents reacted the same way."

"I guess," I said. But I still knew that I was the one that caused everything.

~~~

Emma came back to school the next day, but I wasn't able to see her anywhere else. I wasn't even allowed to give her a ride home anymore. Her dad picked her up every day after Theater.

"My dad's making me see a psychiatrist," she told me one day after class. I didn't have time to reply, though. She had seen her dad at the entrance and had to dash.

It didn't matter because I didn't even know what to say back. I guessed he was trying to figure out how to fix the problem or what caused it in the first place, even though I knew he thought I was the one who corrupted her.

I couldn't even talk to her on the phone. We spent our nights chatting on the internet. I tried to stay positive and reassure her that her dad would come around and the two of us would be together again.

Despite my efforts, I could sense a change. I felt her steadily distancing herself, pushing me away. I told her we'd make it work. I'd wait. I told her I loved her, even though she didn't tell me she loved me back anymore. I tried to convince myself it was because she was afraid her dad might have seen it.

But I guess I didn't realize how ignorant I really was until the next Monday.

~~~

I'd begun to worship Theater class, finding myself counting down the long hours and minutes until the bell rang and I could see her again. When I could be with her for the hour that went by all too fast.

I sat in my usual seat next to her, offering a small smile that she didn't return. I touched her hand and she moved it away. Her actions confused me.

As I gazed into her eyes, I didn't see any love or adoration reflected back. Instead, I found a faraway gaze that was unfamiliar to me.

"Emma, what's wrong?" I asked.

She looked away from me, shook her head. Didn't speak.

I ignored Woodbridge throughout the class and tried desperately to make eye contact with Emma. She was either ignoring me or didn't realize I was trying to communicate with her. I hoped it was the latter.

It wasn't until after class as the two of us were stepping into the hallway that I felt her hand grasping my wrist.

"Charlie, can I talk to you?"

I nodded slowly. She led me down the hallway to the small, empty enclosure near the locker rooms. We stopped next to the trophy case. My eyes ran across the dusty glass before her voice drew my attention to her.

"Charlie." I could hear the hurt in her voice. Frowning, I moved forward in an attempt to kiss her, to try to make her feel better. Or maybe to try to make myself feel better. I wasn't sure anymore. Instead of her lips, I felt her hand hard on my chest, pushing me away.

My heart began to pound against my chest. Something was really wrong. Maybe her dad had taken her computer away, or maybe he was moving her to a different school. I didn't think I could take it if he made her switch schools. I swallowed hard.

"Emma, what is it?" My worried eyes scoped her face for some sort of answer.

"Charlotte," she said. Did she really just call me that? I felt my stomach churn. She took a deep breath. I could hear the slight waver that told me she was about to cry. "I don't think this is going to work."

I wondered vaguely if those words just escaped her mouth or if I was imagining it. Finally, I said, "What are you talking about? Of course it's going to work out. I mean, you turn 18 soon, so your dad can't keep us apart forever—"

"No," she interrupted. "I don't mean that. I mean this. Us." She waved her hands gently, I guess trying to encompass the whole of our relationship in one small maneuver.

"What?" I tried to hold her eyes. She was staring at the ground. "What do you mean?"

She lifted her gaze to meet mine. "I mean we can't be together anymore." The tears were glistening in her eyes. I watched as one slipped from the corner to make a river down her cheek. I wanted to wipe it away for her, but I was so stunned I didn't think I could move my hands.

"Emma, you can't be serious," I said. "We can make it through this."

She shook her head, turning her body away from me. Her hands moved up to her face to swipe at the tears that streamed down her freckled face.

"Emma, please," I pleaded. I was suddenly aware that I was crying too, the tears making a path down my cheek to fall onto the front of my sweatshirt. "I love you."

She turned back towards me, emerald eyes searching mine. She opened her mouth as if to say something, but quickly shut it.

"I have to go," she finally muttered, and I stood, paralyzed, as she turned and walked away with my heart.

Twenty-nine

I had nobody to run to.

I tossed my phone in my hand as I lay on my bed, Wednesday curled at my feet. Every few minutes, I would go to my contacts and scroll through to see if they'd possibly changed. Maybe, if I didn't look, I'd have new friends.

Or my old friends back.

I think I would've been happier with the latter.

Giving up on divine intervention, I turned my phone off and tossed it under my bed. It's not like I needed it. Nobody was going to call.

Nobody important, anyways.

The only thing worse than sitting alone at home feeling sorry for myself was actually having to go to school. I hadn't thought about how awkward it would be with Emma being in one of my classes, but I quickly found out.

What hurt the most was that everything didn't even seem that difficult for her. She walked into the classroom and sat in her original seat on the other side of the circle with her iPod blaring music into her ears. She didn't look the way I felt. It only seemed to cut deeper into the wound she'd inflicted inside of me. I just wanted to scream, *how can you act so normal? What about everything we had? What about everything we could have been?*

The only way I could tell how she felt was when she lifted her eyes. She'd shoot a fleeting gaze at me and I could tell she hurt, too, even if she wasn't showing it. There was no sparkle, there was no life. They'd become the window to her broken spirit.

Maybe that was why they called it breaking up. Inside, neither of us was whole anymore. We were like puzzles missing a single piece.

She was my missing piece.

I just wished so badly she would realize that I was hers.

~~~

I felt like I'd turned into some sort of recluse. I hadn't even bothered to attempt to smooth things over with Kenny, but I had noticed that something was going on with him and Sarah. I vaguely wondered why Sarah wouldn't mention it. Did Kenny instruct her not to tell? Was she afraid I'd run to Bryan?

I started sitting with Cory and some of her friends at lunch. It only seemed to make the mockery worse.

I had officially joined the school's gay crowd. It should have made me feel liberated, or at least like I had other people to talk to about what I was going through.

It didn't.

I still felt as alone as ever.

After school the next Tuesday, I settled down on the couch in my living room. It'd become my routine. My hand found the remote and I began flipping through the channels, resting my head against the cushioned arm of the couch as I watched TV.

I heard the familiar clicking of paws against the floor and looked to the side to see Wednesday ambling over, her tongue dangling merrily from the side of her mouth. Giving her a weak smile, I sat up to reach over and scratch behind her ears.

"What's up, girl?" I asked.

I burst into giggles as she jumped up onto the couch and began licking at my face and neck. Her paws thumped at my thighs. "Okay, okay! Enough." I pushed her off of me. She hopped off the couch and skipped across the living room.

I grinned. It made me feel a little bit better that I could still count on Wednesday to cheer me up.

I watched as she darted across the room and began nudging at my soccer ball with her nose. She glanced up at me with smiling eyes.

Laughing, I rose from the couch and plucked the soccer ball off the ground to juggle in my hands. The husky rose onto her hind legs, her massive body coming in contact with mine as she tried to take the ball away. I nearly fell over.

"You want to play?"

Wednesday barked animatedly.

"I'll take that as a yes," I said.

I tucked the soccer ball under my arm and made a beeline for the door. Wednesday followed, her tail wagging with excitement. I threw on my coat and boots and opened the door. My dog bolted outside.

I shut the door behind me and tossed my soccer ball onto the front yard. Wednesday jumped on top of it and began rolling around in the thin layer of snow on the ground. I ran after her, stealing the ball from between her paws and dribbling it across the yard as she dashed after me.

Wednesday could get the ball away from me better than an actual player. I burst into laughter when she picked the ball up between her teeth and ran across the yard to the side of the house.

"Hey!" I shouted, running after her. "No teeth! Foul!"

She dropped the ball and barked at me, lips curling up in a snarl as she leaned protectively over the ball. I walked up to her to kick at it. It didn't go anywhere. Grinning, I used the ball of my foot to pull it back and picked it up with my hands before she could jump on top of it. Whining, she scrambled into a sitting position and peered up at me.

"Oh, you want this, do you?" I asked, juggling it on my knees. "You've got to come and get it."

Just as the soccer ball rose off my knee and into the air, so did Wednesday. She bounded upwards, the front of her snout coming in contact with the ball and sending it hurtling across the yard.

Straight into the road.

"Wednesday, no!" I yelled as I watched the husky bolt after the ball. She didn't listen.

I didn't even have time to move. Everything happened so quickly. The blare of the car's horn. Me, screaming. The ear-piercing yelp of my dog. The sickening sound of metal against bone, bone against concrete as Wednesday landed hard in the middle of the road. I felt my heart stop in my chest.

Before I knew it, I was at my dog's side. I was vaguely aware of the driver leaping out of his vehicle to rush to my side.

Wednesday was laying still, her whimpers filling my ears. I was in tears as I reached down to touch her. There was blood, so much blood, and it was staining her grey fur and the dark concrete underneath of her. Her legs were so mangled I couldn't even look at them.

"Oh, my God." I turned to see the driver, an older gentleman, staring down at my husky. "I'm so sorry, I didn't even see him. He came out of nowhere."

"Call someone," I begged. "Please, call someone. We have to get her to a vet."

He pulled out his cell phone, but simply looked at it. "Who do I call?"

"Wait with her," I said, rising. Before waiting for an answer, I was running through the front door and into my room to grab my cell phone, cursing myself for not having it on me like I normally did. It wasn't even a minute before I was back outside and next to Wednesday, watching helplessly as tremors seemed to shoot through her body.

"Please be okay," I said as my shaking fingers began dialing Mom's phone number.

~~~

In what seemed like hours, I was able to get Wednesday into the backseat of my car and to the closest veterinarian. A glance at my watch brought me to the realization it had only been maybe 10 minutes when I finally pulled into the parking lot. The phone call the driver had made to the office already had a few technicians in the lobby waiting to usher the convulsing husky inside. I could only stand quietly as chaos seemed to erupt around me. The men pushing the stretcher threw questions. I offered what little response I was able to muster and simply nodded my head at their comments, struggling to keep my composure.

I watched as the technicians disappeared with Wednesday. I was about to follow when the secretary stopped me.

"How old are you, sweetie?" she asked, trying her hardest to sound comforting.

"Seventeen," I replied.

"Is your mother or father on the way?"

"My mom is." I felt tears beginning to spring from my eyes. I had to be with Wednesday. I couldn't leave her alone. I started to move but the woman stopped me once more.

"I need you to have your mom sign these forms, okay honey?"

I had started to reply when I saw Mom burst through the front door of the office in her scrubs. She rushed to my side and I threw my arms around her, crying.

Mom didn't say much. Instead, she took the forms and filled them out before shoving them across the counter. The two of us were in the back at Wednesday's side before the secretary could say anything else.

I could only watch as the technicians tried to stabilize Wednesday while the veterinarian looked over the damage. Everything seemed like it was going by so quickly. Like I was watching a movie. Mom stroked Wednesday's neck, struggling to hold back tears.

"She's not in good shape. We have two choices," the vet finally said. "We can either operate or you have the option to euthanize. However, I'm pretty sure we have a good chance of saving her if we can operate quickly."

I looked at Mom, who didn't seem to respond. I knew she was analyzing in her head just how much an operation was going to cost. Finally, she turned to me. "It's your choice, Charlotte. She's your dog."

"Operate," I replied quickly, speaking more to Mom than the veterinarian. "Please, just save her."

I couldn't lose her.

Wednesday was rushed to the operating room, I was instantly aware of what was going on around me. The splotches of bright red blood on my clothing, the barking of dogs in the veterinary kennel, the sound of voices as technicians and veterinarians talked hurriedly.

Maybe things would be okay. They were going to operate. The vet said they could save her. I felt a flicker of hope ignite inside of me.

Pulling my cell phone out of my pocket, my finger lingered over the speed-dial button for my best friend.

But would he even come?

Would he even *answer?*

Taking a deep breath, I hit send and slowly lifted the phone to my ear. Mom peered at me through the tears in her eyes. "Who are you calling?"

"Someone that I want here with me," I replied.

To my surprise, Kenny's familiar voice answered the phone. For a second, I didn't know what to say. What to do. What had come over me? How did I feel like I had any right to call him and ask for help?

"Charlotte? Hello?"

Finally, I said, "Kenny. I need you."

<u>Thirty</u>

Even though he'd said he was on his way, I was still shocked to see him walk through the doors of the clinic. I leapt from my chair, but withheld the hug that I desperately wanted to give.

"Kenny," I said. "You came."

A tense smile flickered across his face. "Of course I came," he said, glancing towards Mom. "Hey, Ms. Hayes."

"Hi, Kenny." She rose. "You know, I think I'm going to go see what's going on."

Despite the fact that I knew the vet would let us know if anything was happening, I let her go, grateful for the alone time.

"Look, Kenny—" I started.

"Don't." He shook his head. I felt his muscular arms wrap around me and pull my body into his chest. I let myself relax as the familiar scent of Axe surrounded me. "It's all good. I forgive you. I wish you would've told me that you're, well—" He cast a glance down the hall.

I was doing everything I could to keep from crying, but, before I realized it, the tears started flooding down my cheeks. "Gay? I couldn't even admit it to myself." I took a deep breath. "I'm so sorry." I buried my face into the crook of his shoulder.

He took me by the arms and backed a step, holding me out in front of him. "It's okay," he said, giving me a smile that didn't light up his eyes the way it usually did. "Besides, she's happier with you."

I shook my head. "Not that happy. She broke up with me."

"What?" He sounded surprised. I thought he would've been able to tell that there was something going on between us by the way we acted in school, but I guess he was oblivious. "Are you serious? Why?"

"I don't know." I shrugged. I knew, though. It was me. It was my fault.

"I'm so sorry I wasn't there for you." Once again, he took me into a tight embrace.

It's not like I was there for you, I thought. But just as I was about to say how sorry I was for hurting him, Mom appeared from around the corner.

"How is she?" Kenny asked. "Is there any news?"

"She's still in surgery," Mom said. "They didn't give me any information."

She'd been in the operating room for an hour and a half now with still no word. I was getting more worried by the minute. Turning away from Kenny, I craned my neck to peer down the long hallway, hoping somebody would materialize with a smile.

"What happened, exactly?" Kenny asked me, forcing my attention to return to him.

"I was playing with her and she ran into the road."

I took a step over to where Mom sat and lowered myself into a chair. Kenny strode over to sit next to me.

The three of us were silent for a long time. I felt my eyes glaze over as I stared at a painting of a happy black Labrador on the far wall.

"Hey, are you okay?" Kenny stretched one arm around my shoulder and pulled me into a gentle hug. I leaned against his firm frame, closing my eyes.

"Do you think she'll be alright?" I felt fresh tears forming at the corner of my eye.

He hesitated before answering. I could tell he was thinking of the right thing to say to make me feel better. "I'm sure she will be," he said, but the way he tightened his arm around my body made me think he wasn't so sure after all.

~~~

"Charlotte. Wake up."

I felt Kenny jostling my shoulder and my eyes snapped open. I'd fallen asleep. I looked down the hallway, noticing Mom chatting quietly with the vet. In a flash, I was on my feet and at her side to hear the news.

"How is she?" I asked, cutting directly into their conversation and not really caring. I needed to know how my dog was.

"She's going to be okay," the vet said.

I felt myself smiling. I turned to Mom to hug her, but froze when I saw the tears leaking down her cheeks. Something wasn't right.

"What's wrong?" I felt my hand grasp her arm as I turned back to the vet, taking notice for the first time of the aged blood dotting his scrubs. Wednesday's blood.

He frowned, throwing a glance to Mom before answering. "Unfortunately, the muscle and bone of her right front leg was so damaged that we couldn't repair it. We had to amputate."

"What?" I stared in disbelief, whirling to see Kenny standing next to me. I started to ask if I'd heard correctly, but the shock on his face told me it wasn't my imagination. I turned my attention back to the vet, taking my hand off of Mom's arm to swipe at my cheeks. "You had to amputate," I said, more of a statement than a question.

The vet nodded, lifting a hand to place on my shoulder in whatever amount of comfort he had to offer. "She's going to be alright, though. She's going to live."

I pictured Wednesday when we first got her, bolting around our back yard in an attempt to investigate every crevice of her new home. Her first bath, how I somehow ended up more soaked than she did when she dashed out of the tub and began to rub her wet fur all over the carpet in my room. The harmonic ticking of her paws against the linoleum every day after school when she raced to greet me. She'd never do any of those things again, not with three legs.

The feeling of Kenny pulling me close made me realize how hard I was crying. I felt the familiar choke in my throat as I tried to quell my tears.

"Can we see her?" I heard Mom ask.

"Not tonight." The vet glanced in the direction of the operating room. "She's still under anesthesia. Tomorrow, though. Go home and get some rest for now, we'll take good care of her."

"When can she come home?" I pulled myself away from Kenny.

"She'll have to stay here for a few days so that we can make sure everything turns out alright," he said. I nodded, wishing he had said otherwise. I wanted her to be home, where she belonged.

"Will you take good care of her?" I asked.

"Of course." He led us over to the front desk where he handed my mom a clipboard with more forms to fill out. "She'll get excellent care."

I bit my lip as I watched Mom fill out the forms for Wednesday's aftercare, praying that my dog would be able to make it through the night. Praying that maybe, just maybe, things would work out in my favor.

~~~

Our family may have already been what one could call broken, but the absence of Wednesday left our home even more incomplete. I had learned to tune out her familiar sounds, and yet with her gone I noticed the lack of every bark, every whine, and every thump of her paws against the floor. The silence was deafening.

When Wednesday was finally able to return home on Saturday, Mom and I were elated. I suppose we picked her up expecting everything to go back to normal. For our home to be mended. It wasn't the case.

It was hard, but we quickly realized that Wednesday wouldn't ever be the same. She was more depressed than I'd ever seen her. She hobbled around awkwardly on her three remaining limbs, but mostly stretched out in various places throughout the house. I guessed her quiet demeanor was a combination of the loss of her leg and the huge cone-shaped object around her head to keep her from biting at her stitches.

And, despite my hardest wishes, the house didn't return to normal. It was still as silent, still as lonely, as before.

~~~

I called out of work on Sunday to spend the evening with Wednesday. I tried to work on some Theater homework, but it was impossible with the thoughts that pounded ruthlessly inside my head.

Dropping my pencil onto my neglected worksheet, I wandered into the living room to find Wednesday lying in the corner. She tilted her nose towards me as I sprawled across the carpet to wrap my arms around her neck, stretching my face around the large cone on her head to kiss her on the muzzle. She gave me a half-hearted lick in return, but her eyes, once sparkling with life, only read sadness.

My hand traced gently over her back and came to a stop at the spot on her shoulder just above where her leg had been removed. I buried my face into her fluffy neck, tugging her close as I let myself cry into her soft body. It was difficult to register that she wasn't whole anymore, that she might never be the same. I knew exactly how she felt.

"Wednesday," I whispered, pulling my face away to look into her calm eyes, "we're one and the same."

~~~

When I walked into Theater class on Monday, the sight of Emma made my mind reel back to reality. Her birthday was the day before. With all that had happened, I had completely forgotten.

The desk next to her was empty. Should I? I hesitated, pausing in the doorway of the classroom. Before I had a chance to convince myself otherwise, I was walking over and taking a seat beside her.

Emma looked up as soon as I sat down and turned her iPod off.

"Hey," I said. I felt awkward.

"Hi," she replied. Her voice was quiet. I watched her nibble her bottom lip and turn her eyes away.

I analyzed the side of her pale face, suddenly feeling stupid and embarrassed all at the same time. I shouldn't have approached her. Taking a deep breath, I told her, "Happy birthday."

"It was yesterday."

"I know." I swallowed hard and glanced down at my hands when she looked back up. "I'm sorry I didn't get you anything,"

"Why would you get me anything?" she asked. "I don't deserve anything from you."

"Well…" I trailed off. *Because you mean more to me than anything in the world,* I wanted to say. "Anyways, I guess I'll get to my seat." I started to rise, but the sensation of Emma's hand on my wrist made me stop. Made my heart stop.

"You can stay here." She withdrew her hand as though it were shocked. I was disappointed that she took her hand away, but at the same time excited she offered me to stay next to her. I lowered myself back into the chair.

"My dad got me a car," she said, filling the silence that worked itself into the gap between us just like it used to. "It's nothing nice, but I guess he got sick of giving me rides back and forth from school every day."

"What did he get you?"

"A Jeep Cherokee."

Emma driving a Jeep seemed like such a stretch it made me smile. "Good car," I replied, wondering if I sounded as lame as I felt.

She nodded. "What's been going on with you?"

Only heartbreak and loneliness.

I hesitated for a moment before telling her about the week's events. When I finished, I gazed into Emma's eyes to see the tears threatening to slip down her cheeks. She acted as though she was about to hug me, but stopped herself.

"I'm so sorry," she said at last.

"Why?"

She paused, drawing a shaky breath. "I'm sorry that I wasn't there for you." Her eyes searched my face. I turned away. I wanted to say something more, but couldn't seem to think of the right words. *I wasn't there for one of your most important birthdays,* I wanted to say.

The sound of Woodbridge's voice telling us to be silent completely erased the idea of a continued conversation. But, as hard as I tried, it was impossible to pay attention throughout the entire class. The knowledge that Emma was sitting only inches away made my nerves tingle and my mind wander.

~~~

When the bell rang, I didn't say anything to Emma as I gathered my belongings and rose to make my way out of the classroom. She seemed hurried as she threw her things together to follow. Out of the corner of my eye I caught her small frame as she darted up beside me.

"Hey, Charlie," she said. I turned my head to find her green eyes locked on my face.

"Hey," I replied.

"I was just wondering if you wanted to do anything tonight."

I stopped dead in my tracks, narrowing my eyes in confusion. "Hang out? But, well, what about your dad?"

"We had a conversation," she said. Her voice sounded hurried. "And besides, I'm eighteen now. I should be able to do what I want, right?"

"I don't know." I turned my eyes away to watch a few students milling around a soda machine down the hallway. "I don't know if it's really a good idea." It hurt to say it, but it was too hard to just be friends with the one person I was still so in love with.

"Oh." Her voice was nearly a whisper when she spoke. "Alright, well, I guess I'll see you around then."

I watched her hurry off down the hallway, wondering vaguely why she even wanted to hang out with me. Striding towards the front of the school, I pushed the front doors open with a sigh and began the long trek to where my car was parked.

When I finally reached the battered old Probe, I threw my belongings into the backseat and hopped into the driver's side. I slammed my foot onto the clutch as usual and turned the key in the ignition.

Nothing.

I pressed my foot a little harder onto the clutch as I tried to spark my car to life once more. The engine whirred weakly before growing silent once again.

"Are you kidding me?" I said out loud as I tried again and again to start the car. Still nothing. I popped the hood of the car and jumped out to inspect the engine. I didn't know why I was even bothering to look. I knew absolutely nothing about cars and how they worked. All I knew is that Old Reliable got me from point A to point B, usually with no problem.

I let the hood slam shut before delivering a blow with my foot to the side of my car, which only made me cry out in pain and annoyance at the fact that the driver's side door now had a fresh dent. "Why me?" I growled. "Why is it always me?"

The sound of an idling car snapped my attention away from Old Reliable.

A white Jeep Cherokee was sitting next to my parking spot. It was old. Battered. It may not have been the prettiest, but the girl inside sure was.

Emma didn't say anything as she reached across the console and popped the passenger side door open.

Thirty-one

"Thanks," I told Emma as I climbed into the passenger seat of her Jeep. I dropped my bag on the floorboard.

"Old Reliable not feeling so reliable today?" she asked.

I shrugged, leaning back and buckling my seatbelt. "I guess not," I said. My eyes shifted over the inside of her Jeep. She'd only had it since her birthday and it was already messy. Clothes were strewn across the backseat. A few empty water bottles littered the floor. I opened my mouth to make a comment about it, but decided against it.

"What do you think is wrong with it?"

"I don't know," I answered. "I don't know anything about cars."

She shrugged. The silence seeped into the space between us. I felt awkward and out of place, which was so strange because this was where I felt like I belonged.

"So, it's a good thing your dad decided to get you an automatic transmission." I glanced back towards her as my fingers fidgeted in my lap. A smile grew across her face. She was so cute.

"Shut up." She brought the Jeep to a jarring stop at a red light and tilted her face towards me with a smirk. "I wasn't meant to drive a stick."

I felt a blush rise into my cheeks and quickly turned my attention to my hands as the light switched to green. "How are things with your dad?" I asked.

"Alright, I guess," she replied with a sigh. "You remember how he took me to a psychiatrist a couple of weeks ago?" She turned towards me to watch me nod before continuing. "Well, the guy pretty much told my dad to get over it because he can't change me, so ever since then he's been trying really hard to be accepting."

"I told you he'd come around," I said lamely.

She didn't say anything else as she navigated through the streets and finally pulled into my driveway. I sat for a moment with my hand on my bag, noticing that she put the car into park. Did she expect to come inside?

"Thanks for the ride," I told her. "I really appreciate it."

"It's not like you didn't give me a million rides." She smiled. Her gaze settled on my face. I tugged my eyes away to push the door open. I began to step out of her Jeep, but stopped with my hand on the door.

"Do you want to come inside and visit Wednesday, maybe?" I asked. "She'd like that."

I was surprised when her response was quick. "Sure." Her smile widened as she hopped out of the driver's side of her car. Swinging my bag over my shoulder, I slammed the door shut and trudged slowly up to the porch.

"So, when did she have the surgery?" she asked as we walked through the front door. I listened briefly, for some reason expecting the familiar clicking of Wednesday's paws against the floor. I guess I still wasn't used to the dismal fact that things had changed. That things would never be the same.

I stood in place as Emma rushed forward to kneel next to her. "Oh, poor girl," she cooed. Her hands stroked Wednesday's fluffy back. Wednesday's tongue lapped against the side of Emma's face in greeting before she let her head rest against the side of the couch once more.

"You should have called me," Emma said. "I would have been there."

I walked over to kneel down next to her, my hand resting on Wednesday's paw. "I didn't want to bother you."

"You wouldn't have been bothering me." Her voice was a near whisper. I watched as she averted her attention back to Wednesday to gently rub at her shoulder. "Do you think she still hurts?"

"Yeah, it still hurts," I said, but I wasn't talking about Wednesday anymore.

"I'm sorry," she said. "I never meant to hurt you."

"You broke up with me."

"I still love you."

She said it so quickly that I didn't even have a chance to think, much less respond. My heart throbbed in my chest.

"I-I'm sorry," she stuttered, scrambling to her feet. "That was out of line. I should go."

"I—wait, no," I begged. But it was too late. She was through the front door before I could even tell her that I still loved her, too. I still loved her so much.

~~~

Mom and I managed to get my car towed to the mechanic later in the evening, yet even after his twenty minute speech about everything that was wrong with it, I still wasn't exactly sure what the problem was. The mechanical and automobile lingo had me stumped. The only thing I could actually manage to comprehend was the price.

"It's going to be about $825 in overall repairs," the man told us in a gruff voice as he stroked his beard. I heard Mom gasp next to me, covering her mouth with her hand. After Wednesday's surgery, I was pretty sure we were both broke. I bit my lip hard, trying to think of how much I had in my checking account. Thirty dollars, at most, after giving Mom pretty much all of my money to go towards the surgery.

"That much?" Mom asked. "I don't think the car is even worth that amount of money."

The mechanic shrugged, glancing at the Probe and trying to look sympathetic, even though I knew he really wasn't. "There's a lot wrong with it. To be honest, I'm surprised she didn't give out months ago."

With a sigh, I said, "Mom, just forget it. Let's take it home and I'll take care of it when I make the money."

"Alright," she agreed, defeated.

I wanted nothing more than to have my car back, fixed no matter what the cost, but sometimes things are too broken to be healed so quickly.

~~~

When I walked into Theater class the next day, I stood for a moment to decide whether or not I should sit beside Emma. My mind was made up for me when she motioned to me.

"Hey," she said when I took my seat next to her. After a moment, she added, "How's the car situation?"

"Hopeless." I sighed and pulled my binder out of my bag. "The mechanic wants an arm and a leg to fix it, so it looks like I'm going to be a recluse for a while."

"How'd you get here, then?"

"I drove my mom's car today," I told her. "She didn't have to work."

"Oh." Emma turned away from me to tuck a strand of hair behind her ear and began doodling in her notebook. I'd decided that our conversation was over until she said, "You can call me for a ride, you know."

I looked at the most recent notes scrawled across a page in my binder. I read a line, noticing how I didn't remember a thing even though it was all just from the day before. I could only remember how preoccupied I was by the knowledge that Emma was sitting right beside me.

"Charlie?"

"Oh, right," I said, jarred out of my wandering thoughts. "Yeah, I know. Thanks Em."

I let my eyes fall on Zach. It looked like he was showing Jasmine some sort of cheer. The sensation of Emma's leg bumping into me drew my attention back to her.

"Sorry," she said, a blush creeping into her cheeks.

Somehow, though, I didn't think it was an accident. She didn't bother to move her leg, and neither did I.

~~~

After saying goodbye to Emma after class, I started to head towards the front of school just as I did every day until I stopped in my tracks, my gaze falling into a classroom located a few doors down from Theater. A few students mingled about the desks, chatting and goofing off with one another. There were mostly unfamiliar faces among the handful of teens, but the few that I recognized make me realize almost immediately what they were all there for.

The Gay-Straight Alliance. I hadn't even realized it was Tuesday.

Ever since Zach and Cory had approached me with the prospect of attending their meetings, I'd been trying to force myself to at least think about going. Yet, every time Tuesday came around, I always seemed to find some excuse not to attend.

And, when Emma broke up with me, I didn't want to go and have people think I was just trying to use the GSA as a cheap dating service.

I hesitated outside the classroom. A voice interrupted my thoughts.

"Hey, Hayes! Thinking about joining us today?"

Cory was sprawled across a desk towards the far side of the classroom waiting for my response.

I had started to tell her I wasn't interested when I was tackled from the side.

"Charlotte!" Zach squealed, squeezing me so hard I felt my breath slipping from my airway. "I'm so glad you decided to finally come. Come on in, take a seat. We don't bite." He ushered me into the classroom.

"I do, actually. But you should know that, shouldn't you Zach?" A blonde kid I didn't recognize piped up from the desk next to Cory. Laughter immediately circled around the room, Zach's the loudest.

"You wish, Danny." Zach sat down in a chair. I took a deep breath, glancing around one more time before taking a seat next to him. My eyes wandered the room, searching the faces for any more that I recognized. There was a guy from my Literature class, and a girl from my grade I'd seen around in the hallways from time to time.

The other two people, Danny and the girl next to Cory, I'd never seen before. Or, maybe I had, I just hadn't noticed.

"Hey, sorry I'm late guys."

The familiar feminine voice echoing against the cement walls made me turn abruptly in my seat. Veronica was walking across the room, juggling a handful of books. She came to a startled stop when she saw me.

"Charlotte." She glanced around at the other students before bringing her eyes back to me. "Hey."

"Hey," I replied, shifting uncomfortably in my seat. I felt so out of place. Shoving a piece of hair behind my ear, I offered her a weak smile.

Veronica navigated through the rows of desks to claim a chair next to me. "I'm glad you finally decided you come."

I nodded. "I didn't know you were gay," I said.

She laughed, dropping her books onto the floor and straightening up against the back of the chair. "I'm not. I have a boyfriend, remember?"

"She's straight," Danny told me, laughing.

I narrowed my eyes in confusion. "Wait, what?"

"Gay-Straight Alliance," Zach pointed out with a nod of his head. "She's a straight ally."

I glanced back to Veronica. She smiled at me, which only made me feel even more stupid. Blushing, I sank a little lower into my desk.

"It's okay," Veronica said, smiling even wider before scanning the room once more and changing the subject. "Why isn't your girlfriend here?"

I hesitated, frowning. "We broke up," I replied.

"Shut up, are you serious?" the girl next to Cory cut in. "You two were so cute together."

I shrugged. I felt a strong arm wrap around my shoulders.

"Emma's loss," Zach said as he gave me a small squeeze. "My gain. Did I fail to mention to you guys that Charlotte and I are an item now?"

Everyone burst into laughter. Zach grinned, a dreamy expression crossing his face as he brought the back of his hand to his forehead with a sigh.

"I realized I was in love with Charlotte only recently," he said, leaning back so far in his desk that I was suddenly afraid he was going to fall over and take me with him. "Which made me acknowledge the fact that I am, indeed, a—"he paused, exhaling dramatically, "a lesbian."

"Oh, God," Cory moaned, letting her head fall against the desk she was lying across. "Someone get the U-Haul."

I couldn't help but laugh along with everyone else.

Maybe I'll like this after all, I thought, feeling my grin grow wider than it had in weeks.

~~~

I walked to Mom's car feeling glad that Zach managed to intercept me in the hallway. The meeting turned out to be a lot more interesting than I had thought it would be. Not that I had any pre-conceived notions of what a Gay-Straight Alliance would even be like, because I had no clue.

Most of the time was spent laughing and joking, talking about odd girlfriends and boyfriends and how difficult it was to come out to loved ones. While I didn't contribute much, it still felt good to know that there were other people going through the same things that I was. People who understood. People who wanted to hear and share similar stories. People like me.

As I walked through the front door of my house, I couldn't hide the smile that illuminated my face. I heard footsteps and Mom emerged from the living room, a can of diet soda clutched in her right hand.

"You sure are getting home late. Where have you been?"

"I had a meeting after school," I told her, walking past to kneel down where Wednesday was lying near the kitchen table. I began stroking her soft fur. Her tail thumped gleefully against the linoleum floor as she pushed her neck into my hands.

"Oh," Mom said as she took a sip of her soda. "A meeting for what, soccer?"

"No." I shook my head.

"For what, then?"

I took a sharp breath, giving myself a second as I turned my attention to Wednesday's face. "Our school's Gay-Straight Alliance," I said.

"Oh, I see," she said. I glanced up to see her leaning against the counter, a thoughtful smile etched across her lips. "Well, good for you, honey. How was it?"

"It was fun," I told her.

"Good." She nodded. I watched as she took another sip of her drink before turning and taking a step towards the living room. "Oh, right, by the way." She stopped, turning back towards me. "Emma stopped by about an hour ago. She left something in your room for you."

I stared at her for a moment before leaping to my feet and rushing to my room before giving her a chance to say anything more. Emma had come by? I felt my heartbeat quicken as I pushed through the door to my room, my eyes immediately seeking what she left for me.

A single red rose sat against my pillow. Next to it, an envelope. My name was scrawled across it in her neat handwriting.

I climbed onto my bed and gently took the rose by the stem, laying it across my chest as I took the letter from the envelope and read it.

I thought my smile couldn't get any wider. I was wrong.

Thirty-two

"You look happy today," Kenny said as I slid into the passenger seat of his truck the next morning. With his hair flying in every direction and the dark circles underneath his brown eyes, he looked like he just woke up.

I shrugged. "It's a good day," I said.

"It's Wednesday," he pointed out. "No school day is a good day." He grew quiet as he backed his truck out of my driveway. "Are you and Emma back together or something?"

"Not quite," I said. It was the truth. We weren't back together. Yet.

When we pulled into the school parking lot, I felt the butterflies come to life inside my stomach at the knowledge that I'd be seeing Emma soon. As I followed Kenny into our first class of the day, my mind wandered as I thought of what I should say or do when I saw her.

Sitting down at my usual desk, I felt my hand wander to my pocket to pull out the note that Emma left for me the night before. I'd folded it carefully and placed it in the back pocket of my jeans. I'd read it what felt like a thousand times over. It still made me smile each time.

"Charlie,

I know I've hurt you. I know I've done the wrong thing, and as many times as I say sorry I know that it'll never make up for what I've done.

Even so, I'm sorry.

I never wanted to break up with you in the first place. I didn't want to hold you back. I didn't know if my dad would ever let us see each other again, and I didn't want you to have to go through that because I love you so much.

I loved you then, and I love you now. I think I'll always love you.

*I won't beg for a second chance. I don't deserve it, but that's your choice. I just want you to know that you mean the world to me. You **are** the world to me.*

Always yours,

Emma

P.S. I have a surprise for you."

I felt a small blush rise into my cheeks as I folded the note and carefully slipped it back into my jeans. Turning my head, I was surprised to find Kenny behind me.

"I thought you two weren't back together?"

I scowled. "Were you reading over my shoulder?"

"No, of course not." He threw his hands defensively in front of him as he sank back a little further into his desk. I didn't believe him at first, but the expression on his face was an honest one.

Just as I was about to respond, Lancaster began speaking to the class about what our agenda was. Being the last day of the semester before we switched classes, it was probably just going to be a game of some sort. Ignoring her, I lowered my voice to a whisper.

"We're not together," I said.

"Yeah, today." He smirked. "But how's tomorrow looking?"

I grinned.

~~~

When the bell rang and Woodbridge said her final farewell to us, Emma seemed quicker than usual to slip out of the classroom. I had to speed walk to catch up to her at the front of the school.

"Hey, Sonic, what's the hurry?" I said when I finally managed to catch up to her and close my hand around her small arm. She had been unusually silent throughout the entire class, but I hadn't thought anything of it until she rushed away. Worried, I spun her around to analyze her face. I noticed a bright shade of red creep into her cheeks.

"I'm sorry about the letter."

"Why?" I asked. "I'm not." I realized I was still holding her arm and quickly dropped it.

"It was out of line," she said. A horde of students was rushing around us to get through the front doors. A few of them even shoved carelessly into my shoulders. The more polite ones offered a quiet, '*excuse me*'. I ignored all of it. The only thing I found important was the girl standing right in front of me.

"Emma." I reached forward to take her hand in mine, letting a small smile slip across my lips at the slight tingle that started in my stomach. "I love you."

She lifted her green eyes, the worry slowly dissipating. She opened her mouth, but nothing came out. I felt her adjust her hand to tighten the grip of her fingers around mine.

"You would never have to beg for a second chance. You wouldn't even have to ask," I said.

She started to smile, but I didn't let her finish. I closed the gap between us to press my lips hard against hers. I didn't care if there were students, teachers, even parents swarming around. I didn't think I would care if the Pope was standing beside us.

We pulled away. She rested her forehead against mine for a moment before wrapping her arms around my waist and pulling me into her. "Oh, Charlie," she whispered. "I love you, too."

I let us stay connected for a long moment before finally pulling away. "There's only one thing," I said.

"What's that?" she asked. Her eyes searched my face.

"What's the surprise?"

A grin broke across her lips "Let me give you a ride. Then I'll show you."

I let her take my hand and the two of us walked through the front doors of the school. The sun that greeted me had never felt so warm, so bright. So good.

"What's the surprise have to do with?" I asked.

"I'm not telling you," she said with a chuckle, tilting her chin to the side so that the sunlight caught her cheeks in a way that made her freckles seem to stand out more. "That's the point of a surprise."

I started to respond, but the sound of Kenny's voice made me drop her hand and turn on my heels.

"Hey, Charlotte," he said, a quizzical expression crossing his face. "I thought we agreed to meet by our lockers."

Oh, shoot. I had completely forgotten. "I'm sorry," I said. "I forgot."

"Well, do you still need a ride?" he asked.

Shifting my bag on my shoulder, I let my gaze shift from Kenny to Emma. She had walked a few steps away. She shuffled a chunk of gravel with her Vans.

"No, that's okay." I let myself smile, thumbing to Emma as I turned back to Kenny. "She's my ride home."

~~~

"Don't we need to stop by your house?" I asked Emma as she veered her Jeep onto the main road of my neighborhood. "I mean, to get the surprise or whatever."

"No." She shook her head, shifting her hands on the steering wheel and glancing towards me. "I've got it with me, actually. Is your mom home?"

"I don't know." I shrugged. "She usually works Wednesdays, but who knows. Why does it matter? What kind of surprise is this?" I asked.

She blushed. "It's not… anything like that. I was just curious."

Her curiosity was answered when she pulled into my driveway and the only car parked there was my pitiful Probe. She settled back into her seat.

"What's wrong?" I asked.

"Nothing," she said. "This just feels weird. Like a dream."

I blinked. She must have read my inability to speak as confusion.

"A good dream," she clarified with a grin. She leaned towards me and I met her halfway to kiss her over the console of her car. It took a while, but the two of us eventually managed to force ourselves away from one another to push the doors open and jump out of the Jeep. I led the way to my front porch and, after digging in my bag for what seemed like an eternity, pushed my key into the lock to swing open the door.

The unexpected sound of nails against the floor greeted us as Wednesday hobbled from the living room. Surprised, I knelt down to let her walk awkwardly towards the two of us. She veered away from me at the last minute and instead turned to Emma, her long tongue slipping forward to lap at her face. Emma giggled.

"She must've missed you. I can't believe she's even walking."

"I missed her, too." Emma scratched Wednesday's back and gave her a hug before rising. "She looks good."

"Yeah, she's getting better," I said. I watched as the husky sauntered into the kitchen to lie down a few feet away from us next to her food bowl. I slipped down the hallway and into my room, tossing my bag next to my bed.

"So, where's this surprise?"

Emma rolled her eyes. "Geez, you're so impatient," she said. Her fingers began fumbling with her backpack as she dug through her mess of a binder. She pulled out a crinkled piece of paper and handed it to me.

"Wow Emma, you really know the way to a girl's heart. Paper."

"Read it."

Sitting down on my bed, I turned the paper in my hand and began reading aloud. "Dear Ms. Pearson, I am pleased to inform you of your acceptance into the University of Connecticut for the Fall 2011 semester." I immediately stopped reading. My eyes shifted from the document in my hands to Emma, who stood smiling in front of me. I looked back down at the paper again to make sure I was reading correctly. *I am pleased to inform you of your acceptance into the University of Connecticut...*

"I already signed up for orientation," she said.

I hesitated. "But I thought you had applied to some schools down in North Carolina."

She shrugged. "I sent in my application last minute."

"Why?"

"UConn sounded like a better school," she said as she took a seat next me. "Besides, you're going there, right?"

"Yeah," I said. "But, Emma, you shouldn't go to a school because I'm—"

"I'm not," she interrupted. "I want to. Besides, North Carolina is like, wildfire central. All I have to worry about up here is snow," she joked.

I wanted to say something, but decided to kiss her instead. I let my hand slide across her shoulder to gently touch the familiar crevice between her jaw and her neck. "This is incredible." I was grinning when I finally pulled away from her.

"Surprised?"

"Yeah," I replied. I let my upper body collapse onto the bed and she followed suit, turning her head to rub her nose gently against mine. "I've missed you so much the past few weeks," I said after a long silence.

I felt her arm slide across my shoulders. "Just think of all the weeks to come at UConn. We'll make up for it. Hey, maybe we can be roommates."

I smiled and let my eyes drift shut. The prospect of a tangible future, of the two of us together, felt incredible.

~~~

"What's your next class?" Emma asked as we broke away from my locker the next day after our first class. I felt her press against me as she tried to catch a glance at my schedule over my shoulder.

"College Algebra," I said, making a face at her. "You?"

"Philosophy."

"Philosophy? I didn't even know there was a course for that here," I said.

"Yeah." Emma shrugged. "It's down this hallway," she added as she pointed down the English hall. The two of us stopped. She turned her head to kiss me gently on the corner of my mouth. "See you, Charlie."

"Later," I said. I noticed Katie Dillon making a face at us from across the hallway and promptly flipped her the bird before turning to trek down the Math hallway.

As I walked into my classroom, my eyes searched the sea of faces. I recognized only one of them. With a grin, I weaved through the desks to take a seat next to her.

"Hey, Cory."

Her head snapped in my direction. "Whoa, hey Hayes," she greeted, pausing as her gaze shifted over my body. "This is the last place I expected to see you. For someone who can't put two and two together, College Algebra seems a stretch."

"Shut up," I joked. Cory laughed, reaching up with a hand to tousle the few inches of messy blonde hair that she'd managed to grow.

"Alright guys," our new teacher called from the front of the classroom. Everyone grew quiet. "I'm going to call attendance. Throw me nicknames."

I smiled. He seemed cool already. I glanced at the board behind him as he scribbled his name in messy print. Mr. Logan.

He began to call the roll. I glanced to Cory, who waggled a limp wrist in my direction. "He seems kinda fruity," she whispered, grinning. I laughed. *This is going to be a fun class,* I thought to myself.

"Charlotte Hayes," Mr. Logan called. I glanced up.

"Right here." I raised my hand.

"You got a nickname?" He glanced up from the paper in his hands and smiled.

"Yeah," I said, grinning. "It's Charlie."

To the reader:

Please take a few moments to review this novel on Amazon. It will aid other readers in deciding whether this is a novel they might enjoy. Thank you.

About the author:

Jackie Bushore is a recreational writer of young adult fiction. She received her Bachelor's degree in Criminal Justice, Sociology, and Women's Studies from Old Dominion University in Norfolk, Virginia. An avid horse lover, Jackie owns two horses and competes in various equestrian sports.

Made in the USA
Middletown, DE
18 January 2016